CHRISTC
THE CA
COUNTERFEIT COLONEL

CHRISTOPHER BUSH was born Charlie Christmas Bush in Norfolk in 1885. His father was a farm labourer and his mother a milliner. In the early years of his childhood he lived with his aunt and uncle in London before returning to Norfolk aged seven, later winning a scholarship to Thetford Grammar School.

As an adult, Bush worked as a schoolmaster for 27 years, pausing only to fight in World War One, until retiring aged 46 in 1931 to be a full-time novelist. His first novel featuring the eccentric Ludovic Travers was published in 1926, and was followed by 62 additional Travers mysteries. These are all to be republished by Dean Street Press.

Christopher Bush fought again in World War Two, and was elected a member of the prestigious Detection Club. He died in 1973.

CHRISTOPHER BUSH

THE CASE OF THE COUNTERFEIT COLONEL

With an introduction
by Curtis Evans

DEAN STREET PRESS

INTRODUCTION

RING OUT THE OLD, RING IN THE NEW
CHRISTOPHER BUSH AND MYSTERY FICTION IN THE FIFTIES

"Mr. Bush has an urbane and intelligent way of
dealing with mystery which makes his work much more
attractive than the stampeding sensationalism of some
of his rivals."
—Rupert Crofts-Cooke (acclaimed author of the Leo
Bruce detective novels)

NEW fashions in mystery fiction were decidedly afoot in the
1950s, as authors increasingly turned to sensationalistic tales
of international espionage, hard-boiled sex and violence,
and psychological suspense. Yet there indubitably remained,
seemingly imperishable and eternal, what Anthony Boucher,
dean of American mystery reviewers, dubbed the "conventional
type of British detective story." This more modestly decorous
but still intriguing and enticing mystery fare was most famously
and lucratively embodied by Crime Queen Agatha Christie, who
rang in the new decade and her Golden Jubilee as a published
author with the classic detective novel that was promoted as her
fiftieth mystery: *A Murder Is Announced* (although this was in
fact a misleading claim, as this tally also included her short story
collections). Also representing the traditional British detective
story during the 1950s were such crime fiction stalwarts (all of
them Christie contemporaries and, like the Queen of Crime,
longtime members of the Detection Club) as Edith Caroline
Rivett (E.C.R Lorac and Carol Carnac), E.R. Punshon, Cecil
John Charles Street (John Rhode and Miles Burton) and
Christopher Bush. Punshon and Rivett passed away in the
Fifties, pens still brandished in their hands, if you will, but Street
and Bush, apparently indefatigable, kept at crime throughout
the decade, typically publishing in both the United Kingdom

and the United States two books a year (Street with both of his pseudonyms).

Not to be outdone even by Agatha Christie, Bush would celebrate his own Golden Jubilee with his fiftieth mystery, *The Case of the Russian Cross*, in 1957—and this was done, in contrast with Christie, without his publishers having to resort to any creative accounting. *Cross* is the fiftieth Christopher Bush Ludovic Travers detective novel reprinted by Dean Street Press in this, the Spring of 2020, the hundredth anniversary of the dawning of the Golden Age of detective fiction, following, in this latest installment, *The Case of the Counterfeit Colonel* (1952), *The Case of the Burnt Bohemian* (1953), *The Case of The Silken Petticoat* (1953), *The Case of the Red Brunette* (1954), *The Case of the Three Lost Letters* (1954), *The Case of the Benevolent Bookie* (1955), *The Case of the Amateur Actor* (1955), *The Case of the Extra Man* (1956) and *The Case of the Flowery Corpse* (1956).

Not surprisingly, given its being the occasion of Christopher Bush's Golden Jubilee, *The Case of the Russian Cross* met with a favorable reception from reviewers, who found the author's wry dedication especially ingratiating: "The author, having discovered that this is his fiftieth novel of detection, dedicates it in sheer astonishment to HIMSELF." Writing as Francis Iles, the name under which he reviewed crime fiction, Bush's Detection Club colleague Anthony Berkeley, himself one of the great Golden Age innovators in the genre, commented, "I share Mr. Bush's own surprise that *The Case of the Russian Cross* should be his fiftieth book; not so much at the fact itself as at the freshness both of plot and writing which is still as notable with fifty up as it was in in his opening overs. There must be many readers who still enjoy a straightforward, honest-to-goodness puzzle, and here it is." The late crime writer Anthony Lejeune, who would be admitted to the Detection Club in 1963, for his part cheered, "Hats off to Christopher Bush....[L]ike his detective, [he] is unostentatious but always absolutely reliable." Alan Hunter, who recently had published his first George Gently mystery and at the time was being lauded as the "British Simenon," offered similarly praiseful words, pronouncing of *The*

Case of the Russian Cross that Bush's sleuth Ludovic Travers "continues to be a wholly satisfying creation, the characters are intriguing and the plot full of virility. . . . the only trace of long-service lies in the maturity of the treatment."

The high praise for Bush's fiftieth detective novel only confirmed (if resoundingly) what had become clear from reviews of earlier novels from the decade: that in Britain Christopher Bush, who had turned sixty-five in 1950, had become a Grand Old Man of Mystery, an Elder Statesman of Murder. Bush's *The Case of the Three Lost Letters*, for example, was praised by Anthony Berkeley as "a model detective story on classical lines: an original central idea, with a complicated plot to clothe it, plenty of sound, straightforward detection by a mellowed Ludovic Travers and never a word that is not strictly relevant to the story"; while reviewer "Christopher Pym" (English journalist and author Cyril Rotenberg) found the same novel a "beautifully quiet, close-knit problem in deduction very fairly presented and impeccably solved." Berkeley also highly praised Bush's *The Case of the Burnt Bohemian*, pronouncing it "yet another sound piece of work . . . in that, alas!, almost extinct genre, the real detective story, with Ludovic Travers in his very best form."

In the United States Bush was especially praised in smaller newspapers across the country, where, one suspects, traditional detection most strongly still held sway. "Bush is one of the soundest of the English craftsmen in this field," declared Ben B. Johnston, an editor at the *Richmond Times Dispatch*, in his review of *The Case of the Burnt Bohemian*, while Lucy Templeton, doyenne of the *Knoxville Sentinel* (the first female staffer at that Tennessee newspaper, Templeton, a freshly minted graduate of the University of Tennessee, had been hired as a proofreader back in 1904), enthusiastically avowed, in her review of *The Case of the Flowery Corpse*, that the novel was "the best mystery novel I have read in the last six months." Bush "has always told a good story with interesting backgrounds and rich characterization," she added admiringly. Another southern reviewer, one "M." of the *Montgomery Advertiser*, deemed *The Case of the Amateur Actor* "another Travers mystery to delight the most critical of a reader audience," concluding in inimitable American lingo, "it's a swell story." Even Anthony Boucher, who in the Fifties hardly could be termed an unalloyed admirer of conventional British detection, from his prestigious post at the *New York Times Books Review* afforded words of praise to a number of Christopher Bush mysteries from the decade, including the cases of the *Benevolent Bookie* ("a provocative puzzle"), the *Amateur Actor* ("solid detective interest"), the *Flowery Corpse* ("many small ingenuities of detection") and, but naturally, the *Russian Cross* ("a pretty puzzle"). In his own self-effacing fashion, it seems that Ludovic Travers had entered the pantheon of Great Detectives, as another American commentator suggested in a review of Bush's *The Case of The Silken Petticoat*:

> Although Ludovic Travers does not possess the esoteric learning of Van Dine's Philo Vance, the rough and ready punch of Mickey Spillane's Mike Hammer, the Parisian [sic!] touch of Agatha Christie's Hercule Poirot, the appetite and orchids of Rex Stout's Nero Wolfe, the suave coolness of The Falcon or the eerie laugh and invisibility of The Shadow, he does have good qualities— especially the ability to note and interpret clues and a dogged persistence in remembering and following up an episode he could not understand. These paid off in his solution of *The Case of The Silken Petticoat*.

In some ways Christopher Bush, his traditionalism notwithstanding, attempted with his Fifties Ludovic Travers mysteries to keep up with the tenor of rapidly changing times. As owner of the controlling interest in the Broad Street Detective Agency, Ludovic Travers increasingly comes to resemble an American private investigator rather than the gentleman amateur detective he had been in the 1930s; and the novels in which he appears reflect some of the jaded cynicism of post-World War Two American hard-boiled crime fiction. *The Case of the Red Brunette*, one of my favorite examples from this batch of Bushes, looks at civic corruption in provincial England in a case concerning a town counsellor who dies in an apparent "badger game" or "honey trap" gone fatally wrong ("a web of mystery skillfully spun" noted Pat McDermott of Iowa's *Quad City Times*), while in *The Case of the Three Lost Letters*, Travers finds himself having to explain to his phlegmatic wife Bernice the pink lipstick strains on his collar (incurred strictly in the line of duty, of course). Travers also pays homage to the popular, genre altering Inspector Maigret novels of Georges Simenon in *The Case of Red Brunette*, when he decides that he will "try to get a feel of the city [of Mainford]: make a Maigret-like tour and achieve some kind of background. . . ."

Christopher Bush finally decided that Travers could manage entirely without his longtime partner in crime solving, the wily and calculatingly avuncular Chief Superintendent George Wharton, whom at times Travers, in the tradition of American hard-boiled crime fiction, appears positively to dislike. "I generally admire and respect Wharton, but there are times when he annoys me almost beyond measure," Travers confides in *The Case of the Amateur Actor*. "There are even moments, as when he assumes that cheap and leering superiority, when I can suddenly hate him." George Wharton appropriately makes his final, brief appearance in the Bush oeuvre in *The Case of the Russian Cross*, where Travers allows that despite their differences, the "Old General" is "the man who'd become in most ways my oldest friend."

"Ring out the old, ring in the new" may have been the motto of many when it came to mid-century mystery fiction, but as another saying goes, what once was old eventually becomes sparklingly new again. The truth of the latter adage is proven by this shining new set of Christopher Bush reissues. "Just like old crimes," vintage mystery fans may sigh contentedly, as once again they peruse the pages of a Bush, pursuing murderous malefactors in the ever pleasant company of Ludovic Travers, all the while armed with the happy knowledge that a butcher's dozen of thirteen of Travers' investigations yet remains to be reissued.

Curtis Evans

Chapter One
THE CLIENT

I HAPPENED to be alone in the office because Norris, my managing director, had gone out with a client. When there's nothing doing for me as what Scotland Yard calls an "unofficial expert", I spend a goodish bit of time at the Broad Street Detective Agency, though it's Norris who runs the business. I'm only a kind of figure-head—chairman of the company, and, incidentally, the owner. If Norris wants me, and we happen to be short-handed, I sometimes take the place of an operative or do a certain amount of interviewing, and that Saturday morning I happened to be on hand.

Bertha Munney, that brisk old trouper of a secretary, rang through.

"There's a gentleman here, Mr. Travers, who wants to see one of the principals. Shall I send him in?"

"He's in the waiting-room?"

"Oh yes," she said, and guessed that I'd want to know a bit about him. "He's quite a gentleman. Youngish. Speaks well. Doesn't look worried or anything like that."

"He may do when he leaves here," I told her facetiously. "Send him in, Bertha. What's his name, by the way?"

"Clandon. Henry Clandon."

Henry Clandon came in. Bertha was right, as usual, for he certainly looked what one calls a gentleman. There was a level look and an ease of movement, and all those little, scarcely noticeable things that place a man in a certain social category. He looked about thirty, stood about five feet ten, and his broad shoulders were squared like those of a man who's taken his army life seriously. He was quite good-looking in a strictly virile sort of way. His hair was dark brown, the neatly trimmed moustache was dark brown, and he wore horn-rimmed spectacles much darker and much smaller than my own. His clothes were well cut, and he wore no tie of the kind that announces a school or a regiment.

"Mr. Clandon?" I said, and gave him my best smile and waved him to a seat.

"Yes," he said, and his smile was rather tentative. "I've often seen your advertisement, but I never thought I'd be here." He smiled again, this time apologetically. "That sounded rather crude. Perhaps I mean that I'm here because I saw your advertisement."

"Fine," I said. I liked the first look of him, and it never does any harm to have a certain amount of preliminary blether. It puts the nervous ones at their ease—not that this chap looked especially nervous. If he looked anything at all it was what I might call politely diffident.

"And what can we do for you, Mr. Clandon?" I went on. "My name's Travers, by the way. Ludovic Travers. Not that that conveys anything to you."

"I want you to do something that may sound rather peculiar," he told me, and his eyes blinked a bit behind the heavy lenses. "I want you to find somebody for me."

"Why not?" I said amiably. "It's the kind of thing we're often doing."

"But this is different. I mean—well, I only saw the man twice and that was during the war."

"Tell me all about it," I said. "Have a cigarette."

I held the lighter for him and he seemed more at ease when he'd taken a draw or two. To start the ball rolling, I asked him what sort of a time he'd had in the army. He showed no surprise that I'd hit on the right service.

"Not too bad," he said. "I got carved up a bit in Sicily, at a place called Larentza. That's where I first saw the man I want you to find. His name was Seeway. David Seeway."

"And the last time you saw him?"

"The same time. The following week, in fact."

With all the kinks straightened out, his story was this. After an unsuccessful night attack he had been left in no-man's-land with a lump of shrapnel in his belly. A young officer from another regiment had brought him in and had later come to see him in hospital. That officer—the David Seeway whom we were to find—had stayed by the bed only a few minutes, and with a sister fluttering nervously around since the patient was not supposed to talk.

"That's practically all I know about him," Clandon told me. "But I owe him my life and I want to find him. I'm not being sentimental or anything like that, but I feel I owe him something. If he should be up against it in any way or wanting a spot of help—well, I'd like to do something about it. It was a devilish brave thing he did. Heard a bloke groaning out there and didn't know him and crawled out and brought him in. Got wounded himself in the process, too."

"But you've heard nothing about him since?"

It was a shrewd question that implied a whole lot of things. Some of them he spotted, for he frowned slightly.

"You know how it is in a war," he said. "One minute you're alive and then you're dead, and that's the sort of day-to-day mentality. Then when you're out of things, and for me that was only three years ago, you've got to get reorganised and that's apt to take a whole lot of time and thought."

He broke off to give a shy sort of smile.

"I don't want you to laugh at me, but the other day I saw an American war film that dealt with a situation like my own. It sort of hit me. I suddenly knew I'd been most damnably ungrateful towards Seeway and I've been thinking the same ever since. Only I happen to be a rather busy sort of person, so I thought I'd get you people to look up Seeway for me."

"If he's alive."

"Exactly. If he's alive."

"Right," I said. "Let's start off with a description and so on. His regiment?"

He gave a smile that was even more apologetic.

"You're going to find it hard to understand this," he said, "but I was a mighty sick man when he saw me in hospital. I couldn't even tell you his regiment. I just sort of lay there in my bed and listened. I do remember that I thanked him, but I must have said it very quietly. I guess I didn't feel like talking."

"I guess not," I said. "But anything at all about him that you remember?"

He took out his wallet and found a sheet of notes. He said he'd been racking his brains for a week or two—ever since that evening at the cinema—and had jotted things down from time to time. Seeway was definitely an infantryman—that was a certainty. He looked pretty big and strong, and he was somewhere about Clandon's own age, which was thirty-three. That would be now, of course. Eight years ago Seeway would have been only twenty-five. He'd spoken with a cultured voice and had no recognisable accent.

"This is the real clue," Clandon said, and looked up from his notes. "I'm practically sure he came from a place called Bassingford. You know it?"

"I think I've been there," I said. "A quiet little town about twenty-five miles north of London."

Norris came in then and I introduced him. He took a back seat when I'd outlined the case and let me get on with the eliciting of clues which would give us a starting point. Maybe it was the interruption that made Clandon remember something he should have asked.

"You don't mind my asking it," he said, and craned round to include Norris, "but all this is strictly confidential?"

"Most decidedly," I said. "As confidential as between doctor and patient. In fact," I said, as I offered the cigarette box again, "if you'd come here and told us you'd committed a murder, we wouldn't have dreamed of ringing the police."

"Good," he said, and had another look at his notes. "And there's one other thing and I've wondered if it wasn't some kind of hallucination. After he'd gone that day I must have had a bit of a relapse. Slightly delirious, and so on, and all sorts of mad things running through my brain. This one was over and over again, like the noise of the wheels of a train. And it was a man's name. *Archie Dibben*. Archie Dibben, Archie Dibben—over and over again, just like that." He gave a wry shake of the head. "Perhaps that's why I remember it."

"No clue at all as to why the name was on your mind?"

"Yes," he said. "It came to me last night. I seem to remember his asking me what my part of England was, and then his mentioning of Bassingford. I don't know what I said, if anything, but I faintly remember him saying that if I didn't know Bassingford I wouldn't know Archie Dibben. Something like that. It's all very vague and obscure, and it's all I can be reasonably certain about."

"Tell me this," I said. "Who brought you in from no-man's-land? Seeway alone? There wasn't another man with him?"

"That's an idea," he said, and in the same breath was shaking his head. "I couldn't say. It was dark as hell and I was in a pretty bad way. I think I passed out almost as soon as he touched me. I faintly remember a grenade going off—the one that wounded him—and then I came to in the dressing station. But I do see your point. This Archie Dibben may have been with him and the two of them brought me in, and he was sort of telling me so."

"It's an idea," I said. "And it may make things easier. We've got two people to look for and either may lead us to the other."

"Yes," he said. The notes had petered out and he was suddenly gravelled for lack of matter.

"You haven't made any enquiries yourself?" Norris put in from behind.

"None whatever," Clandon told him. "I'm a busy man, and, if you'll pardon the old adage, I never keep a dog and bark myself. As soon as I'd made up my mind—and that was only last night—I decided to get you people to do the barking."

"Very sensible, too," I said. "And you haven't even been to Bassingford."

"Yes," he said. "But not about that. A few weeks ago I interviewed a client there about a manuscript. I happen to be a publisher."

"Really?"

"No one important," he said. "Just the junior director of Halmer and Blate."

"A fine old firm," I said. "And the address where you'd like us to communicate with you, Mr. Clandon?"

He was a bachelor, he said, and had a small service flat—14 Marlow Mansions, Westminster. He gave me the telephone number and said the best, indeed the only time to be sure of him was in the early morning. Any time before half-past nine. Then he was asking about terms. I quoted terms that allowed for eventualities and he seemed perfectly happy. In fact, he had his cheque-book and was signing his name to the retaining fee as soon as the terms were quoted. I filled in the contract details on one of our usual forms, and he took a quick look through it and signed with never a question.

"As soon as there's anything to communicate, you shall have it," I told him. "It might be pretty soon. In fact," I added humorously, "I don't think we're going to make an awful lot of money out of you, Mr. Clandon. Not that we shall spin the case out. We'll get to work at once. Bassingford's pretty handy, which is an excellent thing as far as your pocket is concerned."

He smiled politely, but the smile wasn't there for more than a second.

"And everything's strictly confidential?"

"Confidence is the basis of this kind of business," I told him soberly. "Have no worries about that, Mr. Clandon." He shook hands with both of us. Norris had a last word as Clandon and I went through the door.

"If any additional recollections should occur to you, you'll let us have them at once?"

Clandon said he certainly would. I saw him through to the outer door and that was that. He had a nice little post-war car that must have made a big hole into a thousand pounds, but I wasn't smiling ruefully at the fact that we weren't likely to collect a handsome cheque. I wasn't smiling at all. I think as I went back along the corridor to Norris that my fingers were instinctively at my glasses. That's a nervous trick of mine when I'm at a mental loss or suddenly confronted with something that seems to need a considerable deal of explanation.

"A nice fellow," Norris said casually as I came in. "The sort of client that doesn't do us any harm. Plenty of money, judging by that car of his and so on."

"Yes," I said. "Who're you putting on to the case?"

"Don't know," he said. "I was just about to work it out."

"Mind if I make the opening moves myself?"

He stared: then he didn't, if you know what I mean. We were just a bit short-handed at the moment, but what had brought the quick surprise was that I should want to handle so obvious and routine an investigation. I told him so, and he admitted I was right.

"That car of his," I said. "Did it convey anything to you?" He said it didn't, except to announce money and good taste.

"Anything else strike you while you were listening?" He shook his head. If I was hinting at something peculiar, then he'd missed it.

"Nothing serious," I said. "Just a thing or two to make me wonder. For instance, why all that insistence on secrecy?"

His head went sideways, like a hopping sparrow's on a lawn.

"Why should he mention secrecy at all?" I went on. "He wants somebody found and we're to do the finding. There's nothing fishy about the two people he mentioned—Seeway and Dibben—so why be worried about the strictly confidential?"

"Maybe something to do with himself and his job."

"Now, now, now!" I said, and I made it amusedly. "How on earth could what he wants or what we're about to do be derogatory in any way? It's just curious, that's what it is. I'd like to know why he placed that one particular emphasis. He stressed nothing else. He didn't quibble about terms. And that reminds me. I take it you'd call him the serious type of professional man? Nothing of the spendthrift or playboy about him; yet he's prepared to spend over a hundred pounds—or so I'd say— to have us do something for him that he could do just as well for himself. Don't mistake me," I added hastily. "He might, and he ought, to have done the initial things himself and then have come to us when they'd failed."

"Yes," Norris said slowly, though just a bit grudgingly. "What you mean is that Bassingford isn't all that way away and he wasn't all that busy that he mightn't have slipped along in his car and made an enquiry or two. At the town hall, for instance, to see if this David Seeway was a ratepayer, or on the electoral roll."

"Exactly! Or he could have put an advertisement in the local paper. If for some reason or other he wanted secrecy, he could have used a box number."

"Yes," he said. Then he grinned. "But what're we grumbling about? It'll be just as easy for us as it would have been for him. What we've got to hope is, it doesn't work out too easy."

"True enough," I told him. "And the probability is that it won't be too easy—if I'm handling it. All the same, you know the golden rule in this game of ours. You've got to be sure of the client before you can be sure of the case."

So there we were. When it was arranged that I'd get to work on the case in the morning, I couldn't help thinking to myself that Norris had been patiently or deceptively forbearing. Ludovic Travers, as he was only too well aware, was something of a schizophrenic. One of him couldn't help scenting, or even creating, a mystery, and the other either found a solution or worried his wits till something arose to make the self-created problem of no importance.

When I was thinking things over that evening in the flat at St. Martin's Chambers, I began to find answers to some of the things that had first puzzled me. There *was* a reason, for instance, why Clandon should wish for strict secrecy. Maybe, unfamiliar as most people with the offices of a detective or enquiry agency, he had felt something just a bit shabby or a trifle beyond the pale in being in that office in Broad Street. It was the kind of feeling I used to have in the very early days of the cinema when one sneaked, as it were, into some hideous, grubby, ill-adapted building in a side street and hoped to heaven none of one's friends had seen the furtive entry.

As for that matter of Clandon's wanting to save himself every ounce of effort, even in so personal a matter, so much the better, as Norris had said, for the Broad Street Detective Agency. And then I had to pause and give myself a shake of the head. Wasn't there something wrong about that? Was that attitude of Clandon's quite in keeping with something else he had tried to make clear? He had just been converted, as it were. He had been convicted of the sin of ingratitude and was all agog to put things belatedly right. But surely a convert would want to act for himself and not to pay others to undertake for him the most elementary and trivial beginnings of the business of expiation and thanks.

Then the other Travers—the one who, as George Wharton says, can find an immediate solution to any problem, even if it's generally wrong—decided that Clandon might be genuinely and uncommonly busy and just a bit disinclined to give himself additional work, even in a matter so personal. So both Traverses decided to leave speculation alone. And even then one of them couldn't be content without a last word.

"You can say what you like," he as good as told the other. "Explanations or not, there's still a something that's remarkably peculiar."

CHAPTER TWO
AT BASSINGFORD

I'M NOT proposing to bore you with a full description of Bassingford, but, since the little town has an importance for this story, there are things you have to know. The patience of just one paragraph is all that's required.

It's a little place of twelve thousand inhabitants, with its interests largely agricultural, and it consists of three well-defined parts which are easy enough to memorise. As you come in from London there's a pre-fab-bungalow-council house suburb and then you cross a bridge over the Bassing River to the older part of the town. There you have a terrace or two of Victorian houses interspersed miraculously with bulging, timbered Tudor survivals: their timbering and ancient bricks now concealed beneath hideous pink plaster. Then, and still a part of it, comes the High Street which is the main shopping centre; broken in the middle by the Market Square which has, among other things, a fine early Guildhall, a monstrosity of a Town Hall, and the Royal Cinema, formerly the Theatre Royal. Beyond the High Street the land rises slightly and, after one fairly modern street, you come to a high-class residential suburb, beyond which is the golf course.

I left London after an early breakfast and the Town Hall clock said a quarter-past nine when I parked my car in the Market Square. It was a lovely morning of early June and, once the inner suburbs had been passed, it had been a delightful drive. I was feeling both pleased and complacent: pleased to get away from town, and rather smug about the probable ease with which I ought to get a line on Clandon's missing man or men. Clandon's commission hadn't sounded like a good many that we'd undertaken from time to time. His might be a needle in a haystack, but at least I knew what haystack; I also knew a certain amount about the needle.

Half an hour later I wasn't quite so sure. No David Seeway or Archie—or Archibald—Dibben had appeared among the town's householders or on its electoral roll. Then my eye caught a stationer's shop and I asked if there was a directory of the town, and there was—just published, and the first since the war. I went laboriously through it while having coffee at a nearby restaurant, and again I drew a perfect blank.

I finished a second cup of coffee and made my way to the post office. Business was rather brisk—it was market day—and when I reached the head of my particular queue, I created quite a sensation by asking to see the postmaster. The girl stared at me as if I were in Moscow and had asked for Joe Stalin, and it took another ten minutes before I got behind the Kremlin curtain.

The postmaster, a middle-aged man, was helpful enough, but he knew of no Seeway or Dibben. He called in someone he called Tom—a head sorter probably—who was well over sixty. He wanted to know when Seeway or Dibben had lived in the town. I said it was probably just before the war.

He shook his head. Operation Clandon wasn't going so well, so I asked for advice. I said it was desperately important that one at least of the men should be found.

"Either of these here men likely to've got themselves in the papers?" Tom said. "If so, you might look through the *Gazette*. Ask for Jack Finney and say I sent you."

That was an idea, though I didn't fancy a laborious going-through of several years' files. But I went along to the offices of the *Bassingford Gazette* and asked for Jack Finney. A boy took me down some concrete steps to the usual underground vault which calls itself a library.

Finney was an epitome of every librarian of a small-town newspaper that I'd ever run across: a man of about sixty-five to seventy, thinnish, with shoulders that stooped; peering, rheumy eyes and a grey moustache that straggled over his face like brambles in a long neglected hedge. He was slightly deaf and his voice had as much music as a pneumatic drill.

"Don't know of no Seeway," he told me. "Taint an Essex name. Nor no Dibben."

"That's pretty final," I told him. "You've been here a long time and you ought to know."

"Started here a twelve-year-old," he bellowed at me. "Nothin's ever happened here that I can't tell you about. Rare memory I have for dates and things."

"You a teetotaller?"

"Me?" He looked as if I'd spat in his face.

"Buy yourself a drink," I said, and slipped him a couple of half-crowns. "And if you remember anything about a David Seeway or an Archie Dibben, just let me know."

He made no bones about taking the tip and he flicked a grati-fied finger to his forelock. A mighty independent man for all that. Probably drawing his old-age pension and putting in two or three half-days on the *Gazette* for the sake of old times and a bit of extra cash. That's what I was thinking when I was back on the first of those concrete steps. His yell quite startled me.

"You didn't say nothin' about no Archie. You said Dibben."

I turned back.

"Sorry," I said. "I didn't think the Christian name was all that important."

He wasn't listening. He was tapping his skull and frowning into some private infinity.

"Archie Dibben," he said slowly. "Archie Dibben."

He shook his head.

"Funny," he said, and tapped his skull again. "Somewhere a voice is callin'. Know that song? Archie Dibben . . . Archie Dibben . . ."

He broke off with a gesture of annoyance.

"I know the name, sir, well as I know my own. Just can't think of it."

I couldn't somehow stand any more of that trance-like repetition of *Archie Dibben*.

"Look," I said, "I'll be having lunch at the White Hart. I'll be there from twelve o'clock onwards. You find me something about Archie Dibben and there's a pound note in it for you at the least."

He gave me a nod and I left him frowning away and muttering that name to himself. I took a short walk round the town and had a tankard in the White Hart. I'd almost finished my lunch when the waiter told me a Mr. Finney wanted to see me in the lounge.

Finney had something. I knew that as soon as I saw him. If I hadn't asked where we could go for quiet, he'd have begun bellowing his news in that crowded lounge bar. Five minutes later we were back in that musty, paste-ridden vault of his.

Almost as soon as I'd left him, he'd remembered Archie Dibben. He'd looked through his files and found an advertisement or two, and then as soon as he began to talk I knew he was on the wrong track. And then I didn't know. Surely the world didn't contain so many Archie Dibbens? There was a smoothness of ring about the name: something that spoke of personality. Intuition told me that much was right: the trouble was that everything else was hopelessly wrong. But let me explain.

The Theatre Royal operated as such till the spring of 1940 and then it became the Royal Cinema. In the March of 1939 a touring company in the London success *Under My Thumb* put on a week's show, and billed as one of its stars was Archie

Dibben. The name rang no bell for me, even with that starring. I have a pretty good memory for names, especially in a theatrical context, but the name of Archie Dibben conveyed never a thing. Then when I learned that in the show he'd been the comic uncle, I knew he wasn't my man. And yet something would keep telling me that he had to be.

"Did you see the show?"

"Oh yes," Finney said. "Never used to miss one o' them theatrical shows. Can't stand the cinema, though. Can't hear nothin'."

"What sort of man was Dibben?"

"Littlish man. Pot-bellied. Be about fifty. Looked younger on the stage, though. Rare comical, he was."

"You see him off the stage?"

"You couldn't help seein' them actors when they was in town. Far as I remember, he used to be at the White Hart a goodish bit. I saw him there with Mr. Proden. Him what now own the cinema. It was him that got Miss Ladely what owned it to have it turned into a cinema. Then when she died he come into her money. A nephew or somethin' he was."

So far, so bad, and I was doing a bit of quick thinking. On the face of it, the Archie Dibben of *Under My Thumb* couldn't conceivably be my man. A pot-bellied actor of fifty doesn't get into the army and have the physique or moral fibre to crawl out into no-man's-land and earn a couple of medals. And there arose a something far more insuperable. Why had Seeway that day in hospital mentioned the name at all? Why should Seeway ask Clandon if he knew Archie Dibben? If Archie Dibben had been a prominent citizen of Bassingford—a large property owner, for instance, or a famous local wit—there might have been a certain amount of logic in the matter. But the Archie Dibben of *Under My Thumb* wasn't even a citizen. He was a member of a touring company that spent just that one week in the town. In fact, the whole thing made no kind of sense.

I looked up to see Finney's eyes anxiously on me. Maybe he was thinking of that pound note. I gave him a couple, and he almost spat on them for luck.

"I don't think this Archie Dibben's the man I'm looking for," I told him. "Mine is a much younger man. But you mentioned a Mr.—Proden, was it?"

"That's right. Him what own the cinema and no end more property in the town."

"Maybe it wouldn't do any harm to have a word with him. Your Archie Dibben, for instance, might have had a son, and he'd be the sort of age I'm looking for. Mr. Proden might know about that."

Proden lived, he said, at a house called Beaulieu, near the golf course. I said I'd like to know a bit about him before I saw him, but Finney couldn't add a lot. He described Proden as a gentleman and a sportsman: at least he played a lot of golf and had sponsored a good few boxing shows for the troops during the war. His age would now be about fifty.

"He inherited a lot of property from his aunt, you said?"

I don't know why I asked the question, unless it was that I somehow wanted a bit more time in which to think. But it produced a lot more Proden history when Finney had taken his time over the consulting of his files. Not that the information was of any use to me. Proden had spent some time abroad and had come to Bassingford in 1939, doubtless to see his aunt. He married in 1941 a Bassingford girl of very good family and with plenty of money—a Rosamund Vorne, only daughter of a Colonel Vorne, a widower who was killed in the retreat to Dunkirk. There was a divorce in 1947 and Mrs. Proden left the town, and where she was now living Finney did not know. Proden was still at Beaulieu.

Finney was ferreting round to find more information, but I'd heard more than enough. I had to indicate that I was in rather a hurry and I got away with a promise of payment for any more news. But only about Dibben. Nobody else interested me—I had to make that clear—unless it was the David Seeway about whom Finney knew nothing. By the look on Finney's face I guessed that he'd work through his files with a small-toothed comb.

I came up into daylight and clear June air, and I was blinking against the sudden light. Then I went on to the post office and looked up Proden's number, and all the while I knew that what I was doing was an utter waste of time. I rang the number and I could hear the bell going in the house, and after five minutes of that I replaced the receiver. No one was at home at Beaulieu.

I got in my car and drove out towards the golf course, and one enquiry led me to Proden's house. It was a biggish, red-brick affair in late-Victorian Tudor: high-gabled and set in well over an acre of grounds. Trim lawns, neat drive, bright flower-beds—everything spoke of money. A striped sun awning over a porch door said surely that someone was at home, and I wondered why the telephone had rung unheard. I let the car stay just by the handsome twin gates and went to investigate.

As I reached the end of the fifty-yard gravelled drive I heard the whirr of a lawn-mower, so I went on past the side of the house. A youngish gardener was mowing another expanse of lawn which seemed to have been specially laid out as a putting green, with nine holes and beautiful tricky contours.

"Mr. Proden not in?"

"Not at the moment, sir. He's gone to town. Be back about six, so he told me. You wanted to see him?"

I said I did, and rather urgently. I asked him to ring me at the White Hart as soon as Mr. Proden returned, but he couldn't do that as he stopped work at five. So I wrote a message on a page from my notebook, and the gardener said he'd leave it with the housekeeper. She was at the cinema but would be home before five.

I gave him a tip, drove back to the Market Square, and lingered out tea at a restaurant. Common sense told me I might just as well go home instead of spending the firm's money, and then some other kind of sense kept urging that since I was in Bassingford I might as well make it a day. So I ordered dinner at the White Hart, and six o'clock found me in the lounge within earshot of the telephone. I finished a second tankard and nothing had happened. I was through dinner and thinking of ringing my wife, when at last my call came.

"Mr. Travers?"

"Speaking," I said.

"This is Hugh Proden. You want to see me about something?"

"Yes," I said. "Something private and rather urgent."

"Really?" There was no wonder he was surprised. "Do we know each other, by the way?"

"I don't think so. All the same, I'd be very grateful if I could see you."

"You wouldn't like to give me a preliminary idea of what you want to see me about?"

"If it's all the same to you, I'd rather see you than talk over the telephone."

"Right," he said. "Come along now, will you? Sorry I couldn't ring you earlier."

There are one or two things I'd like to make clear, and maybe because I wouldn't wish you to think I'm assuming any kind of omniscience. If you're sitting with a man in your or his garden and you hear a bird note or two and he suddenly says, "That's a spotted fly-catcher," you don't question the opinion—*if* you know he's an experienced bird-watcher. If an old countryman points to this and that and tells you there'll be rain before the day is out, you'll probably be a fool if you start watering your garden. And, in a way, that's how things are with myself.

For over twenty years I've been working on murder cases with George Wharton—Chief Superintendent Wharton to you—of Scotland Yard. If we're interrogating together, he usually does the talking and I watch the reactions of the suspect or witness. If I'm working alone on some aspect of the case, I do both, and that's why I can reasonably claim to recognise the truth or spot a lie. And that's why—like the bird-watcher I didn't see the bird, I heard only its note—I knew from Proden's voice and even his hesitations that my simple message and very few words had made him distinctly uneasy.

There's just one other thing. One of my hobbies is the study of my fellow men. I like to look at them and listen to them in trains or pubs or buses, and place their accents and guess their professions, and if there's a chance I make an opening to check the accuracy of my observations. I don't say I'm right in sixty per cent of cases, but it's a great game in a job like mine. And after

I'd listened to Proden on the telephone, I could be pretty sure of the kind of man he was. His had been a cultured voice with just a trace of heartiness: the voice, shall we say, of the man of the world plus the man about town.

I accepted that for granted, and as I drove to the house I had to base my opening gambits on that and on the uneasiness I thought I'd discerned. This time I drove my car in. It was a lovely evening, and, though the awning had gone, the door was wide open. Almost as soon as I'd touched the bell an elderly housekeeper was admitting me. From the spacious hall I could see through another door on my right a younger woman clearing a dinner table. Proden, then, had had his meal before he had rung me, and in spite of the urgency of my note. I wondered what it was that he had had to think over.

I was shown into a lounge—a tasteful, comfortable room with a view across the golf course. Papers and magazines were on a large, low table and the bulk of them were sporting publications—*The Racing World*, *Current Form*, *Modern Motoring*, *Golf Illustrated*, and so on. A television set was in one corner and a showy cocktail cabinet in another, and on the walls were old sporting prints. I was looking at a rare one of Jim Belcher when Proden came into the room.

He gave me a quick, shrewd look, and no more. Most people can't help a longer look, for I'm not the usual type. I'm pretty tall, for instance—six foot three in my socks—and my leanness makes me look taller. I've a long, Roman sort of hatchet face and my sight is so bad that I wear special lenses in immense horn-rims. I have a back lock of hair that not even glue can flatten, and since it sticks out well behind my skull, it gives me the look of a secretary-bird.

"So sorry to have kept you," he was saying, and his eyes were wrinkled as he smiled. "Coffee's just coming in, if you'd like it."

It came in as he spoke and I had a cup of black.

"Kümmel or brandy?"

I said it was very good of him, and I'd have a kümmel, and I was taking a good look at him while he fetched it and filled the liqueur glasses. You've seen the advertisements in the glossy magazines for overcoats and waterproofs? The tall, tanned, lean-faced gent with a foot on the running-board of an expensive car, binoculars perhaps in his hands, and at his elbow another highly tailored sahib with the same tanned, lean face and cropped moustache? Either of them would have done for Proden. And he had the voice to match—a perfect baritone, the words just a bit clipped, and an easy heartiness and that solicitude of manner which so contributes to charm.

"Now just what is it that we're going to talk about?" he was asking me quizzically.

My name had conveyed nothing to him, which was just as well. We're a pretty anonymous lot at Scotland Yard, and though I often have to appear in criminal courts, it's in an unobtrusive way. But I told him no more than was necessary about myself—leaving out the Yard—and then came with an intentional suddenness to the name of Archie Dibben. I was watching him like a hawk, and the name hit him like a short-arm uppercut in the lower ribs. But only for a second—if that. He actually pretended not to have caught the name.

"Dibben," I said. "Archie Dibben."

He frowned.

"Dibben . . . Archie Dibben. . . . The name rings some sort of bell. And I'm supposed to know him?"

I made no bones about saying I'd made enquiries; in fact I told him what I knew. It was great to see how subtly he let a recollection steal slowly in. He even ended up with a little chuckle.

"But of course, my dear fellow. I remember him. Down here with a touring company, as you say. Funny I didn't place him at once."

"You don't happen to know where he is now?"

"My dear fellow!" He shrugged his shoulders. "I've no more idea than Adam. Best part of twelve years ago! And I only saw the fellow in a business sort of way. I may have had a drink or two with him, but that's all." He leaned just a bit back with closed eyes, and there was another faint smile of remembrance. "An amusing sort of chap, far as I can think back."

"Ever hear of him since?"

"Never a word," he said, and his face straightened.

"You don't know if he had a son?"

"Heavens, no! I couldn't even tell you if he had a fat aunt."

"That's that, then," I said. "But what was he like to look at?"

"Dibben?" He frowned. His eyes screwed up as he leaned back. "A chap of about fifty. Fresh-faced. About five-nine or so. Dark. Clean-shaved, of course. On the lean side, if anything. Typical comic man. Stage twinkle in his eyes, if you know what I mean." He remembered something else as he leaned forward. "A quite well-spoken sort of old boy. A long way from Eton and Balliol, but he was quite educated, if you get me."

"A capital description," I told him craftily. "But just one other little thing. Do you happen to remember where the company went from here?"

"Lord, no," he said. "Think of it, my dear fellow. Twelve years ago and a company of some sort here every week. Then the war, and a whole lot of family changes as far as I was concerned. Then six years of peace which have been a damn-sight worse. Besides, my aunt died early in the war and I'd induced her to modernise the old Royal and turn it into a cinema. That's one of the reasons why Dibben never came here again. As far as I'm concerned he might be dead." He was asking if I'd have yet another coffee, or more kümmel, and I was courteously declining both. I could see he thought—and maybe hoped—the interview was at an end. But I didn't budge, and then he was leaning forward again.

"Would I be in order if I asked just who it is that is interested in this chap Dibben?"

"Afraid I couldn't answer that," I told him with what I hoped was a nice mixture of apology and professional reserve. "The very basis of a high-class business like ours is absolute secrecy as far as the client's concerned."

"But he's an important client?"

"Is he?"

He laughed.

"My dear fellow, he must be! The chairman of a concern doesn't run about doing ordinary detective work—you'll pardon the term—just for any Tom, Dick or Harry."

I also produced a laugh. I said that was pretty good deduction and that was as far as I was prepared to go.

"And by the way," I brought in as a kind of after-thought, "this client of ours isn't looking for Dibben so much as for quite another chap altogether. I can't tell you the whole story, but Dibben was only vaguely connected with this other and really important man. I asked you about Dibben because I hoped he might lead us to the other man. A bit confusing, but I hope you get the main idea. This chap's name, by the way, and I'm pretty sure you've never heard of it in your life, is Seeway—David Seeway."

He stared. He was trying to control himself, but he couldn't. If the mention of Dibben had caught him clean in the wind, then this mention of Seeway was the very devil of a shock.

"Seeway!" he said. "David Seeway! Twelve years, and you're asking *me* about Seeway!"

CHAPTER THREE
NO HAYSTACK

HE WAS shaking his head as he got to his feet. For a minute or two it was as if I wasn't in the room, for he seemed to have forgotten all about me as he moved across to the door and pushed a bell. Then he mixed himself a long, stiff whisky. The housekeeper came in and took the coffee tray, and he didn't say a word, even to her. He brought his drink back to his side table and he didn't ask me to have one with him. I waited. He'd had plenty of time to do his thinking and I was wondering just what would be coming.

"Let's get something clear," he told me quietly, and took a second pull at the long drink. "David Seeway was a cousin of mine—I'll tell you that to start with—but how the devil could there be any connection between him and Dibben! I doubt if the two ever saw each other. Unless David saw him on the stage."

"I'm just as bewildered as you are," I had to tell him. "But suppose we try to puzzle out a connection. I mean, you tell me— if you'll be so good—all you know about Seeway."

He made no bones about it whatever. Concisely and chronologically, as it were, this was what he told me. And the people and events, as he said, were well enough known in the town.

There were three Ladely sisters. Hilda and Aggie were twins and Maud was ten years younger. Aggie was Proden's mother, Hilda never married, and Maud was Seeway's mother. Aggie married early and Maud late, which accounted for the fact that in 1939 Proden was forty and David Seeway twenty-two.

Hilda inherited the bulk of the money and property. Aggie divorced her husband, who then went to America, and no one had heard of him since. Maud and her husband were killed in an accident and Hilda took over the young David and sent him to public school and Cambridge. In 1939 he was just down and supposed to be looking around for a suitable job. Meanwhile Hugh Proden had long since left his school and gone out to Ceylon with a tea-planter friend of the family. He came home for good in 1939.

David was a bit of a cub with expensive tastes and a bad temper. Hilda, his aunt, was straitlaced and had uttered warnings about his drinking habits and choice of friends. One nasty business in Bassingford itself was hushed up—Proden admitted that he was responsible for the hushing up—but something must have leaked out. There was a stormy scene between David and his aunt and then David simply packed up and left. On his twenty-first birthday he'd come into a small estate, and he'd collected what apparently was left of it—about three thousand pounds— and disappeared. Nobody had heard a word of him since.

"That was why it was a bit of a shock, your mentioning his name," Proden said. "We assumed he'd joined the army, or something, and had got himself killed. Never a word from him from that day to this."

"Maybe he did get killed," I said. "All I'm at liberty to tell you is that he was alive at the time of the invasion of Sicily. He was an infantry officer and my client met him there. My client considered himself indebted to him in some way and—belatedly, as he admits—asked us to find him."

"But this chap Dibben! Where the devil does *he* come in?"

"You know as much as I do," I told him. I added speciously that during the course of general yarning Bassingford must have been mentioned and Dibben's name had somehow cropped up.

"Yes, but what does your client say about Dibben?"

"Just nothing. He faintly remembers the name. We were hunting around for stuff to work on and our client just recalled that name, as I said. It's a long while ago, as you were saying in another context, and all our client remembered really well was the indebtedness. I'm sorry to be so vague, but those are the facts. After what I've heard from you, I'm just as much in the dark as anyone."

He didn't seem to be listening. He was leaning back again with screwed-up eyes.

"Wait a minute," he said. "I may possibly have something." Then he was shaking his head. "Don't think so. I don't think it'd account for it."

"Would you mind telling me, all the same?"

"It was this," he said. "It was just after that *Under My Thumb* company left here that David left, too. And now I remember, he did see Dibben—personally or convivially, I mean. I remember seeing them together in the White Hart." He gave another and almost bewildered slow shake of the head. "Funny how things begin to come back to you."

"Yes," I said. "And do you think there's any clue in it as to Seeway's bolting from Bassingford?"

"Don't know," he said. "The whole thing's beyond me." He gave an exasperated click of the tongue. "Seeway in the army—that's nothing. He either had to join up or be conscripted. It's that other business that gets me. Your client was a stranger to him?"

"Yes," I said. "There's no harm in admitting that much."

"And yet Seeway talked to him about this Archie Dibben who was in Bassingford only a week, and in 1939! It just doesn't begin to make sense." Then his eyes popped a bit. "Wait a minute, though. Is your client by any chance a relative of Dibben?"

"Good lord, no!" I said. "He'd never heard the name before. Dibben's an incidental. My client wants to find Seeway. If he can't, then possibly it might be done through Dibben."

Then I thought of something else.

"Let's suppose Seeway joined up at the earliest moment—in September 1939. You tell me he left here at the end of March. He must have spent those five months somewhere, so why shouldn't he have run up against Dibben again? Why shouldn't he have hooked himself on to that touring company? Did he have any leanings towards the stage?"

"None whatever. He was supposed to be looking around for the right sort of job, and the longer he was finding it, the better he'd have been pleased. He had the most high-faluting ideas."

"There wasn't a woman in the case, by any chance? I mean, to account partially for that sudden breaking with his aunt and Bassingford?"

"No," he said. "The only girl he was what I'd call friendly with was a Rosamund Vorne. I'll tell you that quite frankly because you might hear it in the town and put a wrong construction on it. It was purely platonic, believe me, I ought to know. I married her myself and she was as mystified as I was about his cutting himself off."

"That sounds pretty final," I said. "What sort of a chap was he to look at, by the way?"

"Dave Seeway? Well, tallish and thickly built. Good-looking in a rather peevish sort of way. Supercilious sort of chap, if you know what I mean. Very pleased with himself always."

I got to my feet and began thanking him for letting me take up so much of his time.

"My dear fellow, I ought to thank you." He shook a wry head. "It's been an astounding evening. But tell me one thing. Just what do you propose to do now?"

I saw no harm in telling him. What I proposed was to find out through the War Office if and when and where Seeway was demobilised. That would mean he was alive at that particular time, and I'd pick up the trail from there. I'd also begin looking for Dibben. Theatrical agencies might help me there, and advertisements.

"Obviously you know your job," he told me. "But any chance of keeping me advised?"

"I'd like to," I said. "You're anxious to see Seeway?"

He gave a little grunt.

"Well, I wouldn't say anxious. I suppose I'm his only relative and the war may have done him good."

I thanked him again and said I'd do what I could, but even if we found Seeway we couldn't do more than casually bring in Proden's name and then the rest would be up to Seeway. I thought it was something we might reasonably leave till the occasion definitely arose. I added that Proden had addresses and telephone numbers, and I'd be grateful if he'd let me or the office know if anything further came back to him that might be any sort of clue.

I had to go back to the White Hart, and as I was driving there I was thinking a whole lot of things. I had to revise, for instance, my ideas about Proden. What I had taken for uneasiness when I had first talked with him over the telephone had been merely bewilderment, but two things had arisen during that hour and more I had spent at his house. Firstly, in spite of his pretence of a slow remembering, he had known the identity of Archie Dibben as soon as I'd mentioned his name. If ever I was sure of anything, I was sure of that.

The other thing was that his description of Dibben differed in most ways from that given by Finney. Finney remembered a shortish, pot-bellied man: Proden a man of medium height and not at all fat. But Finney might have been recalling the man he saw on the stage—a man with a couple of cushions under his belt to give a comic air of obesity, and that very obesity would have made him seem shorter than he actually was. After all, an actor needn't be fat to play Falstaff, and Falstaff always looks on the stage a much shorter man than a tape measure would make him.

I was, in fact, inclined to favour Proden's description of Dibben, even at this distance of twelve years. Proden was a shrewd observer and a good judge of men. If his voice over the telephone had told me the kind of man he was, then my voice had given him the same information. We had taken each other for what I'd call members of the same social stratum, and that was why—without even seeing me—he had ordered coffee to be brought in as soon as I arrived. I didn't tell myself, mind you, that I liked Proden. To like a man, even at first sight, you have to have some sympathy in interests, and to move in the same social orbit is far from enough. His interests, as I judged, were a long way from my own, but he was a man whom I could at least respect. Sahibs have the knack of giving me, unreasonably perhaps, a certain private amusement, but Proden wasn't a man with an Asian complex. Neither India nor Ceylon was mentioned except in one strictly necessary context.

It was lucky that I went back to the White Hart, for a message was there from Finney, asking me to see him, that night if possible, at his house in River Terrace. I rang my wife to say I might be very late.

It wasn't quite dusk, and as I drove slowly along the road looking for Finney's number, I heard someone calling, and there he was at the door, on the look-out for me. I got inside quickly, for I didn't want him to bellow whatever news it was to the street. He showed me into the front parlour, and a tall, broad, beefy man got up from the chair.

"Here we are, sir," Finney told me, and waved a hand at the other man. "This is Sergeant Coll."

"Ex-Sergeant Coll," he said, and was smiling a bit sheepishly as he held out a huge, moist hand.

Ex-sergeant or not, I didn't like the sound of things. There seemed something a bit ominous in that presence of the local police. But old Finney was taking charge.

"This David Seeway you was anxious to find out about," he was telling me. "Well, sir, I found it. Not in the files, but Albert here, he remembered. You tell Mr. Travers all about it, Albert."

What I heard was this, and I had to pretend that the whole thing came as a complete surprise to me. I have to expand Coll's story slightly since it's necessary to reinforce some of the things I'd heard from Proden.

Coll had been promoted at the tail-end of his career and during the war. In 1939 he was a constable, and it was as such that he knew something about David Seeway, since he was called in by the landlord of the White Hart in connection with the fracas that Proden had mentioned. Seeway had been something of a nuisance before, and he was a difficult man to handle both physically and what I might call imponderably, for not only was he something of a light-heavyweight boxer but his aunt could pull innumerable strings in the town.

The trouble was that Seeway couldn't carry his liquor. Some people, as Coll ponderously assured me, get maudlin in their cups, or just morose, but Seeway got argumentative and that night in the saloon bar of the White Hart he had struck one of the men with whom he had been heatedly arguing, and had knocked him out, and there had followed something of a free-for-all. No case was made of it because Proden pulled various strings. I wanted to know what strings.

"Well, sir, the aunt was a big property owner in the town," Coll said, "and Mr. Proden—what came into her property when she died—sort of got at the higher-ups, if you know what I mean. And I believe he made Mr. Seeway apologise to the man he'd knocked out. I wasn't supposed to know all that, sir, but I did know. Then it wasn't long after that that Mr. Seeway left the town."

"What was the trouble with Seeway before? The same sort of thing?"

Coll said it was. And there'd been trouble about the way he drove that car of his—a fast little sports two-seater. He'd practically got to blows with a constable who pulled him up one night, but the constable knew of the Ladely influence in the town and didn't make a case of it.

"I was under the impression," I said, "that the aunt was a straight-laced sort of woman."

"So she was," Coll said. "All the same, sir, you have to be careful. You never know how people are going to take things. And she was supposed to be very fond of this Seeway. Practically brought him up, as they say."

"And he had a good friend in Mr. Proden?"

"He did that, sir. Mr. Proden's been a good friend to a lot of people in this town."

"He's a good fellow, is he?"

"Mr. Proden's a gentleman," Coll told me emphatically. "I worked with him a lot on Civil Defence during the war, and I ought to know. Real class is Mr. Proden, and one of the nicest gentlemen you'd want to meet."

"Isn't he divorced from his wife, by the way?"

"Oh, that," Coll said, and just a bit apologetically. "Some reckoned she was carrying on with someone else and some reckoned the same about him, though I must say that if Mr. Proden do any carrying-on—as they say—it ain't in Bassingford, not to my knowledge."

We talked on for a bit and Finney joined in, but there was nothing new to elicit. It was Finney who went with me to the door, and I knew why. Two more notes changed hands, and he promised to let me know at once if anything fresh turned up about either Seeway or Dibben. I got into my car feeling a rather tired man.

It was a beautifully clear night and even before I reached the suburbs I drove quite slowly, and because I wanted to think. On the whole I had every reason to be satisfied. I had at least localised both Seeway and Dibben as in Bassingford in 1939, and that seemed to clear away certain uneasinesses that I'd had about our client Clandon. The only remaining mystery was just why Dibben had been brought in at all, and about that I was proposing to get into touch with Clandon to see if I could stir his memory into shedding a little more light.

Of Seeway I had a fairly clear picture. I knew at least *how* he had left Bassingford—in that car of his, and I could see him after that interview with his aunt pettishly going to his room and packing his bags and throwing them into the car and shaking the dust of Bassingford from his feet. But that, I then knew, was just a bit picturesque and far too sudden. He had had to get that money of his from the bank, and three thousand pounds isn't the kind of sum you can draw out at a second's notice from a country bank. But the main picture was right for that.

I cross-checked Coll's story with Proden's and found never a flaw and, as I said, I'd every right to be pleased. And yet out of those very optimisms there came a slight depression. In a way I was back where I'd started from that morning. I was better off, and worse off. Now I knew an enormous deal more about two men, but those same two men had both vanished into thin air. Maybe both were dead. In any case I no longer had a haystack. I might know more about the couple of needles, but heaven knew where I was going to find the right haystacks.

But by the time I was back in the flat I had the next day's work mapped out. Bernice was in bed and apparently asleep, so I jotted down a time-table and made some urgent notes for Norris. By then I was feeling pretty tired, so I set the alarm clock for six-thirty and got into bed myself, and almost as soon as my head hit the pillow I was asleep, and I didn't remember stirring till the whirr of the bell woke me up.

Ours is a service flat—I'm lucky enough to have inherited the whole block—but we rarely trouble the restaurant for the first meal, but make a continental breakfast for ourselves instead. At eight o'clock I was ringing Clandon. You know how it is. You ring someone at some unearthly hour and you tell yourself there can't possibly be any answer. But there was. Clandon's voice came after a minute or so. I said I'd reserve my news till I saw him, and he said he'd have a quick meal himself and be free at a quarter to nine.

I got out my car and drove round to the office and left those urgent jobs I'd written down for Norris. I was dead on time when I got to Marlow Mansions. They were what I'd call a quiet, somewhat stolid block of flats. Clandon's was one of the smaller ones, but quite large enough for a bachelor. The room we talked in—lounge is the term nowadays—was somewhat crowded with books, but it was a man's room with the smell of good tobacco. I don't know why, but I was surprised to see him smoking a pipe.

I was interested, too, to have another sight of him, and in his own neck of the London woods, and I still liked the look of him. There are men with whom you soon feel at home, and Clandon was definitely one of them. A bit on the diffident side, perhaps, and that's a good fault, if fault you can call it. And arising dimly out of all that, I did a curious thing. Before I said a word about what I'd discovered, I zipped a question at him. I did it in a kind of humorous way, and hoped the answer would finally clear whatever doubts I'd had in my mind.

"Well, we're getting on," I said. "But I still can't for the life of me understand why you didn't nip along to Bassingford yourself and learn as much as I've done."

His quick look was mild and apologetic.

"Far too busy," he told me, and offered me his tobacco pouch. "Up to the eyes at the office and—see that pile of manuscripts? That's my chief headache when I get back here of an afternoon. Evening, I should say. I'm still a good three months behind, and infuriated authors keep writing in, and you can guess how it is. That's why I didn't want even you to ring me except at about this time."

He held a match for me when I'd stoked my pipe.

"I gather that you've already had a bit of luck."

I told him what I knew, and he seemed extraordinarily pleased. But he was perplexed about Seeway. At the hospital he hadn't struck him as the kind of man that Coll and Proden had characterised.

"But I wasn't in a fit state to sum anybody up," he said. "Also my mind has since become what I might call clouded with gratitude."

"That reminds me," I said, and I put up to him once more that question of the actor, Dibben. I said that in the light of what we both now knew, wasn't it fantastic that to what one might call a complete stranger—rescuing a man in the dark didn't make him a friend, even if it gave a warm interest—Seeway should mention a man whom he himself apparently had known, and then far from well, for a maximum of only a single week.

"I see that," he said, "and I still can't help you. I can't remember Seeway mentioning Dibben at all. All I know is this, and it still occasionally comes back to me, that after Seeway had gone I got this mad sort of stuff running through my brain. Like the wheels of a train, as I told you—clickety-click, clickety-click, clickety-click, only it wasn't clickety-click, it was Archie Dibben, Archie Dibben, Archie Dibben, over and over again, hour in and hour out. When I came to think about it afterwards, I could only ascribe it to something Seeway had said."

Then he was staring.

"Good lord! I've just realised something. I was right! It must have been something Seeway said! You found that Dibben *had* been in Bassingford. And Seeway did know him."

"I know," I said. "That makes it only the more puzzling. No use harping on it, but why the devil should Seeway think you'd be interested in a man named Dibben? There are no Dibbens even remotely in your family?"

"Never a one." He frowned as he gave a look at his cold pipe. "There's only one thing I can suggest and that's pretty futile. I was a kind of stranger, as you said, and Seeway was trying to make conversation, and I must have been pretty unresponsive, and the sister was hovering round, and so on. Under those circumstances he'd be mighty glad to talk about anything that came into his mind. I know," he went quickly on. "You don't think that's very satisfactory, and neither do I. But there it is."

He asked what I proposed to do next, and I thought it just as well to keep something up my sleeve, so I merely mentioned that War Office approach in the matter of Seeway.

"And what about Dibben?"

"But it's Seeway you want us to find," I pointed out. "He's the important one. Naturally if the War Office can give us nothing, then we might have to fall back on Dibben."

"I don't know," he said. "Mind you, I'm not suggesting anything or interfering with your ideas. As I told you, I think it a damn-fool policy to keep a dog and bark yourself. But this Dibben business has got me intrigued. I'm just the opposite from you. Mysteries are your bread and butter. I hate 'em. Give me a mystery and I'm miserable till I've solved it." He smiled as he waved a hand at that stack of manuscripts. "No detective novels among that lot. If one falls to my share, it's read by me and back to the author or accepted in double quick time."

I said he was a man after my own heart. A mystery gnawed at me, too, and I was going to be a highly intrigued and restless man till I knew all about that Dibben business. I added that, unless Dibben was dead, it ought to be a reasonably easy job to find him. The stage is clannish. Old troupers still hang, so to speak, around the stage doors.

That seemed to please him and he was asking if there'd be anything extra to pay. I assured him there wouldn't be—at the moment—and that was virtually that. He went down with me to my car and then I went back to the Agency. I hoped that Norris had fixed that appointment with Tom Holberg at the Shaftesbury Avenue office.

CHAPTER FOUR
CURIOUSER AND CURIOUSER

I SUPPOSE Tom Holberg's is easily the best-known theatrical agency in town. My only doubt was that his clientèle might be composed of so many top-notchers that his memory wouldn't have room for a touring company, and as far back as 1939. But I wasn't too dubious. I'd known him for well over twenty years and had never ceased to be surprised at the range of his knowledge. And he'd never take any payment for my use of his time.

I'd once done him a favour which he'd chosen to think much bigger than it was.

I was dead on time and was shown straight into his office. We shook hands and asked after each other's health and said it was quite a time since we'd met, and then I got down to business. He's a quiet-spoken chap; never ruffled and always making one feel that there's plenty of time. Under that bald dome of his he's probably got enough secrets to set Shaftesbury Avenue buzzing like an overturned bee-skep if ever he wrote an honest-to-God book of reminiscences. But he and I trust each other, and that's the main thing. I've told Tom with never a qualm things that might have landed me deep in a libel action.

As soon as I mentioned Archie Dibben, he was cocking an ear.

"You know him?" I asked.

"In a way—yes," he said. "As a matter of fact, I handled him when he first came south."

He explained. Dibben had been one of those comedians who abound in the northern circuits: just the usual middle- or end-of-the-bill kind of comic. Then, in his forties, he struck lucky in a straight comedy part. That got him a London part and he did well in a musical hotch-potch called *Over the Moon*.

"It went to his head," Tom said. "He never was a very nice piece of work, and there was a very ugly scandal to do with a couple of chorus girls. Nothing ever got out, but everybody dropped him like a hot potato. From what you tell me, he must have edged his way back into that touring company. That'd have been two or three years later when things had died down."

I wanted to know what he was like in himself.

"A shortish chap. A bit on the meaty side. His face was his best asset. And he could put on quite a Vere de Vere voice as well as his Lancashire one. He used it with me when I first saw him here."

I said it fitted in with what I'd learned—that he could give an impression of being a man of some breeding and schooling. But what I wanted to know was if he was still in the business. Tom was dead sure he wasn't. He rang Barney French and Barney told him he hadn't heard a word of Archie Dibben for years.

"Right," I said. "What I've got to do, then, is to get back to 1939. I'd like to know the itinerary of that touring company: where, in fact, it went after it left Bassingford."

Tom said that shouldn't be too difficult.

"And I'd like to know, not so much who were in that company as the names of any members who're still in the business and where I could get hold of them."

"You think they could give you news of him?"

"I wasn't thinking of that," I said. "But something mighty peculiar happened when that company was at Bassingford, or so I'm beginning to think."

I told him all of the story that wasn't too confidential, and he found the whole thing as much of a mystery as Clandon and I had done.

"If you find anyone who was with Dibben at Bassingford, you think you might get a line on what it was that happened," he said. "You're in a hurry?"

I said I wasn't, though I'd like the information pretty soon, if only for the sake of the client's pocket.

"I doubt if I could get it before tonight," he told me, and I said that'd be fine. I'd expected him to mention two or three days.

When I'm working on a job I like to keep moving, and I'd hate being involved in a couple of cases at once. But the War Office always takes its time and that was why I wanted to keep busy over the Dibben side. It's true that I had something of a pull at the War Office, but that merely meant that it might take us a week to find out what anyone else might hope for in anything up to three months.

But Tom Holberg did ring me that evening.

"I haven't got quite what you want," he told me, "But I think it'll do. I've contacted a Walter Widgeon for you. He's living at 10 Hatton Road, Enfield, and he'll see you any time in the morning between nine and eleven. He was the butler in that *Under My Thumb* company, so you can get the itinerary from him."

*

I was at Enfield the next morning at half-past nine. I ought to have guessed that Widgeon would not be very young, but I didn't expect to find a man well into the seventies. The little semi-detached house was scrupulously clean, and he told me he'd looked entirely after himself since his wife had died. He seemed the quiet, saving sort, or maybe he'd come into money.

"I remember Bassingford well," he told me. "Not a bad little town—as they go."

"Then there's no need to ask you if you remember Archie Dibben."

"No," he said, and just a bit quietly. "You a friend of his?"

"Never heard of him till a day or two ago," I said. "He's just someone with whom I want to get into touch on behalf of a client."

"Then I can't help you. I never clapped eyes on him or heard of him after that tour."

I said that didn't assume that he couldn't help me. Would he mind telling me, in the strictest confidence, just the sort of man that Dibben was.

It was a pity in a way that he was such a decent soul, for otherwise he might have been far more frank. He hadn't liked Dibben, and that was as far as he'd go. I suggested that Dibben—as a one-time London star—had perhaps thrown his weight about, and he had to admit it, though, as he pointed out, there'd been few contacts except at rehearsals and on the actual stage. Dibben was the star of that show. He'd stayed at an hotel. Dibben could afford to hobnob with the regulars in the saloon bar of the White Hart.

"Just the sort of thing I want to know. For instance, who was the manager of the Theatre Royal at the time? I know it was owned by a Miss Hilda Ladely, but who was the manager?"

He couldn't remember. Then I described Proden and mentioned his name, and he was almost certain that Proden had been acting as manager. I described David Seeway, but he'd never heard the name. And so to the jack-pot question.

"I'd like you to take your time and think it over very carefully, Mr. Widgeon, but did anything happen at Bassingford that struck you at the time as peculiar?"

He could think of nothing.

"Then look at it this way," I said. "Did Dibben himself change in any way after you left Bassingford? Did he behave any differently from what he'd done before?"

As far as he'd remembered there'd been no change at all.

"Then will you tell me where you went after you left Bassingford?"

There was no hesitation about that. From Bassingford the company went to Colchester, then Ipswich, Norwich, King's Lynn and finally Cambridge.

"Now a rather peculiar question," I said. "I mentioned a David Seeway of Bassingford, a nephew of the Miss Ladely who owned the Theatre Royal. There wasn't a possibility that he might have joined your company under another name after you left Bassingford? Say if somebody went sick or dropped out?"

Nothing of the sort had happened. But it gave him an idea. He was so diffident about it that I had to urge him to tell me what it was.

I'm not up in theatrical jargon, but what happened was this. It was at Cambridge and in the middle of the rehearsal a man came bold as brass—Widgeon's own words—on to the stage and called to Dibben. Dibben wasn't at all annoyed: he just asked him to wait a minute, and the man stood in the wings smoking a cigarette and, as soon as a break was called, Dibben went out with him. And he was a quarter of an hour late in getting back.

That was all that Widgeon remembered, except that Dibben had called him Fred and that Fred had looked a bit excited. But Fred definitely wasn't Seeway; he was a youngish man—about thirty-five, Widgeon thought—and with a Cockney perkishness about him.

"He couldn't have been Dibben's son?"

He'd never heard of Dibben having a son. It was common knowledge that Dibben had been divorced, but as far as he knew there'd been no children. And the Fred bore no resemblance to him. He looked—so Widgeon remembered, and just a bit libel-lously—like a go-ahead commercial traveller or insurance agent.

"You never saw Fred again?"

He'd never seen or heard of him again. 1939 was none too good a year for business, and the tour, which should have included Lincolnshire, had been cut short. When it ended at Cambridge Widgeon saw the last of Dibben, nor could he remember hearing of him again, which was almost as good as saying that he must have completely dropped out of the busi-ness. Widgeon himself had worked for ENSA, but still had never heard of Dibben. Then he had dropped out, too, and had gone into a munitions factory and made some good money.

"What sort of a man was Dibben to look at?"

"Well," he said, "sort of shortish and fattish. Quite a fat face; purplish and mottled far as I remember. I know he used to lift his elbow a good deal."

"Easy to get on with?"

"If you didn't cross him. Quite the gentleman when he wanted. And a good mimic. I saw him once get himself up as one of those retired Indian colonels, and he did it to the life." Then he frowned. "Now I come to think of it, I believe that was one of his original music-hall turns. Pretty good at character studies, so I was told."

That seemed to be all I could elicit from Widgeon, and he wouldn't let me pay him a cent, and that made it harder work giving him addresses and telephone numbers and asking him to let me have any remembered thing that he might judge import-ant. And then, just as I was getting into the car, he did remember something.

"I don't know that it's important," he said, "but you were asking me if anything happened to him after we left Bassing-ford, and I just thought of something that did happen. He wasn't with us at Colchester at all. I think his mother was very ill and died early in the week. I wouldn't be sure, but I think it was his mother."

He'd rejoined the company at Ipswich, Widgeon said. The understudy wasn't too good and neither was the Colchester business, and everyone was relieved when things were normal again. Perhaps he saw by my face that that bereavement news wasn't of much use, but I told him not to apologise. I'd be glad to hear anything, no matter how apparently insignificant.

An unusual, likeable sort of soul, I thought him, and as far from a theatrical type as you'd be likely to meet. And though my hour with him had yielded little that was positive, it had at least revived one particular doubt—the truthfulness of Proden's description of Dibben. For Widgeon's description was much the same as Finney's, and that made Proden's wrong. And yet I didn't know. Twelve years were a long gulf across which to look back and claim a certitude. At the moment I couldn't bring myself to believe that Proden had been deliberately deceiving me, since nothing else of what he had told me had proved to be other than implicitly true.

I had coffee at a restaurant and over it I suddenly decided to go on to Bassingford instead of back to town, and in most ways it was merely a resolution of despair. When that *Under My Thumb* tour ended at Cambridge, Dibben seemed to have vanished into thin air. He couldn't have been killed—utterly disintegrated shall I say—by a bomb, for the bombs didn't begin falling till a year later. And, if one could imagine him doing such a thing, he hadn't gone into a munitions factory, for the rearming of Britain hadn't begun. And yet he had had to live; and the heavy drinker at whom Widgeon had hinted would need a deal of money. And I took him for the sort of person whose whole life was the theatre. Unless he had come in for money, I didn't see his finding another means of livelihood.

As I drove towards Bassingford I was trying to make something out of that mysterious Fred, but it was all too vague and remote, and capable of far too many explanations. Fred might have been anything from a distant relation to a bookmaker's runner. And even if he were some tiny factor in the Dibben-Seeway mystery, I had, after twelve long years, no means by which I could trace him. In fact, at that moment I felt the Dibben affair to be so hopeless that I knew myself a fool for not having gone back to town.

I didn't park my car in the Square or go to the White Hart, for I didn't want to run into Proden. What I did was to ask at the *Gazette* office for Finney, only to be told that I'd probably find him at home. I found him in a workshop in his back garden, where he was doing some fretwork. A queer hobby, but it takes all sorts to make a world. He wanted to go to the house, but I told him not to worry, and I found myself a seat on an upturned box with a sack for cushion.

What I wanted was a list of the employees of the old Theatre Royal, and at once he found it a tough bit of remembering. What we finally arrived at was just one single person who was still in the town—the cashier, now married and with a young family. She was a Mrs. Gaul, and living in one of the bungalows beyond the bridge, which was as near as he could get. He said it was a pity I hadn't come earlier. Jim Barnes, the former commission-aire and handyman, had died just before Easter, and he'd spent his whole life at the Royal.

I found the bungalow, and the woman who came to the door was Mrs. Gaul. She looked about forty, and she told me her youngest child was just of school age. But she didn't seem too happy about me. I think she still thought there was some-thing I wanted to sell. But once we got really back to the old Theatre Royal and she'd remembered Archie Dibben we were just a couple of old friends. And her description of Dibben, by the way, was that of Finney and Widgeon. I said I'd heard him called pot-bellied, and she said that that was just what he was. That and his face got him a lot of laughs.

Of David Seeway she remembered practically nothing, and there was quite a bit of thinking before she was sure that Proden was acting as manager. A Mr. Luke, who'd held the job for years, had had a stroke, and, in fact, he never came back to the theatre. About Proden she was almost enthusiastic and her character sketch varied little from that of Sergeant Coll. One thing did seem to puzzle her, that one so obviously a gentleman should have taken over the job and done it so well.

"But there," she said, "everyone got on well with Mr. Proden. You couldn't help it; he had such a nice way with him. Spoke to you as if you were a lady. And the same with everyone."

And so at last to the one important question. Had anything happened, say at the end of the *Under My Thumb* week, that had struck her at the time as in any way unusual? She found it a strange question and it seemed to be bothering her, and I had to put it in different ways and from different angles. All she could finally remember was something that might or might not have been trivial. I took considerable pains to see it against the right background.

There had been a well-attended matinée on that Saturday, and after it May Pollinger, as she then was, had Proden's O.K. as regards the takings. The evening show came on as usual. There were three acts, and at the end of the second takings were made up and Jim Barnes, the commissionaire, took them to the manager's office. The general manager—if that's his title—of *Under My Thumb* would be there, and as soon as May received the O.K., as she called it, she was free to go home. On the Monday Jim Barnes told her of the unusual happening.

The theatre was cleared and everything finished with at about half-past ten on the average night. Jim would be the last to go, except perhaps the manager, and he always went up to the manager's office, got his all-clear, and then went home. As a very old employee he had got into a certain groove. He gave a quick tap at the door, stuck his head inside, and asked formally if everything was all right, but that Saturday night when he tapped at the door the door was locked. But he had heard voices and knew therefore that Proden was there. The voices had hushed at his tap, and he tapped again. Proden came to the door, but he didn't unlock it. He simply told Jim he could go.

"And what did Jim think had happened?"

"Well," she said, and flushed slightly, "I wouldn't have this mentioned for the world—"

I assured her that everything she said was entirely between me and her.

"Well, what we thought was that they had some of the girls up there and were having a bit of a lark."

"That was unusual?"

"Oh yes," she said. "Nothing like that ever happened with Mr. Luke."

"Did Barnes actually hear women's voices?"

"I can't say he did," she said, "but of course they'd be quiet when they heard him on the landing."

"There were always drinks in the office?"

"Oh yes," she said. "There was a cupboard there that Mr. Proden used to keep specially for drinks."

I left it at that and because I saw no point in a further exploration. I did ask if any of her contemporaries at the Theatre Royal were still in the town, but she couldn't think of a single one. Everything had been radically altered when the change-over was made to a cinema—and there'd been the war.

So that again was that. I got into my car and drove back to a side street and had lunch at a little restaurant, and I was feeling like Touchstone when he got to Arden. *Now am I in Arden, and the more fool I. When I was at home I was in a better place.* For what could I do? Who was there to question? And if by a miracle I found someone, what was there to remember? March of 1939 and June of 1951, and between those dates the war of all wars, and the frustrations and bewilderments of peace. Against the epochal, Dibben was less than the trivial. But not to me.

To me he was an assignment, and a client, and the reputation of the Agency, and yet what was there that I could do? Switch back to Seeway and take Dibben as a kind of flanking movement? But I couldn't get to grips with Seeway till I'd heard from the army authorities. Or was that sheer pessimism? Wasn't there something I could do? Try to trace his movements after he left Bassingford and before he joined the army? It might be done through that car of his, and yet I doubted it. Most likely he had sold it when he joined up, but twelve years was far too long and the dealers far too many, and to hunt old files for an advertisement of sale was more than a hopeless prospect.

So I did the sensible thing and drove straight back to town. Later on I was to know, and rather too late, that what I'd done was indeed the sensible thing—and for a queer and paradoxical reason: that, in fact, I'd learned all there was to learn and all that was needed. But that's what I might call both the endless hope and the ever-present exasperation of my sort of game. You see the trivial and think it important, and you listen to the important and shrug your shoulders at the waste of time. You see detached happenings and at the moment there's no flux of logic to make them a whole. All you can do is trust to a good memory, and keep on thinking back, and try to re-appraise, or hope that something may happen to make a first sequence, or bring into focus the blurred and dim.

So for a day or two I left the Seeway-Dibben case at the back of my mind, and I fobbed Clandon off by saying we had a slight lead which might take a deal of following. And then at last we got that information from the army authorities. And if I'd been flummoxed before, it was nothing to how I felt when I read what was on that official document.

I saw Clandon early the next morning, and I never saw a man so staggered.

"But it's fantastic!" he said.

"Maybe," I told him, "but there it is. No David Seeway ever was in Sicily. No David Seeway, spelt with *ee*, was demobilised. There was one spelt with *ea*, but he was a gunner of forty-five. And there wasn't a David Seeway casualty."

"But it's ridiculous!" he said. "I'd lay every penny I have in the world that I heard his name as clearly as I hear your voice now. And not only that. When I was off the danger list, I remember the sister telling me I ought to be grateful to that Mr. Seeway."

"That settles one thing," I said ruefully. "I was half minded to put up to you that you'd imagined the name. Now I can think of something better. I told you that Seeway left Bassingford in a kind of huff. Maybe he enlisted under a different name. He'd cut himself off completely from his relations, mind you. And a question arises there. He looked a decent sort of chap?"

"One of the best."

"A man of breeding, if I may put it that way?"

"Most decidedly."

"Then here's a possible answer," I said. "He was in the same hospital with a minor wound or wounds, and when he was discharged he thought he'd like to look you up. But he was the sort who'd hate to be embarrassed by thanks, so he didn't tell you his army name. He told you the one that first came into his mind—his real name."

"Yes," he said slowly. "It's a good idea. The only one that would fit the case. Even the sister would accept the name. It was a big place and he'd have come from another ward."

"Let's say we accept it," I said. "Then where do we go from there?"

He shrugged his shoulders. He gave me a look of almost furtive amusement.

"Aren't you doing the barking?"

I had to smile, but I had my come-back.

"Most decidedly, if you're prepared to go on paying."

"Don't worry about that," he told me. "Spend what's necessary." He gave a little frown. "This business is beginning to get me. It began with repentance, so to speak, and now it's a kind of Old Man of the Sea. Like being told a riddle, and the chap who asks it dies or something before you've had the answer."

"That's how I'm beginning to feel myself," I said. "I don't mind telling you that if you'd called us off, I might have gone on probing on my own. It *is* a riddle, as you say. Why should Seeway, who'd just given you what was virtually a false name, have mentioned this Archie Dibben? It's bad business to tell you so, but it's beginning to worry me a bit, too. Usually I can find a reason for most things, but I'm damned if I can even begin to find a reason for this."

"Well, go on probing," he told me. "After all, we're both in the same boat."

So there we were. The fact that Clandon was an excellent client whom I liked better every time I saw him was not necessarily a help. Failure always has to be envisaged, and I didn't like the thought that he and I might go to our graves without an explanation of that Dibben-Seeway business—and after we'd taken his money. Then out of that new and none too needful pessimism I did get an idea. There was one person connected years ago with Seeway whom I might profitably see—the Rosamund Vorne with whom he had been friendly, and who had later married Proden.

The first thing to do would be to discover her present where-abouts, and, if possible, without a direct approach to Proden, and it was while I was thinking about that in the early evening that the telephone rang. It was Tom Holberg.

"Sorry to disturb your leisure," he said, "but I've been making various surreptitious enquiries into that business you were in about the other day. I've got the most extraordinary lead for you."

"Just what I'm needing," I told him.

"You know Monty Orville?"

"Of him, of course, but I can't say I know him."

"Well, I've told him you'll probably be getting into touch with him. He's on at the Majestic, by the way. He'd probably see you after the show. He knows everything will be confidential, but I'd like to hear what happens."

I said I'd certainly let him know. And at once I looked up the Majestic. Monty Orville was co-starred in a farce called *Chins Down*, and the show looked as if it might be over in the neigh-bourhood of ten o'clock.

Chapter Five
WITH HIS BOOTS ON

ON THE stage Monty Orville looked about thirty-five. In his dressing-room with the grease-paint just removed, he looked his fifty. He'd asked me to have a drink, and I hadn't seen why I shouldn't.

"You're a friend of Tom Holberg's, I take it," was how we got down to the point.

"Yes," I said. "And of pretty long standing. Your agent, is he?"

"Agent, extortioner—call it what you like," and he gave that wide-mouthed grin of his which the cartoonists always exaggerate. "You want to know about Archie Dibben—if he was Archie Dibben."

I said I certainly did. I thought it would do no harm to tell him a client of ours wanted urgently to get in touch with him. I added that his own name would on no account be mentioned.

"Don't worry about that, old boy," he told me. "But I knew Archie, of course. And, by the way, did Tom let on at all about that scandal Archie was involved in? I was in the same show with him when it happened. A pity, really. Not that he wasn't a nasty piece of work. But about this extraordinary business at Hurst Park."

He wasn't in any way a racing man, he said, but he did like an occasional day at the races, and a week or two back he'd arranged such a day with a stockbroker friend named Harwell. They went down in Harwell's car. Orville was what he called incognito.

"Didn't wear any war-paint, old boy. Don't like people spotting me and autograph hunters and all that. But we did ourselves quite well. Went in the enclosure and all that, and it was just after the second race—might have been the third, not that it matters—that I caught sight of this cove. A middle-aged chap with a beautiful middle-aged spread, and got up to the nines. Lovely binoculars and topper and the whole rig-out. I looked twice at him because he looked like a Frenchman—nice little white beard and so on—and there was a French horse or two going that day. Then I had another look and all at once I said to myself, 'Damned if that chap isn't the spitting image of Archie Dibben!' I hadn't seen Archie for fifteen years or so, but you know what I mean. Beards don't cut any ice with me. I've put too many on."

And then came a real coincidence. Orville pointed the man out to Harwell and Harwell said he'd seen him somewhere before. In a minute or two he remembered where. Harwell lived at Stapley Green, one of the more outlying and exclusive of the suburbs, and usually went to town by Tube, and the man whom Orville thought was Dibben also used the Tube from that same station, though not regularly. Harwell had seen him there from time to time, and the natural inference now was that he, like Harwell, lived at Stapley Green.

Orville had another good look. He sauntered past the man and quietly had an even better look, and he was dead sure the man was Dibben. And he simply had to do something about it. He contrived to meet the man head-on.

"Pardon me, but aren't you Archie Dibben?"

The man seemed taken aback. Then he drew himself up to his full five foot eight, and with an immense dignity.

"Sorry, sir, but I'm afraid not. My name's Marquis, sir. Colonel Marquis."

"But he was!" Orville told me. "I was dead sure he was. And I knew that plum-in-the-mouth, colonel-wallah accent. I gave him a grin. 'Come off it, Archie! You can't fool me.' And then damned if he didn't draw himself up again and tell me either to make myself scarce or he'd call the police. 'That's all right with me, Archie,' I told him. 'But don't be surprised if I'm seeing you again.' But I didn't see him again. I don't know what he did with himself, but when I got back to Frank Harwell, there wasn't a sign of him. Pretty fishy, don't you think?"

I said it certainly was.

"But why precisely were you so sure he was Archie Dibben?"

"Fifty reasons, old boy. I could know what he'd be like after fifteen years. Everything was there, only just nicely aged in the wood. And Archie had a mole, just above his right eye, and this chap had a mole. Pretty convincing—what?"

"Yes," I said. "Not only convincing but absolutely clinching. But you don't happen to know if Harwell has seen him again at Stapley Green Station?"

"I don't," he said, "but I can soon find out."

He told me to help myself to another drink while he telephoned. In a couple of minutes he had his number and his man.

"Hallo, Frank. Monty here. Sorry to rout you out at this ungodly hour, but you remember that cove we saw at Hurst Park? The one I swore was an old pal of mine? . . . You seen him since? . . . Oh, you have! . . ."

"There we are," he told me, with the famous grin. "He didn't probably see me with Harwell, if that's any help to you."

It wasn't, though I didn't tell him so. I said I was extraordinarily grateful to him and I thought there'd be no difficulty now in running Dibben to earth. If he really *were* Dibben. But my client would know as soon as I could contrive to let him set eyes on him.

"I hope he gets ten years."

"Nothing of that sort," I said. "Just a friendly meeting between a couple of people who haven't seen each other for ages."

He gave me a wink to indicate he'd taken that for so much eyewash. As we shook hands he was wanting to know if I could drop him a word if anything happened. I said that at least I'd let him know if our mutual friend definitely turned out to be Dibben.

So far, so more than good. As I waited for sleep that night—the time when I do all my really knotty thinking—I was wondering how I could induce Dibben to talk. That he almost certainly *was* Archie Dibben was no particular help, for it was no use running to earth a man who might draw himself up and talk about calling the police. If he were living at Stapley Green it was almost certainly under that other name, and as I lay there I was worrying my wits for a means of applying sufficient pressure to induce him to part with the information we needed. I could promise, of course, to respect his privacy. If that didn't help, I could hint that things could easily be made awkward, but that was a form of blackmail that went against the grain.

I woke in the morning and found the problem still unsolved. Then I thought I'd ring Clandon and see if he had any bright ideas, and, after what I'd have to tell him, I didn't see that he could very well accuse me of suggesting a bit of barking from himself.

"Promising news for you," I said, "and I thought you'd like to have it at once. I'm almost sure we can lay our hands on Dibben."

"My God, no!"

It was a curiously vehement reaction.

"Yes," I said. "But I ought to tell you that he's almost certainly going under another name, and he's grown a beard. Calls himself Colonel Marquis. Also I'm in possession of information"—a fine bit of jargon, that—"which tells me he'll indignantly deny that he's Dibben. He may even cut up rough about it. So where do we go from that? You got any ideas yourself?"

"No," he said slowly. "I don't think that I have. I couldn't identify him myself because I've never seen him. But what about that actor chap you were telling me about?"

"Widgeon?"

"That's the chap. Couldn't you scheme somehow for him to have a good look at him?"

I had to point out that that didn't help. The crux of the whole matter was that Dibben had probably been living at Stapley Green—I hadn't meant to let that slip out—ever since he'd disappeared twelve years ago. He would have an identity card and ration book and maybe a car registration book to prove he was the Colonel Marquis he was claiming to be, and whether he cut up rough or was merely blandly ignorant, we'd get never a word about Seeway. Or the minor mystery of why Seeway had mentioned his name that day in hospital.

"He's living in Stapley Green, you said?"

"So I'm guessing."

"Then you don't know the actual address?"

"Not yet," I said. "But I'm proposing to find it. Probably this afternoon."

It was quite a time before he spoke, and I even wondered if he'd gone off the line.

"Been trying to think," he said. "Everything had best be left to you. You scout round and get what you can. Perhaps you'll be so good as to let me know what's happened."

That was how we left it. I couldn't get out to Stapley Green till the afternoon. If there'd been an operative available I'd have had him do the spade-work, and then when I got out at the Tube station I was rather glad I was still doing everything myself. As it was, I wasn't wondering what to do when I simply knocked at a door and came face to face with Dibben. I had to find where Dibben actually lived, and I was optimistically telling myself that by the time I'd got as far as that I should probably have solved the problem of what I had to say.

It was 9th June, a fine, hot afternoon, and even the main shopping centre by the station was looking rather drowsy. Just by the exit on the left a newspaper seller lounged against the wall. I bought an *Evening Record*. I gave him his penny and there was still some silver in my hand.

"I'm trying to find the whereabouts of a man," I said. "I'm not sure about his name but this is what he looks like."

One eye was on me and the other on the silver.

"I know him, sir. Don't know his name, though. Usually goes to town about three times a week by the nine-thirty."

"You've no idea of his address?"

He had no idea. But he knew the way by which he approached the station or went home. As that was on foot, the house ought to be close.

"Did he go to town this morning?"

He didn't remember seeing him. I gave him a half-crown and took the side road that he'd pointed out. I was wondering if I might do better at the police station, and then I saw a postman. Another minute and I was telling him the tale.

"Ah, that'll be Colonel Marquis," he told me. "Straight on, sir; turn left facing the golf course, and it's just round the corner. A house called Redgates. Can't miss it."

Colonel Marquis. Now I was dead sure, I could say the name a couple of times, and I was feeling remarkably good. That colonel business was one of Dibben's old acts, and Widgeon had thought he had once had such a role in some play or other, or used it in one of his earlier music-hall turns. It was the sort of thing he'd know by heart. Maybe he'd have found himself a regiment and a record and had learned a lot of new patter, and when I knew that I wasn't feeling so uncommonly fine. For twelve years he'd played a part. He'd acquired an environment. What chance would I have of shaking him into an acknowledgment of anything resembling the bogus.

I was almost at the house. The road was Links Avenue, and facing it was the wide, undulating sweep of the golf course. I stood by the chestnut fencing and watched a couple of men approach a green. I watched them putt out and move on to a tee hidden behind a mass of gorse. I squinted round over my left shoulder and took a look at Redgates.

It was a smallish, detached house; built, I was thinking, between the wars. Trees and a narrow shrubbery screened it on each side from its neighbours. Its front lawn was well kept and a wide crazy-paving path led from its gates to the front, porched door. At the far side twin gates led to a garage, brick-built and matching the modified Tudor of the house. A long bed of what looked like antirrhinums made gay colouring beneath the wide twin windows. Those windows were shut. It seemed an indication that no one was at home.

I heard the crack of a ball and turned back to the links. A four-ball was coming down the long fairway, and I watched for the next five minutes. I watched the four appear behind the gorse and move along the next fairway. The course was then clear, and I had a tentative idea. I crossed the road, walked a little way along it, and then turned back.

If the Colonel was out, maybe a maid or housekeeper would be in. If not, I could have a look at the back of the house. And if the Colonel did happen to be in, then I was visualising a scene. With my own cropped moustache and air of reasonable good health, I didn't look so antiquated that I couldn't have been in the war.

"Colonel Marquis?" I would say, and then add quickly that I was sorry to have troubled him; that I'd been staying with friends and had happened to hear his name mentioned, and as an old major of mine had been called Marquis, and had probably got a step up. I'd thought I'd look him up for a yarn about old times. But now I could see that I'd found the wrong man with the right name.

"Come in, my boy, in any case." That ought to be the right reaction as I'd worked things out. I might be offered tea or a *chota-peg*, and there'd be talk. And that was as far as I'd got, except that out of the talk I was hoping that something might reasonably emerge.

But it didn't work out that way. No one answered my ring at the front-door bell, so I went between house and garage to the back. Through the garage window I could see a smallish car that looked like an early war-time model. Then at the side, tradesmen's door, I saw something that made me pause. A bottle of milk was on the step, and a newspaper just protruded from the letter-box of that back door.

I rang that back door bell and I listened, and the house had the quietness of emptiness itself. I moved on to the back garden. There was another lawn and then a tall screen of hedge through an arch of which I could see a small kitchen garden and beyond it a miniature orchard. I went through, but there was never a sign of a gardener.

I came back and then I noticed the flower-pot set in the lawn, and I suddenly knew that the Colonel must have taken up golf and there was his putting-green. A flagged path ran along that back of the house and there were french windows from which one could step straight to the lawn. I moved along to the front again. I crossed the road to the fence. A woman was just putting and I waited till her ball just skimmed the hole and back went the flag.

"Excuse me," I called, "but do you happen to know if Colonel Marquis is on the course? I don't seem to find anybody at the house."

It was the elderly male partner who answered me. He didn't think the Colonel could be playing or he'd have seen him during the round. In the summer he usually played only of an evening.

A minute or two and I was at the house just beyond. A smartly dressed, youngish woman didn't know anything about the Colonel, but she hadn't heard his car go out, and usually, as she told me amusedly, it made a great deal of noise.

"Not a soul in at all," I said. "Isn't there a housekeeper or anything?"

"He's just lost his old housekeeper," she said, "but there's a new woman who comes in at about five."

"No gardener?"

"He shares a gardener," she said. "I expect this is one of the days he doesn't come."

It was a quarter to four, and if I wanted to see the woman who came in at five, then I had an hour to wait. So I walked back to the shopping centre and found a place for tea. At a quarter to five I was back, with one eye on the golf and the other on the house. It was on the stroke of five that the woman arrived.

She went in at the garage gates and I overtook her by the garage. She was a tall, thin woman; a cut above the ordinary type that just comes in for an hour or two's help.

"If you don't mind waiting at the front door, I'll let you in," she told me. "The Colonel ought to be in at any time now. Usually he's in long before this."

Then she caught sight of the milk bottle and newspaper.

"That's strange," she said. "Why, he hasn't even taken his paper in!"

I saw her put the Yale key in the lock, then went to the front door. In a minute she was letting me in. There was a hall with a cloakroom, and she showed me into a lounge on the right. I must have an honest face, for she had taken me entirely at my own word.

"The Colonel must have been away early this morning," I said.

"Yes," she said. "That must have been it. But he didn't say a word about it last night."

"You come in of evenings only?"

"Every other morning, and every evening," she said. "Just see to his evening meal and wash-up and then go. I'm glad to do it since my husband died."

If I looked out of the window, she said, I'd see the Colonel when he came in. Then she left me to myself and I let my eyes wander round the room. It was what I'd call sumptuously furnished. The chair-chesterfield suite was large and superbly sprung. The radio-television-gramophone cabinet looked the latest thing. A cocktail cabinet was a miniature bar; the carpet was deep-piled; and in the air was the faint scent of expensive cigars. The one blemish were the prints on the walls: they looked as if they'd been bought as a job lot. Money—that was what the room told me: money and very mixed taste.

And then I heard the shriek. I was at the door in a flash and there was that housekeeper just coming into the hall. She was blundering in, uncertain of her steps, and her hand was at her mouth, and her eyes were screwed up in horror.

"Dead!" she said, and was trying to point back. "He's dead!"

Then she began to cry. I went on through the open door. I caught a glimpse of the kitchen and made for another open door on my left. The room was a kind of office and its french windows were those that opened on the back lawn. I saw that, and no more, for I couldn't miss what lay towards those windows on the grey carpet just beyond the desk.

I went carefully forward and got down on one knee. Colonel Marquis, as he called himself, was deader than mutton, and he'd died with his boots on. Embedded in the fat of his neck was something green that looked like picture cord. I raised his head and on the back was a contusion that had just drawn blood.

I left him there and went back to the hall. The woman was peering my way and she drew back as I came in.

"He's dead. . . . Really dead?"

"Yes," I said. "But you—you're feeling all right?"

"I'm all right now," she said. "It was the shock of it—that's all."

"You stay here," I told her. "Or get yourself some brandy from in there. I'll have to call the police."

"The police?"

"Always have to when there's a sudden death. You sit down in there. I'll be back in a minute."

It was when I was just at that office door that the telephone went, and in the quietness of that house and a dead man on the floor it was like that knocking on the gate in *Macbeth*. I gingerly used my handkerchief as a glove and gently lifted the receiver.

"That you, boss?" a man's voice said, and it seemed to have an urgency.

I didn't actually speak. That was a lesson I'd once learned the hard way.

"Uh-huh."

"Been trying to get you all day, boss. Everything's all right. He'll pay."

I could do nothing but grunt again—and hope.

"Be all right if I slip along about eight?"

I grunted again, listened for just a moment and then hung up. If the speaker had taken me for Marquis, then I'd had an extraordinary piece of luck. Then I was trying to remember the voice—brisk, slightly cockney, a bit excited, perhaps, and a bit gratified. The voice of a man of forty or fifty. A debt-collector, maybe. Someone had decided to pay, and at eight o'clock he was coming to give a detailed report. If I hadn't scared him off.

Then it was as if I noticed the telephone again. I picked up the receiver and dialled 999.

A couple of minutes and I was back in that lounge. The woman was sitting rigidly upright on the edge of one of the chairs, and she was looking pretty pale.

"You'd better have some brandy," I said. "You've had a nasty shock. The police'll be here at any time now, and they'll want to ask you some questions."

The cocktail cabinet wasn't locked but there wasn't any brandy. I looked in the neo-Sheraton sideboard and there was brandy there and other bottles besides. There were three or four boxes of cigars—the kind that nowadays leave little change out of a ten-shilling note. There were tumblers and the whole range of glasses.

"You drink this," I said as I took the brandy over. "What's your name, by the way?"

"Spiggott. Mrs. Spiggott."

She coughed a bit over the neat brandy and I waited till she'd got it all down. I took the glass and gave her my best smile.

"You worked here long, Mrs. Spiggott?"

"Only about a month," she said. "He used to have a house-keeper, but she died and I answered his advertisement. I had to do something after my husband died."

"You liked it here?"

"Yes," she said. "I liked it—and it was something to do."

"Nice to work for, was he?"

"Very nice. Always seemed grateful for anything you did."

"Fine," I said, and then was cocking an ear. I saw the car shoot just past the gate and then suddenly halt.

"The police," I told her. "Probably only the local inspector."

CHAPTER SIX
A NIGHT'S WORK

I WENT down the path to meet them: Summer, the chief inspector, and his sergeant, a thickset, youngish man named Killner. Summer said he knew me, or of me, which was lucky under the circumstances and saved some awkward questions. He'd probably picked up more when he rang the Yard. And he had some news for me. Wharton was on the way.

It puzzled him a bit that I should have asked for a message to be put through to Wharton. A Chief Superintendent of the Yard doesn't concern himself even with murder cases, unless they turn out particularly hard nuts to crack.

"As a matter of fact," I told Summer, "I've got some inside knowledge. I doubt if everything here is going to be open and shut."

He raised his eyebrows.

"You'll be hearing about it pretty soon," I said, "but this Colonel Marquis may be someone else altogether. I believe he's an ex-actor of the name of Dibben. At any rate I think I know someone who might make certain for us. Another ex-actor—a chap called Widgeon. I'll give you the address and perhaps you could send someone to bring him here in double-quick time."

Killner went back to the station to fix things. Summer, a bit anxious not to put a foot wrong with Wharton, was asking what else we could do. I thought he might at least see the body and then we might take a statement from that acting-housekeeper. Even then Wharton would probably want to see her himself.

As I stood just inside that office-study with Summer, I was having my first good look. It was an untidy room. Against the right-hand wall was a large, old-fashioned roll-top desk. By it was a side table with so many oddments of papers that there was scarcely room for the telephone. In the corner by the windows was a handsome bag of golf clubs: a matched set by the look of them, and each of the three woods in its woollen jacket, and on the floor by it was a carton filled with practice balls. In the opposite corner beyond the windows was a stout safe, on the top of which were more papers and an unopened box of golf balls. Along the third wall ran an old-fashioned sofa. The fourth wall had, besides the door, quite a good-class easy chair. In front of the desk was a swivel chair, probably bought to match.

"Getting pretty fashionable, this strangling business," Summer said, and nodded down at the body.

"Clean, and quiet," I said. "Just a crack on the skull and a twist with a cord and there you are."

"Called himself Colonel Marquis, did he? Can't say he looks much like any colonels I've ever met."

"Takes all sorts to make an army," I said. "What he is now doesn't give a clue to what he might have been twenty years ago. That's what he was probably banking on. Between you and me, I wouldn't be surprised if one of your jobs tomorrow is to interview any members of the local golf club whom he generally played with, just to see what his line of patter was."

"What about these photographs?"

He meant the dozen or so hanging on the walls. All were a bit faded, all framed to match, and all seemed to have an Indian background. Practically all of them were groups, both officers and civilians.

"If he's a fraud he probably bought them as a job lot," I said. "Most of the books here seem to be about India."

There wasn't a bookcase: the books were here and there and added to the general untidiness. A couple were on top of the desk: *Forty Years of India* and *Tales from a Bengal Bungalow*. Some were on the floor with old copies of *The Times* and *Sporting Life*. Most had something to do with army life in India, though one or two dealt with sport or travel. Most looked pretty old.

"Probably picked up from time to time in Charing Cross Road," I said. "They were his scripts. If he was a dud, then he had had to learn a part."

"There *is* an if?"

"Only till Widgeon's seen him," I said. "He ought to know."

I made as if to go. Summer was still looking down at the body.

"Curious he should be just there, don't you think? Almost looks as if he were trying to crawl to those french windows."

"If he was, then he nearly made it," I said, and gave a pointed look at my watch. "Perhaps we'd better be having a talk with Mrs. Spiggott."

She was still in that lounge. I told her she ought to be making herself a meal. She told us she didn't feel like eating. Or even like being in the kitchen with that room alongside. I asked her just what the arrangements were between her and Marquis. She seemed glad to talk.

"Mondays, Wednesdays and Fridays he always went to town," she said, "and then he got his own breakfast and had his lunch in town and got back about four or half-past. I came in about five and washed his breakfast things and made his evening meal and tidied up a bit. Half-past six, or a bit earlier, his meal always was, and I usually got away about a quarter-past seven. Sometimes a bit earlier."

"What about the other days?"

"Then I was here all morning and got his lunch. Afternoons I went home because I have an invalid daughter, but I always dropped in again at five, the same as I did tonight. Sundays I didn't come at all. I left a cold supper and he used to get his midday meal out at the golf course." That was plain sailing. Summer pointed out that she was probably the last person we knew—she missed the significance of those last two words—who had seen him alive, and that was at a quarter-past seven the previous night. He wanted to know what he ate at his meal.

"Well," she said, "there was cold ham and salad—"

"Ham? Lucky, wasn't he, to get ham?"

"That wasn't my business," she told him sharply. "Then I'd made a redcurrant and raspberry tart and some real custard with egg. He had some of that, and then some cheese. And a glass of port. He always had a glass of port."

"He didn't seem in any particular hurry last night?" I asked her.

"No," she said. "Nothing different from usual."

"He didn't happen to say he expected a friend?"

"He didn't. He just said good night in the usual way when I left."

"The telephone didn't ring while you were here?"

"I wouldn't know," she said. "Sometimes I heard it and sometimes I didn't."

"Did he ever talk to you about himself?"

"There wasn't time for that. I was always too busy. This is a big house to keep clean, even if a charwoman does come in on Saturdays."

"He never mentioned India?"

"Oh yes," she said, as if that hadn't counted. "He was very fond of curries, but he said they didn't do his heart any good." She leaned forward slightly. "Was it his heart?"

Summer gave a little grunt.

"That was about it. Just stopped beating. But how did you guess he was dead?"

"He was so still," she said. "He just looked dead. I was sure he was dead. My own husband died like that. I came home and found him lying in the passage. That's why it was such a shock to me."

A car was drawing up outside. A second was just behind it.

"That'll be the London police," I told her, "and the doctor. Another few minutes, Mrs. Spiggott, and you ought to be able to go."

I closed the door behind us.

"She didn't get near enough to see that cord," Summer said quietly.

"All the better," I said. "If we'd talked about murder we might have had a worse witness."

I opened the front door. George Wharton came in, and Cave, the police-surgeon, with him. George was looking a bit tired. His huge shoulders were more hunched than usual, though that might have been an act, and his vast moustache was more straggly than ever. He shook hands with me and Summer. George is a great one for shaking hands. He'd have made a first-class deacon. Maybe he is. I wouldn't put it past him, for I'm none too sure what he does on his spare Sundays.

"Well, where is he?" he asked me, and he gave me a glare as if I was capable of making away with the body.

"He'll keep for a minute," I said, and was opening the door to what turned out to be a dining-room. "I think you'll find it quicker in the long run if you hear what I know. No reason why Cave shouldn't have a look at him. He's in a kind of office, just round at the left."

"Make it snappy," Wharton told me.

I said the snappier I was, the less he'd know. And he might as well sit down, for I'd need a good five minutes. I could have added that putting on a high-executive act for Summer's benefit was all right so long as it didn't make me an office-boy. I've been working with him for over twenty years. I don't say it wouldn't upset me to part company with the Yard, but it wouldn't go near to financially embarrassing me. I'm under his orders, mind you, but, all the same, I work my own way or I don't work at all, and there's no doubt about his knowing it.

I didn't tell him the name of my client, but I told him practically everything else: about Seeway, Dibben, the Seeway-Dibben mystery, Tom Holberg, Monty Orville and Widgeon and Mrs. Spiggott. He didn't ask a single question till I'd finished.

"I've got it," he said. "It boils down to this, or am I wrong? For some reason or other this Archie Dibben disappeared twelve years ago and reappeared here as a Colonel Marquis. Just as you're on his tracks, someone does him in."

I said that was it. He seemed pleased that we'd sent for Widgeon. And then I told him about that voice on the telephone in the dead man's room.

"What I'd suggest is this," I said. "I think the cars and the ambulance, when they arrive, should be moved further along the road. If the caller, whoever he is, had his doubts about who was on the other end of the line, he'll probably have a preliminary scout round. The cars might give the game away. Also I'd have a man at the T-head just to collar him if he comes snooping round."

He gave a grunt and a nod and asked if that was the lot. I told him what we'd learned from Mrs. Spiggott. Cave could work at the stomach content and we'd know the time of death. I said Wharton might like a quick word with Mrs. Spiggott, and then the house, so to speak, would be free.

Summer went out to arrange about the cars and the man at the T-head. I opened the lounge door for Wharton.

He fancies himself with women. Nothing in the Lothario line, but as an extractor of information, and usually he's uncommonly good. Had I the physique I could do him to the life and all the old tricks were there that evening: the quiet, eye-wrinkled smile, the out-stretched hand, the deft mixture of the genial and the forlorn. If necessary he'd soon be bringing out those antiquated spectacles of his with the plain glasses, and peering at her sympathetically over their tops.

"Don't get up, Mrs. Spiggott. This has been a nasty shock to you, and you'll be wanting to get away home."

A minute and he was going over some of the ground we'd covered, but that was only for show. What he'd wanted was a good look at her, and when he'd had it and—for the sake of her finger-prints—had got her to write down her address, he was getting to his feet. He said he might want to see her again—just a matter of form—and he might not. He almost took her arm as he went to the door. He watched her go out by the front gate and along till the shrubbery hid her.

"A bit obvious," he said, "but reliable. Now let's have a look at this body."

From just inside the door he let his eyes run slowly round. They narrowed a bit as he went forward. Cave had been standing at the french windows looking out at the lawn. The house faced south to the golf course, and the early evening sun threw long shadows across that back lawn. It looked as peaceful as Eden, and there was even a twittering bird or two.

"Everything straightforward?" he was asking Cave.

"Yup. Quiet, neat job. No mess; no nothing."

An elderly chap, Cave; cynical, flippant and ironical. To him and Wharton corpses are just corpses.

Wharton got down on one knee and had a look.

"Same as that Hampstead job," Cave said. "A crack on the back of the skull and then quick work with the cord."

"Yes," Wharton said, and got to his feet. "Wonder why he's facing the windows."

"Just because," Cave told him amusedly.

"You think so?" He gave a grunt. "Why not roll him over out of sight?"

"You're losing your touch," Cave said. "Maybe he wanted the body found. Maybe he guessed we'd know when the dirty deed was done and he's cooked up a nice little alibi."

"Sure it was a he?"

"A hundred to one on. It was the devil of a crack on the skull. Look at that fat neck of his. Took some strength to tighten that cord."

A couple of minutes and the circus was in. The three of us sheered off till the room would be clear again. Cave, who had to wait for Widgeon, stoked his pipe and said he'd stay in the dining-room. Wharton and I had a look in the kitchen. He even opened the door of the tall refrigerator and had a look inside. He unwrapped a corner of the greaseproof paper and grunted at the ham. There was a nice slab of rump steak and pots of this and tins of that.

"Did himself well," George said. "Wonder where he got it?"

In the smallish pantry were more pots and jars and tins. Plenty of butter, foreign cheese, sugar galore, and packets of tea. There was also the unfinished half of that fruit tart. We went on to the lounge. He had a look at the cocktail cabinet and the inside of the sideboard. He even smelt one of the cigars.

"Where'd he get his money from?"

"Don't ask me," I said. "Maybe he had a rich aunt. Or knew how to pick the winners. What I'd like to know is if the house is his and when he bought it."

"Ought to be easy," he said. "Let's have a look upstairs."

There was a remarkably handsome bathroom and four large bedrooms. Two had dustcovers. One, in process of being covered, was almost certainly the late housekeeper's room. The other was Marquis's room. It had a beautifully sprung double bed, and a suite, handsomely inlaid walnut, to match. George had a look in the six-foot-wide wardrobe. It had everything, from plus-fours to tails. Every pair of shoes was treed, and there must have been forty or fifty neckties. There was a fur-lined overcoat that had been dusted with some anti-moth preparation, and a couple of lighter coats.

"Must have spent money like water," George said. And then there was a call from the foot of the stairs. Widgeon had arrived.

The finger-print sergeant drew back as we came in. Wharton waved a hand at the body.

"Like a light on, or do you think you can see?"

Widgeon didn't seem to have heard. He was looking down at that face and I was watching him. His eyes narrowed. He gave a slow shake of the head. Regret? Or didn't he know?

"It's him," he said. "If he was shaved he wouldn't be all that different from when I last saw him. And there's that mole against his eye."

"Right," Wharton said. "Then we won't keep you any longer, Mr. Widgeon. It was extraordinarily good of you to come."

We went with him to the door. Widgeon was still a bit bewildered. Dibben masquerading for years as a retired colonel and, by the look of things, remarkably well off for money. He couldn't see what was behind it all.

"Neither can we—at the moment," Wharton told him.

"Dropping the stage altogether: that's the curious thing," Widgeon said. "No matter how much money they get, you don't find them dropping right out. Of course, it may have had something to do with that scandal he was mixed up in. Not that I know the details. It was just one of those things that got around."

"Tell me if this is right," I said. "Dibben had reached the West End and was looking on top of the world. Then he got himself involved in a very nasty scandal and found himself out of a job. Then he managed to get back, but only as star in that touring company. Whatever face he put on things, he'd be only too aware of the come-down. And he probably knew he'd never make the West End again. So if he came into money—a very big if, mind you—he'd be only too glad to drop out."

"That's all right as far as it goes," Widgeon told me doggedly. "But if a man like Dibben came into money, he'd be only too keen on swanking in front of his old friends. If there was anyone he had a grudge against, he'd want to show them he'd done pretty well for himself and didn't care a damn. That's only human nature."

Wharton cut in with a request for secrecy. At the moment he was preferring to leave the dead man as Colonel Marquis. When Widgeon had gone, I asked him why.

"You can't trust one identification," he told me. "Pretty fools we'd look if Widgeon was wrong. I'll get your friend Orville to have a look at him, and clean-shaved. If he's as emphatic as Widgeon was, then we'll get the story splashed."

We went back to that office. Cave said there was nothing new. The photographers had finished and the contents of the pockets were on the table. So the body went out, and nothing was left of Colonel Marquis but a chalk outline.

"What about prints?"

"Plenty of his and a few of the woman's," the sergeant told him. "An extraordinarily good set, though, on the outside knob of that door."

It was one of the french windows he meant. Wharton stared at him.

"On the outside? The key's in the lock, isn't it? And both windows are bolted?"

I saw what he was getting at. The murderer must almost certainly have been admitted by Marquis, so why should he try the outside window? And he hadn't gone out that way, for the window was locked and bolted. And supposing the windows had been unlocked or even open while Marquis was having his evening meal, even then the murderer couldn't have concealed himself in that room. The curtains that ran across the glazed half of those french windows came down to only just below the glazing. If he hid behind the sofa, then Marquis must have heard him when he moved out, and the room showed no signs of a struggle. And why should the murderer, who'd left never a print in the room, be so careless as to leave a perfect set on the outer knob which apparently he'd had no reason to use?

"Take the knob right off," Wharton said, "and get it along to the Yard."

"These all the contents of his pockets?" he was asking Summer.

"This is the lot," Summer said. "No wallet, sir, as you notice."

"At any rate we've got his keys. Let's have a look in the safe."

He found the right key, turned it, pressed the handle, and pulled the heavy door open. Summer and I had squatted down to look. But there was nothing to see. The safe was empty. It had the bleak bareness of a long-deserted house.

"Give me a torch," Wharton said. "Too dark inside here."

I gave him a torch from his case and he flashed it inside. He grunted. He held it for Summer and me to have a look. A thin steel shelf divided that safe in two. On it, and on the bottom, was dust, and in the dust were patterns. Wharton got to his feet.

"That safe's been cleaned out. And last night, or my name's Robinson. Let's see what's in the desk."

He unlocked it and pulled the roll top down. That desk wasn't empty, but it had been hurriedly searched. Four pigeon-holes were at the top, and under them two rows of four small drawers, with a tiny central cupboard that broke the drawer and pigeon-hole sequence. The key was in the tiny lock, but the door wasn't shut. Edges of paper were visible in the hastily shut drawers, and papers in the pigeonholes were askew.

The desk itself had two short drawers and two long ones. Their contents had been looked through, but they seemed to contain no papers. There were more golf-balls, two pairs of binoculars, old magazines, a ball of string, some old guides to the turf, a long box of envelopes and two packets of notepaper embossed with the Redgates address, and, in one of the long drawers, a miscellaneous collection of what I might describe as Indian knick-knacks—carvings in bone and ivory and wood, none of them large and none of any great value.

"All part of the background," I said. "He probably used to show them to his pals. 'No great value, old boy, but I like to keep them for sentimental reasons—what?'"

Wharton didn't comment. He glanced at his watch.

"Not too far off eight o'clock. You might have a look at that man of yours, Summer. I've got a hunch that man who telephoned is a bit of a slippery customer. I'd like to shake hands with him."

Summer went out. Wharton scowled at the desk.

"Looks as though we've got an hour or two's work," he told me. "A cup of tea wouldn't do any harm. What theatre did you say that Monty Orville was at?"

I left him to his telephoning. Inside ten minutes I'd brewed a big pot of tea and I'd found some packets of biscuits. And all the time I'd been half listening for the return of Summer and with him that man whose voice I'd heard on the telephone. No matter who he was, he was our first contact between Marquis and what I might call the outside world, and what he had to tell us might make a deal of difference.

But Summer wasn't back by the time that tea was ready. George and I had our snack in the kitchen and lighted our pipes and went back to that desk. But we hadn't time to get down to work. There were quick feet in the passage and Summer came almost bursting in.

"Yes?" Wharton said, and he'd only to look at Summer's face to know something had happened.

"A bad business, sir. That man of mine. Had the fellow under his nose and then let him get away."

CHAPTER SEVEN
LABOURING ON

HAD it not been tragic, the bare-facedness of it all would have made it amusing. The plain-clothes man was called Mallins, and he'd been placed strategically just beyond the T-head. That other road led to the club-house and ran along the ninth green, and he, too, had had one eye on the golf and the other slewed round for his man. Various people came along, and it was not till about a quarter to eight that one fitted the bill. He was a man who came briskly round the corner and then suddenly stopped. He peered ahead at the two cars. He stood where he was as if wondering what to do. Mallins was quickly across.

"Excuse me, but aren't you the man who rang Colonel Marquis up on the telephone this afternoon?"

The man stared at him.

"Never heard of him. And who are you?"

Mallins showed his warrant card, and he repeated the question.

"Sorry, officer, but I never heard of him. My name's Brewer. I live here."

He waved a hand at The Hollies. Mallins apologised.

"That's all right," Brewer said, and went on the yard or two to the gate of that corner house. But he didn't go to the front door. He went by the garage to the back. Mallins watched him that far and went back to his waiting.

"Soon as I heard his tale I guessed what had happened," Summer said exasperatedly. "There's no one at The Hollies of the name of Brewer. The people are called Harris, and only Mrs. Harris was at home. What this so-called Brewer did was nip along to the back garden and into somebody else's garden and out at their front gate bold as brass. Probably miles away by now."

"Can't be helped," Wharton said. "No fault of yours. But what about a description?"

Mallins had furnished one. Brewer was about forty-five, of medium height, dark, clean-shaven, and with a foxy kind of face. He was brisk in his manner, spoke with all the assurance in the world, and had a slight cockney accent—just enough to make him a Londoner. He was dressed in . . .

"Clothes don't matter," Wharton told him.

"To this extent they do, sir, if you'll pardon me. Mallins noticed his black shoes and the man had remarkably small feet for his height. Probably fives or sixes."

"Yes," Wharton said. "That's certainly something."

I said that he seemed to fit the bill as far as what I'd heard was concerned. Wharton said there was no use crying over spilt milk. Summer had better be going through the miscellaneous oddments that strewed the room, and a finger-print man ought to be with him. We'd get busy at the desk.

You want to hear results, not a tedious record of slow progress. An hour and a half later we had two things only. The first was straightforward and the other far from it. It was, in fact, three things, and dramatically discovered. But about that first discovery.

There were two cheque books. One was personal and the stub markings showed nothing unusual, and the bank was the local Barclay's. The other cheque book had written on its outside—WEEKS, LTD., and the bank was the Midland at Spenser St., W.1. The first was a small book of twenty-four crossed cheques; the Weeks one a business book of sixty cheques. Its stubs showed no names, but only letters or initials.

"Weeks, Ltd.," I said. "The name's familiar enough. Isn't there an employment agency of that name that advertises extensively?"

Summer and I had a quick look through some of the old newspapers, and there were the advertisements. Weeks, Ltd. seemed a specialist firm, and the address was 8 Spenser St., W.1. These were the details of one advertisement in a fairly recent issue:

CHEF—country hotel. £10-£12, all found. Kitchen help. Good refs. required.

VEGETABLE CHEF—for town. £10-£12.

SECOND CHEF—Home Counties hotel. Excellent post, good prospects. £8-£10.

HEAD WAITER—seaside hotel. First-class experience essential. Salary mutual arrangement.

MARRIED COUPLE—man waiter, woman help kitchen. High-class country hotel. £8-£10, all found. Good refs.

WEEKS, LTD.; 8 Spenser St. W.1.

"So that's where his money came from," George said. "That's why he went regularly to town. And kept his own fingers on the till."

It was an excellent find. No need to add that in the morning we'd be calling at 8 Spenser St. If we'd found nothing else, we wouldn't have wasted our time. And we found nothing else till after everything in that desk had been looked at and finger-printed.

"Suppose there couldn't be any secret drawers?" George said, and far from hopefully.

We'd gone over many a desk in our time and we began on the drawers themselves. A favourite trick is to shorten a small drawer in depth and have a tiny compartment behind it: so tiny, in fact, that the shortness is never suspected. There was nothing of that sort there, so we tried the thicker wood, and couldn't find a sliding panel. Then we tried the uprights of that middle compartment.

A little door ran from top to bottom, as I said, and the door was fastened and closed on two neatly made uprights, just as the door of a house is hinged to one upright and shuts against another. But these uprights were beautifully made, with little carved capitals and fluting, though they were only half an inch wide. I gave one capital a gentle pull and the whole thing came out in my hand like a narrow box. Something was inside it, and I gave it a tap on my hand and out fell a couple of photographs and a piece of paper. I gave a pull at the other capital and when it came out I had to steady it, for the door was hinged to it. I looked inside and nothing was there. I tapped it for certainty's sake, but nothing fell out, so I put it back, and its door with it.

We had a look at the photographs. Each was unmounted. The first was half-plate size and it had faded almost to white at its edges and then to a chocolate brown. It might have been taken as an illustration for a work on medical jurisprudence, for it showed what looked like the body of a man. It lay with the head across one arm with the other arm loosely by the side. If one discounted the fading, then the clothes were light in colour, and their texture seemed to be close, like worsted or hard tweed. There was a darkness across the man's mouth that looked like blood. We looked at the face through a glass, but the features had almost gone with the fading. The centre of the picture, where the fading was less, showed that the body was lying on a vaguely patterned carpet or rug, and in the background was a foot or two of the bottom of a door.

"When was it taken?" George was asking me. It's curious how at one minute he can credit me with omniscience, and then be regarding with a smug commiseration an ignorance of something of which he happens to have private knowledge.

"Don't know," I said. "Perhaps Summer is a photographer."

Summer admitted the hobby, but couldn't guess at the age of that print.

"Better get it to the back-room boys," was all I could suggest. "They might even bring the features up. The man's a bit short, whoever he was, and on the fat side." And then my fingers went suddenly to my glasses. "Isn't the build rather like that of Dibben? I know the hair's dark and Marquis's is badger-grey, but this print was made quite a time ago."

"Plenty of people about with that kind of shape," George told me. "Let's have a look at that other one. That might tell us something."

But on the face of it, it had no relationship with that first print. It was of postcard size and quite modern, and it showed a woman leaving a room and a man just behind her in the half-open door. The woman was young and attractive looking, with a slightly retroussé nose and a biggish mouth. The face had character and a peculiar charm, and maybe because she was smiling back at the man behind and her lips were parted as if she were speaking. She looked just above medium height, and her hair was shortish and curled up at the nape of her neck. She was wearing a high-necked jumper that was lighter than her skirt.

The man looked about thirty, and was the sahib type: tall, wiry, tweed-coated and with a close-cropped moustache. His head was cocked on one side as if he was listening, and one hand was out to hold open the door.

George gave a grunt and reached for the sheet of paper. One look at it and he was giving it almost contemptuously to me.

"There we are. No argument as to what that photo's about."

That sheet of paper that had been with the photographs was a hotel bill, and not the original but a duplicate. It was made out to a Major and Mrs. Rome who had stayed at the Downland Court Hotel, Bickhurst, Sussex, from the night of Friday the twelfth of May till the morning of Monday the fifteenth. There was a garage charge which showed that the couple had come by car, and the extras included one double breakfast in bed, two early morning teas, and various drinks including three bottles of wine. The year was 1947. The address of the couple was vaguely given as London.

"What're we up against?" George said, and gave me a glare. "Blackmail?"

It looked remarkably like it.

"Where does that faded print come in?" I said. "There must be a connection or the two prints wouldn't have been hidden together."

"Don't know," George said. He pursed out his lips and scowled at that second print. "I'm wondering. Something's beginning to tell me that these are what our friend Marquis was killed for."

Everything seemed to point to it. Someone had been looking for something, and that someone had been in a hurry. He hadn't had time to hunt through the contents of the safe, so he had taken them all away for a later look. What he had taken from the desk there was no means of telling, or what he might have found and taken from elsewhere in the house.

"But why the hurry?" I said. "We've assumed that Marquis let him in, and therefore he presumably knew the household arrangements and that he'd have the place to himself when he'd killed Marquis. Every indication is that he opened the safe with the keys, grabbed the contents and put them into, say, a bag, then had a quick look through this desk and then left. He didn't even ensure that he'd got these prints and the hotel bill, or else he'd have turned the whole place upside down."

"If those were what he came for," George said. "But no use theorising. Better finish with this desk and get to work in the rest of the rooms."

It's curious how one can be more concerned in our job with what one might call the imponderables than with the matter-of-fact. We'd found plenty of the latter. We knew the dead man's bank: we had his paying-in book which showed that a good many deposits had been in cash, and we had a statement for his private account which showed that a week before his death he had had a balance of over eight hundred pounds. That statement also showed the receipt of certain dividends from industrial investments. It is true we hadn't the name of his lawyers who might possibly have the deeds of the house, but we knew about the employment agency. We'd had cases where from the very first moment we'd been at a loss for information and clues, and now we had enough to employ us for days. And yet I couldn't help feeling that those prints and that hotel bill had in them something far beyond facts. There's much of the humdrum about facts. But they were different. They were like the vital cryptogram that had to be read: they were the urge and the stimulant: the things to which one's thoughts were always coming back.

We went laboriously through those other rooms and it was getting on for eleven o'clock and we were having another cup of tea when the telephone rang. It was only Cave. Orville had seen the body and had had no doubts whatever that the man was Dibben. As for the time of death, Cave made it after seven o'clock and before half-past.

"That clears the decks," George told us. "First thing in the morning, Summer, you'd better start a house-to-house enquiry about a man seen entering or leaving. Emphasise that he was probably carrying an attaché case or bag."

"There's one thing I've been thinking of," I said. "What the foxy-faced man told me over the telephone—that someone was going to pay. Doesn't that tie up with the blackmail idea?"

I went over that one-sided conversation again. The man had been excited, as if he'd accomplished something. He'd pulled a trick and he wanted Dibben—no need now to call him Marquis—to know it. And he'd intended to come and make a personal report.

"Might have been a blind," Summer said. "Why shouldn't he have done the killing and then rung up to see what was happening?"

"If he had, then he wouldn't have had the nerve to come back," Wharton said. And then the telephone went again.

It was the Yard. There was no record of those prints on the outer knob of the french window.

"Never thought there would be," George told us. "Probably some pal of his. Couldn't make anyone hear, so he came round to the back for a look. Just tried the handle and found it locked and went away."

Summer caught my eye. I said it for both of us.

"Then he must have seen the body. Anyone looking through that window couldn't help seeing it."

"Then he tried the door and didn't look in," George said blandly. "Another job for your people, Summer. Get a list of his pals at the golf club-house. Get all about him that you can. Make a regular dossier."

If there was nothing else, he thought I might as well be going. He'd be staying on with a man or two, and he might doss down later in the house. First thing in the morning he'd give me a ring.

"There's just one thing," I said. "The Broad Street Agency gets a commission from a client of apparently unimpeachable integrity to find a man named Seeway, and that man seems to have been connected in some way with another man called Dibben. I go to Bassingford and make enquiries. Almost before I've completed them, Dibben is found murdered. Either there's some connection or there isn't. If there is, then Bassingford might be a good place to go on making enquiries."

"You mean that someone in Bassingford suddenly wanted Dibben out of the way?"

"I wouldn't go so far as that, Summer," I said. "As far as my enquiries went, I came across nobody who might conceivably have wanted Dibben out of the way. As far as everybody there was concerned, he was practically forgotten. You might say he didn't exist."

"Plenty of time," George said. "We haven't even begun this case yet. My hunch is, we'll know a devil of a lot more after we've had a look at that employment agency."

A police car took me home. I was so tired that I'd forgotten about food, and I hardly remembered getting into bed. It was half-past six and I was still sound asleep when the bedside extension woke me. It was George Wharton. He said he'd drop in on me at nine and then we'd go on to Weeks, Ltd. I got out of bed at once. Before I even shaved and dressed, I rang Norris at his private address and told him to lay off the case till further notice. Then after a quick breakfast I rang Clandon. He said he was just dressing.

"I'd like to see you, and rather urgently," I told him. "I'd just as soon not mention it over the telephone."

"Come along," he said. "Come and have breakfast."

I said I'd had it, but I'd be along at once. I left it as late as I dared and it was just short of half-past eight when I got to the flats. He was in his room. He'd had his breakfast brought there.

"Something mighty serious has happened," I told him, "and I thought I'd better call and see you personally. Dibben's dead."

I checked his question and went on.

"Remember how I told you we had a line on him, and he was living at Stapley Green and masquerading as a retired colonel? I went to confront him there last night and found him dead. Someone had hit him over the head and then strangled him."

"My God!" he said. "And what happens now?"

"Let's keep to our side of things," I said. "There's no secret of the confessional about an enquiry agency like ours. I'm trying to keep your name out of things, but if I'm directly asked, I shall have to give it. There'll be no publicity, of course. All the same, you may have to tell the police everything you've told us. I thought I ought to warn you. Not that you've anything to worry about. Yours is a straightforward story and I think the police will be grateful."

"Yes," he said slowly, and seemed to be thinking it over. "A pretty horrible business, though—I mean about Dibben. And it cuts off a source of information."

I told him of my own connections with the police. I said if I were he I'd let the case rest for a bit. After all, there wasn't any extreme urgency about finding Seeway. But while I couldn't now serve two masters, I could at least use what he'd told me, and it looked almost a certainty that the police themselves would be as intrigued as we'd been about a connection between Seeway and the murdered Dibben. They'd be looking up everyone even remotely connected with Dibben. It was just possible that they'd solve that mystery and find the whereabouts of Seeway if Seeway was still alive.

"It's the old story," he told me, and gave that wry smile of his. "When I've paid for advice, I take it. If the police should want to see me, they know where I am. All I can tell them is what I told you."

I was glad things had been settled that way. There'd been no duplicity on my part, but I was going to ensure that Wharton had a word with him. If Wharton felt about him as I did, then Clandon's name would be kept out of things. And I'd had the idea that George had found it hard to credit what I'd told him about Clandon, and a personal interview might make that story of Clandon's as credible to him as it had been to myself.

I liked Clandon. It was only too true that I was almost old enough to be his father, but as I was driving back to the garage I was thinking it was a long time since I had run up against a man I liked so much. It's the kind of thing for which you can't account, for beyond pure business I'd had no talk with him. But a gesture can sometimes be eloquent, and there was this and that that I'd noticed about his room. I claim sometimes to have as little snobbery as any man alive, but I did happen to wonder with a personal brand of snobbery if, like myself, he was a Cambridge man, and I made up my mind to ask him when I saw him next.

I got back to the flat just before Wharton arrived. Nothing had happened after I'd left Stapley Green, he told me, but plenty ought to happen before the day was out. Sergeant Matthews had been sent to that Downland Court Hotel to try to get a line on that Major and Mrs. Rome of the photograph. Summer would be busy, trying to compile a Marquis dossier.

"What about the theatrical agencies for a dossier of Dibben?" I said.

George said it mightn't be needed. At the moment he wasn't releasing to the Press anything that even hinted at Marquis's former identity. As he pointed out, those golfing friends ought first to be interviewed by Summer. A man isn't likely to talk so freely if he knows he's going to look very much of a fool, and Marquis had been fooling a considerable number of people for a considerable number of years. Give Summer just the one day, George said, and then the story could be released, and if it didn't produce splash headlines, then his name was Robinson. After that the job would be to cope with the information that would come pouring in.

I make no apologies for any little tricks I may play on George. He has to be handled rightly. Sometimes it pays to blurt out a theory and stand to it doggedly. Sometimes it's the other way round and hints have to be obscure, or you put a theory practically into his mouth.

"About that Bassingford idea of yours," I said, "and all this business being tied up with that Seeway affair. I've been thinking things over, and it mightn't be a bad idea if you saw our client. I think he'd be prepared to see you and trust your discretion about unnecessary publicity."

"Mightn't do any harm," George said.

So I told him about Henry Clandon, and I made it impersonal. He said he might fix it after we'd been to Spenser Street. Then he was looking at his watch and saying we might as well be getting along.

Spenser Street is one of those queer little side streets that make up the maze between Regent Street and Soho. It's only ten minutes' walk from my place, and it took us less than no time in George's car. We went slowly by Number 8, a three-storied building probably honeycombed with offices. The car went on into Mullingar Street, turned at the top and came back to Number 8. George and I got out.

On the wall was the usual list of occupants of floors. Weeks, Ltd. was on the first floor, and shared it with two other firms.

"Better have a look round first," George told me, and began moving up the stairs.

We came up to a fairly spacious landing and looked about us. The tapping of typewriters was coming through doors, but there wasn't a sound from the twin doors of Weeks, Ltd. One door was marked PRIVATE and the other ENQUIRIES. George gave me a nod, moved across to that second door, rapped smartly and then walked in. I was at his heels.

Chapter Eight
AN OLD FRIEND

THERE turned out to be just the two rooms, but the room in which we were was a cubby-hole partitioned off from the main part, which was a kind of waiting-room or room for unimportant interviews. Behind a desk-counter sat a gaunt-faced woman consulting some shorthand notes. Between the counter and the outer door there was room for just two small chairs. On the left was another door.

"May I see the proprietor?"

"You mean Mr. Unstone, the manager?"

There must have been something unusual about us, for her fingers slid from the pad. The off-hand look was suddenly one of interest.

"He'll do," Wharton told her.

"Have you an appointment?"

"He'll see us," Wharton said. "Tell him it's urgent, and private."

She pressed the buzzer and picked up the receiver.

"Two gentlemen to see you, Mr. Unstone. They say it's urgent and private."

Another minute and she was opening the side door and we went through that waiting-room to a door marked STRICTLY PRIVATE. She gave a tap and a voice called a "Come in!"

This was a larger room, efficiently furnished and reasonably light. A man was working at a flat-topped oak desk, and he got to his feet as we came in. I'd call him dapper and for want of a better word, for he wasn't particularly short or neatly trim; but his reddish face fairly shone from a recent razoring; his sleek black hair was smoothed flat and beautifully parted; his black moustache was waxed to a couple of needle points, and there was something finicky about the set of his dark city suit.

"Mr. Unstone?" George said. "Sorry to break in on you like this, but I'm Chief Superintendent Wharton of New Scotland Yard. This is Mr. Ludovic Travers."

Unstone was staring. He took the warrant card that George held out, but barely glanced at it.

"Scotland Yard?" he said. "I'm afraid I don't understand."

"Perhaps we'd better sit down," George said. "We might be here quite a few minutes."

Unstone came fussing round. He almost dusted the seats. And when George had told him why we were there, he was looking like a man who's had a nasty shock.

"Incredible!" he said. "And murdered! . . . It's dreadful. . . . It's beyond me. Or was it someone who broke in? You know the kind of thing that's been happening lately."

"We don't know," George told him frankly. "That's why we're trespassing on your time. We know practically nothing about him. Except that we happened to discover he was the proprietor of this agency. How long had you known him yourself?"

"Let me see," he said. "Ever since he came into the business."

The more he explained, the less happy I was. I had no reason to doubt his word, and the more he told us, the more theories were collapsing about my ears. Dibben had *not* abandoned the theatrical profession because of anything that had happened at Bassingford. There was only one slight discrepancy between what Unstone told us and what I had learned from Widgeon. Dibben had indeed been absent from the tour for the week at Colchester, but not because of the illness and death of his mother. It was his sister who had been ill and had subsequently died. But Widgeon was thinking back to 1939, and the mistake was only reasonable. Unstone was certain. What he said had to be true.

The employment agency had been founded by a Mrs. Weeks and her husband. The husband died in 1938 and Unstone was then engaged as manager, since the widow herself was in poor health. She died in May 1939, and her brother—Colonel Marquis—inherited the business. He confirmed Unstone's managership even though he took an increasingly active part himself.

"That's clear enough," Wharton said. "But let me put a confidential question. You're a man of the world and a man of integrity, but did you ever have reason to suspect that Marquis wasn't his real name?"

"Never in my life!"

"You'd heard about him from Mrs. Weeks?"

"Never," he said. "I didn't even know she had a brother. Everything between me and her was strictly business. I was just her manager."

"You never by any chance heard her mention anyone of the name of Dibben?"

"Dibben?" He shook his head. "Don't remember ever hearing the name in my life."

I think my eyes must have narrowed. There was something wrong about the way he said it. And he was shifting unnecessarily in his chair. But Wharton, it seemed, had noticed nothing. He was always a chameleon: bland, deferential, dignified, jocose—anything to fit the occasion. And with Unstone he was being just quietly and somewhat perplexedly enquiring, and admitting tacitly a considerable indebtedness.

"You don't happen to know his solicitors? I take it he had to have solicitors?"

"Oh yes, I know of the solicitors," Unstone said. "A small firm just off Chancery Lane. Cleaver and Hewes of 27 Raglan Court."

Wharton felt for his notebook. He patted his pockets and came out with a damn!

"Just jot it down for me, will you?"

Unstone pressed the buzzer.

"Miss Ball, type out Cleaver and Hewes' address, will you, and a rough map of how to get to Raglan Court. . . . No, you needn't bring it in."

"You can collect it on your way out," he told Wharton amiably. "Raglan Court's none too easy to find."

"Very grateful to you. But I wonder if you'd mind telling us about your relationships with the late Colonel. How you got on with him, and so on."

"Well, it's a bit awkward," Unstone said, and shifted once more uneasily in his seat. "You're supposed to speak well of the dead—"

"But you can't?"

"Oh yes. But he was getting a very difficult man to handle, if you know what I mean."

It took some explaining, at least in the way he told it. Marquis had gradually taken more and more of the business into his own hands. He signed all the cheques and he kept the main ledger. Abstracts of everything would be kept, and after one of his usual days in the office Marquis would take them away and doubtless enter them in the ledger.

"Just a minute," Wharton said. "You mean he kept that ledger at his house?"

"But of course!"

He was smiling puzzledly as he leaned forward.

"I don't want to sound rude, but aren't you keeping me in the dark? I mean, if he was killed—murdered, I should say—you people would have searched the house. If so, you should have found that ledger. There wasn't any place he could have kept it except at his house."

"No ledger there," Wharton told him. "You've been there yourself?"

"Not more than twice. The last time must have been about a couple of years ago."

"That house in Stapley Green," I said. "How long had he had it?"

"Let me see now," he said. "Oh yes. He bought it in 1941. Property was cheap then on account of the bombing. Up to then he'd had a flat just outside Bromley."

George began asking about the business. Unstone said he couldn't actually say, but his own idea was that there was quite a good margin of profit.

"The Colonel didn't grumble a lot," he said, "and he gave me a fifty pound rise this year."

"Making how much? Just between ourselves."

"Well, it mayn't sound a lot to you gentlemen, but—well, six hundred a year."

"Not to be sneezed at," Wharton told him and got to his feet. "I take it you're always here, Mr. Unstone? We'll probably have to get some kind of official statement from you, but you won't mind that."

No one apparently would be more pleased. No one could have been more ready to help. Or more grateful to be confidentially told how the enquiry was progressing.

"Whoever did it, I hope you catch him, sir. And I'd like to see him hung."

"Maybe I'll arrange it," Wharton told him with an ersatz chuckle. "Goodbye, Mr. Unstone, and many thanks." He looked round at me. "If all witnesses were as frank, our job'd be easier."

"Yes," I said, and took the dampish hand that Unstone was holding out.

We went back through the waiting-room. Miss Ball had an envelope for us and I could almost feel her eyes on our backs as we went out to the landing. I didn't speak till we were almost down the stairs.

"Things aren't quite so good, George."

"No use grumbling," he said, and he said it so off-handedly that I knew he had something pleasant on his mind. Somewhere in that half-hour there must have been something I'd missed. And then as we came out to the pavement I was suddenly nudging his elbow.

"Don't look round, George, but there's a man across the road I'd like to have another look at. I'm going to slip back. You get in the car and wait."

I turned back and kept my eyes away from that watching man. I went up the stairs, waited a moment or two and then came down. The man was still lounging against the wall and reading his newspaper. I went on to the car. Bruff, the plain-clothes driver, moved the car on. We stopped just round the corner in Axton Street.

"Did you get a good look at him, George?"

"Not too good," he said. "He was dug well in behind that newspaper."

"I know," I said. "But I had a good look at his feet. I think he's our friend Brewer—the foxy-faced gent who gave us the slip last night."

A couple of minutes and Bruff was out of the car and I at the wheel.

"You'd better go into an office a little way beyond," Wharton was telling him. "Don't ask me how. Flash your card and keep your eyes open. If he went in at Number 8 he'll have to come out."

Bruff moved off. I moved the car on.

"Where to now, George?"

"Might as well drop in at the Yard."

He said it with such a forced dejection that I knew more than ever there was something pleasant in his mind. I wouldn't say that he loves to be secretive: what he likes is to keep a trick or two up his sleeve or a couple of rabbits in the hat. What he's after is the showy curtain and the snap ending: the old master dramatically proving to a onetime apprentice that the younger generation has still a few things to learn.

As soon as we were up in his room I rather spoiled that particular curtain.

"How're we going to get Unstone's prints?" I asked him. "Prints?"

"Yes," I said. "It was pretty obvious he recognised that little trap of yours. He took good care not to write down the solicitor's address for you. Got that receptionist to do it."

"Oh, that," he said. "As a matter of fact, I don't think we'll need 'em. I've a pretty shrewd idea I've seen him before." He was ringing down for Chief Inspector Jewle. I was trying to think if I, too, had ever seen Unstone, but the face hadn't been familiar and whatever it was that George had remembered had probably been beyond my range. George often boasts that he never forgets a face. He may be right: he has that kind of memory. He closes his eyes, touches a private switch, and a spool of film runs across the screen of his mind. I have a memory that's more like a sieve. Faces and names often fall through the mesh, but what remains are snippets of general information. It's what I call a cross-word-puzzle sort of mind.

Jewle came in. We've often worked together in the past, and he gave me a smile and a nod.

"You handled a blackmail case in Guildford in 1933 or '34," Wharton said. "It was a pretty nasty business and almost turned into a murder case. What was the fellow's name?"

"You mean Stringer?"

George raised hands to heaven.

"Dammit, I must be getting old! Stringer—that's the chap. Lucky to get off with four years, or was it five? Running a private hotel, wasn't he, and making a bit on the side. Think you can find me his picture?"

"Funny," George told me when Jewle had gone. "Remembered everything except the fellow's name. Clapped eyes on him only once, though."

"But he didn't clap eyes on you?"

"He certainly didn't," George said. "A bit of luck for us. But I bet he had some pretty bad moments before we came into that room. Wonder what would have happened if it'd been Jewle instead of me."

"But he was expecting someone."

"Of course he was. And he'd warned that receptionist. You don't think two perfect strangers without an appointment would have been allowed to walk into that room of his? Not on your life."

"Foxy-face must have given him the tip," I said; and then Jewle came in again. He spread the dossier on Wharton's desk. George picked up the personal sheet and I was looking over his shoulder.

"That's him," he said. "No moustache and hair parted the other side, but it's him. I knew somehow the Old Gent was right."

That's the deprecatory way he sometimes smugly alludes to himself. Jewle caught my eye and gave me a wink.

"Better get the main facts," Wharton went on, and took out his notebook. "Nothing like ammunition when you're dealing with a man like Stringer. . . . Four years, eh? That means he was taken on by that Mrs. Weeks almost as soon as he got out. Wonder why he decided to go straight?"

"Mr. Justice Treen scared the living daylights out of him," Jewle said. "Told him what'd happen if he ever came up again."

Wharton went on taking notes. Over a cigarette I told Jewle what it was all about.

"There's no certainty," I told Wharton, "that everything in that agency was run straight. The Weeks woman may have been a crook for all we know. Or Stringer may have had something on her."

"He was a smooth, plausible devil," Jewle said. "He'd have made a first-class con man. If he answered this Weeks woman's advertisement he'd have got the job. I'll bet he had a beautiful set of testimonials."

"I think he went straight while she was alive," Wharton said. "What he did was spot this chap Marquis as a bird of a feather, then they began introducing a few variations. It's a lovely scheme, you know, running an hotel employment agency with a side-line in blackmail."

It *was* a lovely scheme. Unstone, *alias* Stringer, would interview applicants for jobs, and much practice would have made him an adept at choosing the right sort of man. There'd be a man who badly needed a job, or a man who looked as if he had a record, and all that would be needed would be to drop the right kind of hint. And there was probably a specialising in the blackmailing of unmarried couples. The new employee would keep his eyes open and get on friendly terms with the reception and bedroom staffs. A quick word on the telephone to Unstone, and he'd take over. And if the employee himself got into any kind of trouble, Unstone could work him in for another job.

"You're in no hurry," Wharton told Jewle. "While were at it, let's go into this a bit deeper."

He stoked his pipe. I stoked mine. Jewle lighted a cigarette. And then the buzzer went.

"Who?" Wharton said, and, "Right. Put him through." A moment and we were hearing grunts and an occasional "Good" or "Fine". Then the someone was told to report back. Wharton rang off.

"Bruff," he told us. "He followed our foxy-faced friend to Crane Street, Soho. Who do you think he is?"

If we had a guess, we'd too much tact to make it.

"A chap named Rappham. Runs a little private detection business. Calls itself Rappham Investigations Limited."

"I get it," Jewle said. "The employee rings Unstone, Unstone rings Rappham, and Rappham trots off to wherever it is and gets on the job. Takes a photograph if he can, gets an hotel bill, and follows the couple when they leave."

"It can't end there," Wharton said. "Who puts on the bite? Not Unstone. That'd be too dangerous. His agency'd have to be kept well clear of things. Wonder if that was Marquis's end?"

I doubted it. Marquis's days in town had been regular. Apparently they'd never varied, nor had his days at home. But if he'd handled the pressure side he couldn't have enforced any regularity. You couldn't say, "Mondays, Wednesdays and Fridays I'll see people I'm about to blackmail." That sort of thing would have happened at odd times. It wouldn't fit into a schedule.

"Well, that's something we have to find out," Wharton said. "Looks as if we've got to find some third party. Jewle knows all about Marquis?"

I said I didn't think I'd left anything out.

"Right," he said. "Then let's see if we can lick any sense into that dual name business. Mrs. Weeks is Dibben's sister. He comes into the business and whatever else she leaves when she dies. He has to do so under the name of Dibben. Agreed?"

It was obvious.

"But then he suddenly blossoms out as Colonel Marquis. Unstone wants us to believe he never knew him under any other name. Wait a minute," he said, as Jewle made as if to speak. "Let's try to visualise things as Unstone wants us to see them. The new owner pays a visit to Spenser Street. 'I'm Colonel Marquis, the new owner.' 'Glad to see you, sir,' says Unstone, and that's that. But does it make sense?"

"You mean," I said, "that Mrs. Weeks must have mentioned either her maiden name or her brother's name some time to Unstone?"

"Why not?"

"But *was* her maiden name Dibben?"

Wharton stared at nothing. Then he stared at Jewle. "You mean?"

"Just an idea," Jewle said, "but why shouldn't the family name have been Marquis? Why shouldn't Dibben have been Archibald Marquis? After all, stage and music-hall people change their names more often than not. Archie Dibben's a nice, slick sort of name."

"Yes," Wharton said, and made a note in his book. "That's something we ought to find out."

"I'm not exactly throwing a spanner into the works," I said, "but there's a point I'd like to make. When you mentioned the name of Dibben this morning, George, I'm pretty positive Unstone had heard of it."

"Nothing in that," he said. "The two got pally, didn't they? Or Unstone may have seen Dibben and spotted who he really was."

"Maybe," I said. "But just one other question—the missing ledger. Was it in the safe and did the murderer take it? Or was that yarn of Unstone's about Marquis butting too much into the business all a pack of lies? In other words, has Unstone made away with the ledger?"

"Plenty of time for that," he said, but made a note nevertheless. "It ties up in a way with the fact that there weren't any names but only initials or private marks on the stubs of that office cheque book we found in Dibben's desk. Anything else while we're at it?"

I could think of nothing. George had a look at that old-fashioned turnip he calls a watch and did a bit of pondering.

"That client of yours—Clandon," he said. "Think he might see us at about two o'clock? And we'll just have time to slip along to see that solicitor. Might be interesting to know if Dibben left a will."

He went out with Jewle. I rang down for the Halmer and Blate number, and in a couple of minutes had Clandon on the line.

"It's come," I said. "Chief Superintendent Wharton would like a word with you at two o'clock if you can manage it."

"Where?"

"I'd prefer it to be at your flat. Makes a nice friendly kind of milieu. He shouldn't keep you more than a few minutes."

"Absolutely all right," he told me. "What sort of a chap is he? Gimlet-eyed?"

"He's that all right," I said, "but he won't be so with you. Just tell him the plain truth and you'll find him as nice as ninepence." I remembered something. "If you get a chance, play up that Seeway-Dibben mystery. If Scotland Yard find the answer, it might save you a whole lot of money."

That was that. A minute and Wharton was back and impatient to be away to Raglan Court. The car was moving along the Embankment when I asked him if he had that receptionist's map. He grunted and glared. That's another of George's boasts: that there's not a side street or court to which he couldn't find his way in the dark.

"Tried her prints on that paper," he told me. "No record of her. Not that Unstone wouldn't be sure of that."

We came into the Strand and turned up Chancery Lane. A few yards and we turned right and into a kind of square. The car drew up, but George sat on and looked about him. It was one of those Dickensian backwaters and one side of it had been blasted out by a bomb or two. Of what was left, there wasn't a house that wasn't shrieking in agony for a coat of paint.

"Why the devil do lawyers love cobwebs?" George said, and manipulated himself out. "Number 27. That'll be this way."

It was a rickety kind of building, a maze of rooms and passages and stairs. Cleaver and Hewes were on the ground floor, and even then we had to peer about us before we found the right door. CLEAVER & HEWES was in black letters on the frosted glass, and underneath it—*Please Ring*. George rang.

Chapter Nine
THIRD MAN IN?

It was a man in the early forties who admitted us, and what his status was in that office I couldn't guess. There was about him an indifference to smartness and even to tidiness, for he wore an open-necked shirt, his tweed coat was worn round the button-holes and the cheap flannel trousers bagged at the knees. There seemed a faint irony in the look he gave us.

"Superintendent Wharton," George said. "I think Mr. Cleaver is expecting me."

"Just a moment, sir. Perhaps you wouldn't mind waiting here."

He went through the far door. The room seemed to be his office, but it wasn't packed to suffocation as such rooms usually are: no piles of dusty papers, no shelves with tin cases and still more papers, no filing cabinets and no safe. There was a desk with two typewriters—one a brief-sized—and a stationery rack. There was a side table on which was a small pile of documents tied with red tape. There were no less than four chairs. The floor was covered with coconut matting.

"Reception room?" I whispered to George.

He shrugged his shoulders. The door opened.

"This way, gentlemen, please. Mr. Cleaver will see you at once."

We went through a narrow passage to a baize-covered door that sound-proofed a door a foot or two beyond. Cleaver got to his feet, leaned across his flat-topped desk and held out a hand.

"Superintendent Wharton? I'm John Cleaver."

Wharton introduced me. Two chairs had been placed for us, and we sat down, and I was still rather dazed at the sounds that had come from Cleaver's throat. He was of medium height and immensely fat, but the voice had had nothing of an asthmatical wheeze. It was a kind of piping treble that lost itself in an occasional shrillness and had to be recovered with a clearing of the throat. His black coat had still the fallen ash of a cigarette. The old-fashioned wing collar just gave room for the ample chins, and the black bow was definitely ready-made. He looked about sixty; hair white and drawn as camouflage across the whitish-yellow of the skull.

"We won't take up too much of your time," Wharton told him. "We've just called about a client of yours—a Colonel Marquis."

"Indeed?"

For all its fatness, his face was curiously mobile. It was like an instrument on which he played. There had been a smile; then came a shade of concern.

"Nothing serious, I hope?"

Wharton told him. I was watching that face—the consternation, the growing horror, the personal distress.

"Incredible, my dear sir! A man so harmless, so amiable." He leaned as far forward as that spread of his would admit. "What was it? A burglarious attack?"

"Burglars don't strangle," Wharton told him grimly.

"No," he said. A fat hand slowly caressed his upper chin while he pondered the matter.

"Strangled," he said. "Incredible. The sort of man one could never imagine having an enemy in the world. Surely the work of some maniac?"

"Maybe," Wharton said. "But we'd like you to tell us all you knew about him. In the strictest confidence, naturally."

Cleaver smiled tolerantly.

"I don't think that should take long. I'd always acted for his sister and I had the pleasure of acting for him when he came into her small estate. And over the purchase of his house at Stapley Green. Since then he's consulted me from time to time about various small investments." He gave a Whartonian purse of the lips. "I'd seen him once or twice a year perhaps. There was certain legal business, of course, in connection with the employment agency, but Unstone, his manager, usually saw to that. You've seen Unstone?"

"As a matter of fact, we have," Wharton said. "It was he who gave us your name."

"A most efficient person, Unstone. Reliable—and trust-worthy."

Three adjectives, and he wasn't prodigal with them. Each had come almost tentatively, and he had been watching Wharton's face.

"Yes," George said. "That's how he struck me. But this sister of the late Colonel Marquis. Her maiden name was Marquis, I take it?"

A quick narrowing of the eyebrows and Cleaver was back to his smile.

"Yes. There's no harm in saying that it was."

"Why should there be harm?"

Cleaver forced a chuckle.

"My dear sir, just a figure of speech. Just the habit one has of respecting the affairs of a client."

Wharton was just the least bit worried. He, too, was finding Cleaver a something out of the rut of experience.

"The late Colonel's will," he said. "You could tell us the main provisions?"

"Will?" he said. "We have no will."

The hands rose and fell. One dropped a hint, he said, and the client agreed. One hinted again and an appointment would almost be made. Then, as in the case of Colonel Marquis, it was too late.

"I know," Wharton told him. "Like appointments with a dentist. Or everyone's mortal except themselves."

He let out a breath, made as if to get to his feet, then sat on.

"Am I right in saying you can't help us, Mr. Cleaver? You can't think of a single person who had any reason to kill him?"

"Unhappily, not. I knew him as a client and any opinions I had were formed as such. I may say that they were very high opinions. Who his friends were, or his enemies, I couldn't say. After all, we do make enemies. No human calculation or way of life can guard against that."

"True enough," Wharton said, and really got to his feet. Cleaver hadn't finished.

"Providence, my dear sir, is inscrutable. I say it with all solemnity, but it behoves us all to realise we're in the hands of a Higher Power."

He was holding out his hand. Wharton took it like a man bewildered. I was keeping in the background, but the hand sought me out.

"Goodbye, gentlemen. I only wish this brief interview had been on a more pleasant subject. And I could have been more helpful. But don't hesitate to make any demands on me if there's anything I can do. Goodbye, sir. And to you, sir."

The baize door closed behind us. The man took us over, and for the life of me I couldn't help seeing a something supercilious in the suggestion of a smile. George strode on to the car. What was bottled up inside burst out as the car moved off.

"Him and his god-palaver! Who the hell did he think we were?"

"I think he knew only too well who we were," I told him and just a bit placatingly. "He knew all about Marquis. A thousand to one Unstone had rung him up. And—if you don't mind my saying so—it was he who was really asking the questions, not we."

"Yes," he said, still smouldering. "I'll have a question or two to ask before I've finished with him, or my name's Robinson."

He even snapped the head off the driver who'd asked if it was back to the Yard. And back to the Yard we went.

"Two o'clock we're seeing this Clandon," he told me when we got out of the car. "You'd better be here at about ten to. I've got an idea about that Cleaver. Wouldn't be surprised if the Law Society couldn't give us a quiet tip."

I was thinking that over while I had my lunch. Everything about that Raglan Court office had been queer, and in our time we'd called on a good many score of solicitors. Even Unstone had tactfully—or was it with a craftiness of precaution—referred to it as a small firm. In that room of Cleaver's there had been only a very few deed boxes and precious few papers. There had been a safe and a small library of law books, but by and large that room had looked more of a reception office than the private room of the head of a firm. But maybe there was a third room in which they kept the legal lumber. I didn't know, but I did know that Cleaver himself had been as astute a bird as I'd run across for a number of years.

It was as if he held all the cards and worried very little about his opponents' hands. The man was an actor, and a better one than even George Wharton. I recalled the look on his face as he'd gently presented to Wharton those glowing testimonials to the likeableness of Marquis and the trustworthy competence of Unstone. The way he'd covered that question of Marquis's enemies by that god-palaver screed that had so infuriated Wharton, and how that all the time his eyes had never left Wharton's face. And what, in my mind at least, it all boiled down to was this. *Was he the third of the triumvirate, or was he not?* I wasn't dead sure, but I'd have been prepared to bet a nice little sum that he was.

I'd had precious little time for lunch, and I only just made the yard in time for George. Clandon's place was so near that I thought we'd have walked, but we went in the car. George was himself again. His bark is always worse than his bite, and his rare volcanoes brief and erratic in their eruptions.

I thought he was pleased with Clandon and appreciative of the room. I was guessing that everything would be friendly, and it was. Clandon pleased me, too. His manner had just a nice touch of the apprehensive, and Wharton had to put him at his ease.

"I don't say that Mr. Travers here is unreliable, but it's always as well to hear a story at first hand. Suppose you tell me all about it."

Clandon told him. The story was practically word for word the one that had been told to me. George listened and grunted. Then the rabbits began coming out of the hat.

"I've got it, Mr. Clandon. And, if you'll allow me to say so, I see no reason to question a word. And let me see . . ."

He took out his notebook, donned those antiquated spectacles, looked at nothing in particular, then peered over their tops.

"Your regiment was the Third So-and-So's?"

"That's right, sir." He was looking rather surprised.

"You joined them on the eight of September 1939. You were recommended for a commission in 1940. You were severely wounded in Sicily when you were a first-lieutenant. You were discharged from hospital two months later and convalesced in Egypt. You were then transferred to Intelligence and were finally demobilised in 1947 with the rank of major."

"Everything correct, sir."

Wharton put away the notebook. The slightly magisterial became friendly again.

"Glad to see you weren't huffy about all that. Can't always trust people's word, you know, and the sheep have to suffer for the goats. But what were you doing before you joined up, Mr. Clandon?"

"Actually I was in Chile."

Wharton's eyebrows lifted.

"That's a devil of a way off."

"It is—rather," Clandon told him. "I'm an orphan and I was with an uncle in Santiago. He was a mining engineer and I was hoping to be something of the sort, and then he died in the spring of 1939 and I didn't think things looked too good here at home, so I came back. Just got here in time to join up."

"And now you're a publisher."

"Not too good a one," Clandon said diffidently. "I'd always had rather a hankering for that kind of thing, and Peter Halmer happened to be in my particular corner of Intelligence, and we were friendly, and then his people put a proposition up to me and I happened to be able to put some money into the firm, and that's about all."

"I get you," Wharton told him. "But about something else. You've been told what's happened to this Dibben?"

Clandon gave me just the right look.

"Well, if it isn't an indiscretion, I have. Mr. Travers gave me an idea. In strict confidence, of course."

It wasn't an indiscretion. I'd put those words into his mouth. Now I was telling George I'd thought we could afford to trust Clandon.

"Agreed," he said. "But what were your reactions, Mr. Clandon? Did anything come back to your mind?"

"Never a thing," Clandon told him. "Everything's even more of a mystery than it was before. Seeway mentions Dibben to me, and Dibben isn't Dibben at all. He's masquerading as a Colonel Marquis. And why should *I* have anything to do with him? Why did he think *I* should be interested? The more I think about it, the more the whole thing seems crazy."

"You've never been connected with the stage?"

"Never."

Wharton grunted. He hauled out his notebook again. "And you don't know Bassingford?"

"Mr. Travers may have told you I went to it recently only to see a client of ours about a manuscript. I was in and out again, so to speak."

"Yes," Wharton said gloomily. "It's certainly something of a teaser. I can generally see through brick walls as well as most people, but this one hasn't got any cracks."

"Mind if I say something?" Clandon asked him, and almost nervously.

"Why not?"

"Well, it's bound to sound presumptuous, but I'm convinced myself that everything's connected with this place Bassingford. Seeway did come from there, and Dibben did some acting there. I even wonder—"

He was sheepishly shaking his head as he broke off. "Wonder what?"

"It'd be damn cheek if I told you," he said. "I just wondered if Seeway mightn't have had some reason to kill Dibben, or Marquis, or whoever he was."

"Strange to say," Wharton told him with quite a gentle irony, "that fact hasn't altogether escaped us, but Seeway mayn't even be alive."

"So Mr. Travers was telling me."

"Ah well," Wharton said, and got up from his chair, "we'll be doing our humble best to find out. You staying on here or going anywhere?"

Clandon said he was going back to Sussex Street, Strand. Wharton offered him a lift, and Clandon said he'd be glad of it. When we got to the publishing office, Wharton shook hands and was pretty profuse in thanks. When Clandon had gone he was running his eye over the building.

"Prosperous-looking place," he told me as the car moved off. "And a nice chap, that Clandon. One of your Oxford and Cambridge men, but not so lah-di-dah as a good many of 'em."

That's the sort of remark that makes life with George Wharton well worth the living.

Sergeant Matthews was back from Bickhurst. He's a quiet, even-tempered sort of chap with a sense of humour: he has to be to live at Wharton's beck and call.

There was nothing but the negative to report. The hotel had changed hands in the last twelve months and most of the staff was new. Not a soul remembered a Major and Mrs. Rome. That meant nothing was known about their car, but Matthews had tried the only garage in the village, just in case, and had learned nothing there. The only positive thing he had learned was that that four-year-old hotel bill was a genuine duplicate.

"Any employees there now who were taken on through the Weeks Agency?" Wharton wanted to know.

"Never a one, sir," Matthews told him.

"A pity," Wharton said. "That means we've got to find some way of putting the squeeze on Unstone. I doubt if it'll be enough to let him know we've got his record." He clicked his tongue annoyedly. "A smart move that—getting rid of the books. A thousand pities that bloody fool of a man let Rappham slip through his hands."

"Any chance of making Rappham talk?"

"I don't want to jump too soon," he told me. "Let him have a bit more rope."

He took out his notebook and ran his eye over those hieroglyphics he calls shorthand. I think they're his own invention.

"Has anything particular occurred to you about that solicitor fellow—Cleaver?"

I said I'd a vague idea that he might be the third of the black-mail gang, leaving out the dead Marquis as one who merely kept a general eye on things and took a big lump of the proceeds.

"My own idea, too," he told me. "The three of 'em—hand in glove. Unstone planted the right men in the right place, Rappham got the evidence, and then Cleaver wrote one of the parties a nice little guarded letter. Who actually collected the money doesn't matter, but you bet your life Marquis didn't. And that's what we're up against: not three individuals but three of them together. Everything's been covered up and every man-jack's got his own story ready. I don't think one of 'em would crack under pressure. That means we've got to find something that lines the whole three of 'em up."

He put the notebook back.

"We'll find it. Don't worry about that. Maybe Summer'll have something for us at Stapley Green."

"I was wondering if it mightn't pay if I slipped along to Bassingford again," I told him. "My hunch is still that there's something in that Seeway business."

"Might be," he said. "See you here later tonight."

He and Matthews went off. It was ten minutes to three and that didn't leave me much time, with the banks closing at three. So I rang down and asked for some urgent calls to Bassingford. I wanted the bank that had handled the affairs of the former Mrs. Proden, *née* Rosamund Vorne. When the right one was found I wanted an appointment with the manager at about four o'clock.

It seemed a good move to me. Somewhere in the background of things was the mysterious David Seeway: the man who had thought it necessary—and for heaven knew what reason—to mention to a sick man who even knew nothing about Bassing-ford the name of an Archie Dibben. And now the Archie Dibben had been murdered. If Seeway were alive, he ought to be found. As Clandon had suggested and as both Wharton and I had thought, he was a man who might conceivably fit the bill as the killer of Dibben-Marquis. And the only remaining source of information untapped by me about Seeway was Proden's former wife, the woman who, before her marriage to Proden, had been at least Seeway's friend. Proden had frankly told me as much.

It was on the stroke of three, and then the buzzer went. The bank was the Midland, and the manager, a Mr. Trew, would see me at four o'clock. Five minutes later I was on the way to Bassingford.

I found the bank and drew the car up outside. I rang the side bell and was shown into the manager's office. I showed Trew my warrant card and he asked what I wanted to know.

"Almost everything you can tell me," I said. "In the strictest confidence, of course. And to keep it from being one-sided, I'll tell you what it's all about. You'll be reading some of it, by the way, in your morning paper."

The version was closely edited. All I told him, in fact, was that we had reason to believe that a murdered man named Marquis had been connected with a David Seeway who had left Bassingford in 1939 and had not been heard of since. Enquiries in the town had given me practically nothing, and as a last resort I was thinking of interviewing the former Mrs. Proden who'd been, or so I was authoritatively informed, a friend of Seeway's in 1939.

"I've only been here a matter of six years," he said. "I didn't know Seeway, but I seem to remember the name. Was he by any chance a nephew of old Miss Ladely?"

I said he was. And, of course, a cousin of Hugh Proden.

"But about the former Mrs. Proden," I said. "What I was hoping for was merely her address. You don't happen to have it?"

He left me for a minute or two while he consulted his files. When he came back he said he hadn't the address, but the account had been transferred to the Midland at Canterbury. I'd get what I wanted there.

"I'm practically sure she married again," he told me. "I remember seeing a notice of it in *The Times*. Someone with a double-barrelled name as far as I can remember."

"Pretty well off, wasn't she?" I caught the look of withdrawal in his eye. "I only ask because I like to know the kind of person whom I'm going to meet. It makes things all that much easier when you're talking."

"Yes," he said. "The Vornes were quite wealthy. And she was a very charming woman. Very charming indeed."

"Does Proden bank with you?"

"No," he said. "But the Vornes were always clients of the Midland."

"Then tell me this," I said. "The divorce, by the way, must have made quite a local stir."

He gave a man-of-the-world sort of smile and a shrug of the shoulders.

"Not so much as you'd think," he said. "These things can be more or less hushed up, but I own there was a bit of surprise when it did come out."

"And who divorced whom?"

"Well, strictly between ourselves, she divorced him. I wouldn't have a word of this repeated for the world, but he was carrying on with an ex-usherette. A devilish pretty girl, too. She's left the town now, but I've heard the rumour that he's got her installed somewhere." He gave another shrug of the shoulders. "The trouble with those things is that you never know what to believe and what not."

"You know him pretty well?"

"Quite well. A nice chap, Proden. Very well liked."

"But he must have missed his wife's money?"

"I doubt it," he said. "I've heard he came in for quite a big sum of money when his aunt died. He owns a lot of property locally, you know."

"Well, that's about all," I said, and got to my feet. "To sum him up, you'd call him a man of absolute integrity."

"Decidedly so." He gave yet another shrug of the shoulders. "About that woman of his—well, that's beside the point. We all have our little weaknesses and mine don't just happen to be women."

Chapter Ten
FRUITFUL JOURNEY

I MOVED the car on to those tea-rooms I'd patronised before, and over a pot of tea and cakes I was wondering if there was anything else I could do in Bassingford. Then it struck me that I at least owed it to Proden to tell him something about the Marquis-Dibben affair. After all, he'd be reading about it in his morning paper. And though I was pretty sure there was nothing else that Proden could usefully tell me, I knew it was always good policy to keep on amicable terms with someone who had conferred even the slightest favour. So I thought I'd drop in on Proden for just a minute or two and give him the Dibben news, and then get back to town.

It was a hot, almost sultry afternoon. As I drew the car up outside Beaulieu I saw the gardener clipping the front hedge. He saw me as I stepped out, and he came along to the car, shears in hand.

"Afternoon, sir. Were you looking for Mr. Proden?"

"Just wanted a word with him," I said. "Is he in?"

"Afraid he isn't, sir. He's up near Doncaster. Went there the day before yesterday."

"By car?"

"Yes, sir. In the little Austin."

I'm interested in cars. It struck me that Proden ought to have had a fine big car—even a Rolls.

"As a matter of fact, sir, there was a Lanchester, but it belonged really to madam and she took it when she left. The guvnor didn't bother about replacing it. He reckoned the Austin was quite good enough. And it didn't use all that petrol."

"Sensible fellow," I said. "And when's he coming back?"

"Tomorrow, sir. I'll tell him you called."

I slipped him a half-crown and then, with my hand at the car door, I thought of something. Proden had left Bassingford on the day when Dibben had been killed. That was merely a fact and nothing to do with the actual killing. And yet something—a dislike of loose ends or a shameless curiosity—made me ask the question.

"What time did Mr. Proden leave?"

"Round about six-thirty, sir. He had a business appointment he was grumbling about."

"A longish journey. He wouldn't make it that night." He smiled.

"He'd make it, sir. He always did say he preferred driving at night."

I don't dislike it myself. I'd rather see headlights round a corner than some fool who's cutting in. And with regard to those loose ends I mentioned, I was thinking something else as I moved the car off. By no conceivable chance could Proden have been on the way to Doncaster at six-thirty and at Stapley Green at a quarter-past seven. Not that I had any reason to connect Proden and Marquis. For over twelve years Proden had neither seen the man nor even thought of him. He'd be as titillated as the rest of its readers when he saw in his morrow's paper the sensational story of the Dibben-Marquis murder.

As I came to the southern outskirts of the town I wondered if I ought to look up Finney, and on a sudden impulse I slewed the car round. I found him in his garden, digging up a row of peas he'd stripped of their last pods.

"Just passing," I said, "and I thought I'd look you up."

"Got nothin' fresh for you," he said. "If I had I'd have let you know. Might have somethin' in a day or two, though."

He was tapping his skull with a finger.

"Got somethin' in here about that Seeway. Can't sorta remember what it was. Almost had it last night, and then, in a manner o' speakin', I didn't."

"Can't stay," I said, and held out a hasty hand. "If anything does come back to you, let me know."

It was half-past six when I got back to the Yard. I wasn't expecting Wharton in from Stapley Green, but he'd just returned. Summer had a whole mass of information about Marquis from the half-dozen men of his own age or handicap with whom he'd played golf, and not a word of it, according to

Wharton, was of the slightest use in the case. All it proved was that Marquis had played a part and played it fantastically well. Never a man had doubted that he'd soldiered all his life—chiefly in India—and was spending his retirement in a suburb handy for golf and town. Every one of them had been at some time or other in Redgates for a drink. Two of them said that Marquis had a throat weakness, which was why he had had, by specialist's orders, to wear a beard. But for speaking well of the dead, Summer thought some would have called him a bit of a bore. All described him as a free spender with private means that must far have exceeded his pension.

As for that other business, of a man seen entering or leaving Redgates on the evening of the murder, nothing whatever had emerged. The road, after all, was very much of a backwater, and came to a dead end some two hundred yards past the house. Each of those houses had been built at the same time, and the gardens laid out with the same twin shrubberies for privacy. All the murderer had to do was to look from the upper window of Redgates and see a clear fairway, and then a quick look from the garage gates would show if the road was clear. If it wasn't, all he had to do was nip into the shrubbery till the passer-by had gone.

The shrubberies and garden had been searched in the hope of finding the blunt instrument, but nothing had been found. According to Mrs. Spiggott and the Saturday charwoman, nothing was missing from the house, and it looked as if the murderer had brought with him whatever it was that had stunned Marquis just as he had brought his own length of cord.

"One thing I couldn't quite understand," I said to George. "Why didn't we find a gun in the house? Surely Marquis must have lived in a state of alertness? I don't say alarm, but he must have been ready for the arrival of some victim of the gang."

George didn't agree. He thought Marquis's tracks were too well covered. He was the founder and perpetual president, so to speak, and all he had to do was keep well in the background and collect his share of the spoils. George didn't claim that he mightn't have had a gun. It might have been in a handy drawer in the room, and the murderer might have known it and used it as a blunt instrument. Not that it mattered. The finding of the kind of man for whom we were looking would never depend on the finding of that blunt instrument.

I told him about my afternoon at Bassingford and it was agreed that in the morning I should interview the former Mrs. Proden. George was proposing to see Unstone with a view to interpreting those initials and private marks on the stubs of the office cheque-book.

"Putting any pressure on?"

"Oh no," he said. "Just asking for his help."

"You think you'll get it? Some of those payments were almost certainly to Rappham and Cleaver."

George said it would be largely a blind. Unstone had told us that the office kept records of business and that Marquis took them away for entry in the ledger. But there ought to be duplicates.

"What I want," George said, "is the name of every person placed in employment for as far back as I can get. If he claims the duplicates weren't kept, I'll threaten him with the Commissioners of Inland Revenue. Or before I do that, I might make him and that Miss Ball produce everything from their memories. Haven't quite worked it all out yet. All I know is, I'm going to make him feel mighty uncomfortable before I leave Spenser Street."

I was asking about those cash sums paid into Marquis's private account, when a letter came up for George. I saw his eyes pop a bit as he began to read it. He was chuckling as he passed it to me.

"Just what the doctor ordered!"

It was a private and confidential chit from the Law Society with reference to John Cleaver. His real name was John Clare Smallcraft and he had been a member of the firm of Clare, Smallcraft and Clare at N— in the Midlands.

On the death of his father he was really the firm. In 1922 he was struck off the roll. Certain irregularities were proved and other more serious ones were suspected. He left N— and in 1925—he was then forty-five—was employed by Harries, Mavin and Co. of Birmingham. Ten years later, his conduct having been exemplary and on the recommendation of his employers, he was restored to the roll. In 1936 he acquired a partnership with Alfred Hewes of Cleaver and Hewes, and, on the death of Hewes in the following year, he changed his name by deed-poll to John Cleaver.

"What's the meaning of that piece about being employed by that Birmingham firm?" George asked me. "If he was struck off, how could he be employed?"

I said that probably the firm knew him, and his father before him, and had been willing to give him employment for the sake of old times. Being struck off meant that he couldn't do legal work for himself, or quote himself as a solicitor on any note-paper. He wasn't even allowed to do what might be called solicitor's work for the Birmingham firm like conveyances or probates—but merely general work.

"And he went straight for ten years?"

"So it seems. And saved enough money to buy a partnership."

"A pity," George said, and it was the going straight that he meant. "Not that this isn't some pretty good ammunition."

Matthews came in then, so I left. It was best part of eight o'clock and it seemed to me we'd had an uncommonly good day.

I was up early in the morning, and as soon as I was dressed I went down to the hall and bought a selection of papers. *The Times*, of course, merely printed the Dibben-Marquis affair with a certain distasteful regret, and *The Telegraph* with a definite decorum though far more fully, but there wasn't any doubt about the delight with which it had been seized by the rest. The banner headlines were there, and plenty of photographs. And in the few hours at their disposal the news ferrets had certainly driven quite a few rabbits from the deepest of holes. Things might need checking, but there we were, gratuitously provided with the life story of the man who'd been born Archibald Marquis.

And that had been at a Manchester suburb where his father kept a newspaper-tobacco shop, plus a small local employment business. Arch—the name by which he appeared to have been locally known—graduated to the music-hall in the usual way, through a choir-boy voice and local concerts, and so to smoking concerts and Saturday-night do's, where, after the breaking of his treble voice, he became quite a good baritone and then discovered himself to be a wit.

"Of course, I knew Arch Marquis," said Mr. Ramsbottom of Chorley Lane. Charlie Ramsbottom, I may say, is very much of a wit himself. "Arch and I were at school together, just down the road there. . . ."

That was the kind of thing: interviews galore, from the, "E-eh, he was always a rum 'un, was Arch," to the staidly obituarial. Behind it all was often a slightly ironic chuckle that reminded me of Goering's cyanide and the comment of the German man in the street—*Der alte Hermann!*" For Dibben, like Goering, had been a character to the last. And that, of course, was what most of the papers played up: Dibben, fooling the world with a real-life presentation of what had once been a music-hall turn. In spite of myself I couldn't help chuckling. There'd be some mighty self-conscious people for quite a few days in the clubhouse at Stapley Green. And Summer would have his work cut out to control the curious that would be now on the way for a look at Redgates.

But if I had to be at Canterbury at ten o'clock, I had to be on the move, for the fifty-five miles included quite a stretch of suburb. I drove my own car, and once I was in reasonably open country I was thinking, of necessity, about the case. I recognised, of course, that it had hardly begun, for it was still not more than a day and a half since Marquis's body had been discovered. And it's rare that there's any tremendous urgency about the opening of a case. The Yard is a kind of supreme authority. No one barks at our heels when we fail to get results. And there's no time limit at the Yard. I've known a case reopen after ten long years. To some, the mill-stones may seem to grind slowly, but, believe me, they grind exceedingly small.

In the matter of Dibben-Marquis, after only thirty-six hours, I knew that we had an enormous amount of data, but the one thing about which we were by no means sure was motive. That

Marquis was a blackmailer seemed a certainty, and therefore, on the face of it, his murderer should have been one of his victims. But it wasn't so easy as that. I agreed with George Wharton that Marquis had kept himself well behind the scenes, and I saw no immediate way in which such a victim might have been aware of his activities. If anyone should have been murdered, it was probably Rappham, and possibly Unstone or Cleaver. Rappham, judging by that telephone communication which he was supposedly having with Marquis that afternoon at Redgates, was the one who made the vital connection between the victim and the gang, but Rappham was still hale and hearty. Then there was the matter of the intrusion of that queer Seeway business, and the mystery of the apparent bond between him and the dead man. If Seeway were alive, and the murderer, what was the motive? And was he in any way connected with that dubious trio of Unstone, Rappham and Cleaver?

I didn't know. All I could do was ask questions and hope for answers. And in that context, the further I drove, the less hopeful I was about the answers I was likely to get when I talked with the former Mrs. Proden. Why should she be able to tell me any more than I had learned from her ex-husband? A man should know more about a man, just as a woman knows infinitely more about a woman. It was suddenly striking me, in fact, that I was rushing to Canterbury rather like a bull at a gate. Passivity was never in my line, and I'd wanted to be doing something. And now, at various pessimistic moments, I was telling myself that I was wasting my time. But I kept on driving. And it was as well that I did.

The bank manager was waiting for me. I could have got the information over the telephone, but there's always a hope of the unexpected about the personal touch. Not that the unusual eventuated that morning. I learned that Rosamund Proden had re-married at the end of 1947 and that her husband was a Colonel Caverly-Hare of the Old Grange, Maddenham. He was now a fruit farmer, and the Grange itself was a fine old place. Maddenham, by the map he drew for me, was rather out in the long grass, though only six miles from Canterbury. I assured him the bank would not be mentioned, and the information I gave him in return was that I was seeing the lady on a matter of comparative triviality. She, in fact, had been to school with a someone with whom we were anxious to get into touch, and we were just hopeful she might have news of her, and no more.

I drove on along narrowish lanes through hop gardens and orchards and stretches of undulating farmland. I went through a couple of hamlets and came at last to Maddenham. It looked a place of about five or six hundred people, with a tiny main street and scattered houses along still narrower side lanes. I pulled up at the post-office-shop. I had to manoeuvre my car past an almost new and expensive and very shiny coupé that stood plumb in front of the door.

It was the usual country shop, counter and shelves piled with tinned goods, and even the floor so chock-a-block as to leave scarcely a gangway to the post-office counter. A woman was there, talking to an elderly woman assistant, or maybe she was the owner of the shop. The younger woman would be the owner of the coupé, and as soon as I heard her voice I put her in the top stratum. She was youngish and, even to a man and from the back, her clothes had an air of distinction. She seemed to be discussing the affairs of the local Women's Institute. I cleared my throat, not as a hint that I was waiting to be served, but just because there was a slight tickling, but she turned and I saw her face. And then she was going.

"I'll see you on Thursday morning, then, Mrs. Porter. Everything shall be ready."

A smile and she had gone.

"A half-crown book of stamps," I said, and slid my half-crown under the wire partition that fronted the counter. I put the book in my wallet.

"The lady who just went out," I said. "Isn't she Mrs. Caverly-Hare?"

"Yes," she said. "That was Mrs. Caverly-Hare."

I gave a nod and a smile, said I thought I'd recognised her, and went out to the car. The coupe was just in sight ahead and I shot my car after it. By the time I was within a hundred yards it was turning into a drive on the left. I drove just on. A moment or two and I got out and walked back.

The Old Grange stood on a slight rise about a hundred yards back from the lane. It was a spacious, half-timbered house and the tiles of its ancient roof were indescribably lovely in that morning sun. Before its front the garden was terraced and a flagged path across the lawn ended in stone steps that went up to the house. Through the trailing, yellowish branches of a tall weeping-willow, I could catch the colourful line of a long herbaceous border. It was the sort of place that made one wonder why fools like myself still herded in flats.

I went back to the car. Fifty yards ahead a man was coming out of a field gate.

"This is the Old Grange, isn't it?"

"Yes, sir," he said. "That's the Old Grange."

His eye went quickly over me. He asked if I was wanting to see the Colonel.

"You'll find him down the road, sir. In them strawberries, about three or four hundred yards on the left."

I passed a field of raspberries where two or three women were at work tying, then a field that was planted out with chrysanthemums, then a field of peas, and there was the strawberry field. There looked about five good acres of it, and at least a score of women were working along the rows. Just inside the gate was a long shed that would be used for packing and weighing, and through its windows towards the road I could just see a movement and no more. I drew the car up about twenty yards beyond.

I sat there for a good five minutes, and I was thinking hard. Then I had an idea. I looked back, and the man to whom I had spoken by the Grange had definitely gone the other way. I let the car run gently downhill to the gate, and I got out. I walked round to the front of that shed.

A cindered track led to it and beyond, and under the lee of the tall hedge was a thirty-hundredweight truck. In the shed a couple of women were weighing punnets of fruit. In the near corner was a roughly made desk on four tall legs, and a man was working there, checking invoices and making entries in a book. Except at its ends, the front of that shed was open to the weather and my shadow fell across and caught his eye. Maybe he took me for one of the women, for he made a movement of the head and went on with his checking. His neck was smooth, and red as the tiles of his house. Below the khaki shorts the backs of his legs were a leathery brown. I gave a little cough, and he turned.

"Sorry," I said, "but you don't happen to sell fruit to passers-by like myself?"

"Afraid not," he told me frigidly. "Wouldn't pay us."

His eyes—they were a cold blue against the almost white blondness of his hair—went over me from shoes to hat.

"Sorry." There was a shade less curtness. "If we once began that sort of thing we'd be pestered."

"No harm in trying," I told him amiably, but my smile was wasted. He was back at his invoices and I might have been elsewhere.

I went back to the car. I had to drive a good mile on before I could reverse it, and as I came back past that field, I caught a glimpse of Colonel Caverly-Hare, in the field itself now, and talking to the pickers. A hundred yards past the Grange I stopped the car again. There was a telephone kiosk outside the post office and I wondered if I should use it. Somehow I didn't like the idea, and I moved the car on. It was about a quarter to twelve when I got back to Canterbury.

I rang the Yard from the local station and was told that Wharton was out. Matthews was in and he told me that Wharton was expected back by one o'clock at the latest. I said I'd ring again at one o'clock to the dot, and, if he got the chance, would he tell Wharton it was urgent.

I found a place for lunch and lingered the meal out. One o'clock found me ringing the Yard again. Wharton was on the line almost at once.

"I'm ringing from Canterbury, George," I said, "and I've got a facer for you. I picked up Proden's ex-wife and saw her husband. She's now the wife of a Colonel Caverly-Hare and they're at a village about six miles from here."

"All right," he told me impatiently. "What'd she have to say?"

"I didn't speak to her," I said. "That's what I'm ringing you about."

"Didn't speak to her! What made you change your mind?"

"Just this," I said. "You know that photograph of the couple at the Downland Court Hotel? Well, they're it. They're Major and Mrs. Rome."

CHAPTER ELEVEN
THE LADY TALKS

THERE were at least three choices: Wharton could bring that print and hotel bill with him and we could confront the Caverly-Hares together, or he could send it down to me by a man and let me do the job, or he could have me come back to town. He chose the latter. And I admit he was most apologetic. When I'd had another look at that print and reaffirmed that the Caverly-Hares were Major and Mrs. Rome, he was a nice mixture of the exultant and the cautious.

"You don't remember the date of her divorce?" he was asking me.

"The spring of 1947," I said. "We can easily look it up and make sure."

I said he was cautious. He rang down and gave some instructions.

"Now," he said. "Was only one of them being blackmailed, or both?"

I thought it practically a certainty that Rosamund Proden, as she then was, would be the only one. Explanations may sound a bit ponderous, but in case you shouldn't happen to be familiar with the law as affecting divorce, this is how things must have concerned Rosamund Proden. In that spring she obtained her decree *nisi*, and *nisi* means what it says, which in Latin and law jargon simply means *unless*. But it's a tremendously big *unless*. It said, in so many words, that six months after the granting of that conditional decree, the divorce would be made abso-lute, *unless* during that period new facts came to light or she committed adultery. And she had committed adultery. She had spent that weekend with the man she later married. And if that fact was brought to the notice of the King's Proctor, he would intervene and the petition would be squashed.

It was up to us to discover what the procedure had been as far as concerned the blackmail gang. At the hotel was the employee—spotter, if you like—with his chance of making a nice little sum on the side. Reception staffs of any experience can usually spot unmarried couples and word would be got through to Unstone or Rappham. Rappham would go to the hotel armed with a camera. He would get the number of a car, or follow the couple when their stay was over. There would be cases, of course, where all that led to nothing, but not in the case of Rosamund Proden. Cleaver would handle the legal side, and maybe it was he who would apply the first pressure. Conjecture, of course, and it was our job to get it verified.

"I know," Wharton said. "And that's the question. Will she talk, or won't she?"

I said it wasn't only that. There was the complication of whether or not she'd subsequently told her husband. And if she had, then he'd have to be included in our interview.

"Just what were they like from what you saw of them?"

"Very much off the top shelf," I said. "She looked and sounded quite nice, but him I didn't cotton to at all. A mighty tough nut to crack. Looked the sort of man you'd find it hell to soldier under."

He grunted.

"Wonder if there's any way of finding out whether she told him?"

I didn't make it too ironic, but I said there was something else that was pretty important. Hadn't we better find out whether or not she'd paid?

"We can have a shot at it," he told me, and brought from the safe the statements furnished by the bank that handled Marquis's private account. We began early in 1947, and it was not till the

July that we found a likely entry. On the tenth of that month Marquis had paid in a sum of seven hundred pounds in cash.

"Might be it," Wharton said. "It'd take a couple of months for Cleaver to get everything fool-proof and apply the pressure and so on. Wonder what she actually paid? There'd be four of them to take a cut before Marquis got his share. The spotter wouldn't get a lot, but Cleaver'd want a pretty big cut."

"Let's take it for granted she paid," I said. "She was a wealthy woman and a couple of thousand wouldn't have embarrassed her. It was worth that if she badly wanted that divorce."

"But what a fool!"

"There must have been some reason for taking a chance," I said. "Maybe he'd been ordered abroad and she relied too much on things being carefully planned. But about seeing her. I've got an idea."

The idea was to see her, and possibly with her husband, and confine the enquiries to the matter of David Seeway. It was information we needed, in any case, and it would give me a good chance to see how the couple reacted to an enquiry that was quite innocuous.

George thought the idea was reasonably good.

"Why not take that other print?" he said. "Get her to look at it and spin some yarn about wondering if it was Seeway. Work the Dibben business in. They'll have seen this morning's papers."

We'd been disappointed over that faded print. Nothing could be done about restoring it, and to bleach it and try to re-tone might have ruined it altogether. All that could be told us about its age was that the Rapidox paper had been on the market in 1926. It might be that old or it might date to 1940 when the paper had been taken out of manufacture. Everything depended on the amount of light to which it had been exposed, and the lack of thoroughness with which the print had been washed and developed.

"There must be some connection between those two prints," Wharton said exasperatedly. "Together in that secret drawer and nothing else found. But maybe she'll know something. Try her, in any case."

We left it at that. I was to go down to Maddenham in the morning, and I proposed to get there early, before Caverly-Hare went to the fruit fields. George began telling me how he had prospered with Unstone.

"Everything ready and in apple-pie order. Duplicates of every bit of business over the last two years."

"Wasn't that a bit risky of him? I mean he was presenting us with the name of every man they put in employment."

"Risky, my foot!" he told me. "You bet your life that every man-jack of the spotter type has been told to lay off and act dumb. That'd be one of the first things Unstone did."

"What about those stub initials?"

"Very smooth," George said grimly. "All those that referred to wages and rent and bills and so on he spotted at once. Put on a bewildered act about the rest. Blamed it all on that business of Marquis taking things so much into his own hands. But I wasn't worrying. I even pretended I didn't know that a scrawled R. referred to Rappham and a C. to Cleaver." He gave what I call his Coliseum smile—that of a lion who spots a particularly plump Christian. "Great pals, Unstone and me. Like two bugs in a rug." Then he was saying he couldn't sit there talking. And maybe I'd better run along to that old block of flats where Marquis had lived before he bought Redgates. The Press hadn't been on to that and he had a couple of men making enquiries. So I put in an unprofitable hour at that flat near Bromley and then went home and wrote up my reports. And I was in bed early. In the morning I was proposing to be at Maddenham at the latest by soon after nine.

A grandfather clock was striking the hour as we drove up to the house. I'd thought it might give me more of an air to have a police car and driver, but the flourish was wasted, for there seemed never a soul about when I got out of the car. The front door was open and I rang twice and knocked before a soul appeared, and then an elderly maid said the Colonel was out and she thought Mrs. Caverly-Hare was in the garden. I gave her one of my private cards and was shown into a lounge-drawing-room. I waited quite ten minutes and I spent my time totting up the rough value of its major contents. I made it over two thousand pounds. There was a small Queen Anne bureau-bookcase that would have fetched five hundred, and a Swansea dessert service well worth four hundred more.

The door had been left open and I heard voices somewhere in the rear of the house.

"But why not, Mummy?" a boy's voice said.

"Because Mummy's busy, darling. You run off to Ethel and Mummy'll do it as soon as she can."

The steps were nearing. I was getting to my feet and I was remembering that Trew at Bassingford had thought there was a child. Then Rosamund Caverly-Hare was coming in. Perhaps you follow me when I say the name was what she looked like—beautiful poise, just the right smile, the sort of clothes one likes to see on a woman of one's own.

"How do you do, Mr. Travers. You wanted to see my husband? I'm afraid he's out, but we can fetch him if it's urgent."

There was a quick look: polite enough, but definitely puzzled. I put her at ease.

"We've actually seen each other before," I said. "I think we were in the local post office at the same time yesterday morning."

"But of course." She smiled, and it might have been relievedly. "But do sit down."

I said there was no need to disturb her husband. She took a chair that faced mine from across the old open fireplace. She sat almost demurely, hands in lap. An attractive woman, and still only about thirty. A face that you could fault in almost every feature, and yet the whole had charm and character and distinction.

"I'm afraid I've rather misled you," I began, and gave her my warrant card. "As you see, I'm here from Scotland Yard."

There was a quick movement in which she froze into immobility. The warrant card would have dropped from her fingers if I had not held it. She forced a smile.

"Of course . . . I mean—well, you're from Scotland Yard. Isn't that very unusual? I mean, how can Scotland Yard be concerned with anyone like myself."

She had gathered confidence as she went along.

"But of course we're not," I said. "The fact of the matter is that we're concerned with someone quite different. Someone we've gathered, after enquiries in Bassingford, that you might possibly have heard from. A David Seeway."

The colour flared across her face. She was saying she should close the door. There was a draught.

"David Seeway," she said as she sat down again. "It must be twelve years since I heard a word about him. He left Bassingford very abruptly, you know. Don't tell me poor David is dead?"

"We don't know," I said. "It's all very involved; a sort of A, B and C. We're investigating a highly suspicious individual whom we call A. B is David Seeway, and we know that those two knew each other in 1943, so we want to find Seeway and get him to tell us what he did know about A. We've tried various sources of possible information, as at Bassingford, and they haven't got us anywhere. But you're C. You knew David Seeway and we hoped you might be able to help. And may I add a word or two to that. I give you, on behalf of Scotland Yard, of course, my most solemn assurance that not a word of anything you may tell me will ever go beyond us two."

"I wish I *could* tell you something," she said, and was frowning away in thought. "But he just went. No one, as far as I really know, ever heard a word from him since. We didn't know if he were alive or dead."

I made a gesture of hopelessness.

"Mrs. Caverly-Hare," I said. "Please at least do something for me. Tell me everything you knew about him up to the day he left."

What she told me was what I already knew—family history and the Bassingford aunt and Seeway's being down from Cambridge and looking round for a job.

"Seriously looking round? I mean, he wasn't just content to sponge on his aunt?"

"Of course not," she told me with just a touch of resentment. "David wasn't like that."

"What *was* he like?"

The face flushed only slightly.

"He was charming, in a way. A bit irresponsible because his aunt had spoiled him, but absolutely right at heart. She was very strait-laced, of course."

"You were very friendly with him?"

"But of course."

"It wasn't anything more?" Her tongue was suddenly moistening her lips. "Bearing in mind that everything said is strictly confidential?"

"Well, it was more," she said, "and it wasn't. We were tacitly engaged. I don't think now we were ever really in love with each other, but we went about a lot together and we were quite good friends, and that's how it was."

"Yes," I said, and gave the word a certain solemnity. "I was told that in Bassingford, but naturally there was nothing about your being engaged. But what did Seeway tell you when he was going away?"

"Nothing," she said. "Or practically nothing. He went, as you might say, in the morning and I had a letter by the afternoon's post. What it said exactly I forget, but it was that he was tired of loafing in Bassingford and he was going away for a time to think things over." She raised a quick hand. "No, that wasn't quite it. He talked about roughing it. There might have been a mention of the colonies. I think there was."

"And that tacit engagement?"

"That," she said. "I remember that. He said he thought that neither of us had been too serious, and if I'd been serious, then he asked forgiveness. That sounds very novelettish, but perhaps you know what I mean."

"Not a bit of it. It sounds like the letter of quite a decent sort of man."

"David was," she told me quietly.

"More and more curious," I said, and gave a Whartonian pursing of the lips. "That doesn't tally with what I heard in Bassingford. I was given the impression that Seeway was a young cub and sponging on his aunt, and that he drank and couldn't stand his liquor and had been in trouble with the police, and was quarrelsome, and heaven knows what."

Her lips had clamped grimly together.

"You assure me this is confidential?"

"It's a confessional box," I said. "It's a doctor's surgery. Didn't I give you my word?"

"Then tell me something. Who gave you that information at Bassingford?"

"Your late husband," I said bluntly. "Hugh Proden."

She was upright in the chair. The tongue moistened the lips again.

"I knew it," she said.

There was a pause, and I waited. She was asking if she might tell me something.

"This is not spite," she said. "I was finished with Hugh Proden long before we were divorced. I'll tell you what I've thought about him and David—and myself. I hope you'll understand it. My husband knows about it. He always did know."

I had to picture a trio. There was the aunt, oldish and bigoted. David Seeway and Rosamund Vorne: two young people, expensively educated but still unformed and, in the things that matter, practically unsophisticated. Into that circle came suddenly Hugh Proden: older, travelled, with suavity and *savoir faire* and an infinite charm, deferential to the aunt and even ingratiating, and fascinating in the experience of the younger two. Within a few weeks of his arrival from Ceylon he dominated that small circle, and everyone was only too pleased to be so dominated. David hung on his words and aped his manner and copied his clothes. And then David went away. Proden had tried to dissuade him, but he went. The aunt was grim-lipped about it all. Rosamund, who had never cared too much, proceeded to forget. And she had Proden to help her. She married Proden. The aunt died and the Prodens were the heirs. They'd already been living at Beaulieu and they went on living there. And that ought to have been all.

But it wasn't. There was a woman married to a man who was old enough to be her father. For her it was a marriage of infatuation, and it wasn't long before the inevitable revulsion. Now she had to live with the charm.

"What was it?" I said. "A sort of veneer?"

"No," she said slowly. "I met a distant relative of his some time later and he told me Hugh had always been the same. It was his only real asset. Delightful manners and positively fascinating charm. I found it like gorging one's self on chocolates."

"Nothing behind the charm at all?"

"Nothing. Except self-interest and a kind of frightening hypocrisy, though it naturally took me some time to find all that out. Then I could see everything. He'd come home from Ceylon without a penny and he'd set himself to win the confidence of all of us, especially his aunt. I'm absolutely sure his objective from the very first was her money, and that meant discrediting David. I'm positive it was he who got David in such a dissatisfied frame of mind that he left Bassingford."

"Just one definite question there," I said. "There was a scene in the White Hart where David was said to be drunk and to have struck a man. You don't happen to know if that was true?"

"It was, and it wasn't. The man was a communist and insulting and David knocked him down. Hugh pretended to get it all hushed up, but I'm sure that he privately told Miss Ladely about it."

I couldn't tell her that everything she was telling me had a bearing on the case. But I had to keep the ball rolling.

"In a way it's frightening," I said. "But for one thing, I might almost have begun to suspect that Seeway never left Bassingford at all. It's a terrible thing to say, but Proden really ought to have murdered him and faked all that disappearance business. But he didn't. I know that Seeway was alive and in the Army in 1943."

"I knew before that," she said. "Just before we were married I was sure I saw a letter in David's writing, and he pretended it was something else. Now I know I was right!"

Was she unbiased? She had claimed to be, and yet I didn't know. It was as if for years she had dammed her feelings and now the hatreds and even the venom were being poured into my only too willing ears. Novelettish perhaps, as she had said in another context, but there it was. You couldn't get away from the fierce intensity of her voice and the deadly viciousness with which she had almost spat out her words. Nothing unladylike, mind you: just the sheer woman, so to speak, who had good reason to hate.

"I think you're entitled to be told more than I originally intended," I said. "You've been so frank with me, and so helpful. But another question first. Do you recall a name like Archie Dibben?"

A quick shake of the head, and then she was staring.

"Not that dreadful person who was in the newspapers? The man who was murdered?"

"That's the man," I said. "The man who'd been masquerading for years as a retired colonel. He, I ought to tell you, is the A I mentioned."

It took her a moment or two to grasp the full inferences. She was staring again.

"But what could David Seeway have had to do with a man like that?"

I leaned forward even more confidentially. I told her about Dibben in Bassingford: that Seeway had disappeared just afterwards, and that years later in Sicily Seeway had mentioned Dibben's name to a perfect stranger.

It was merely bewildering. She recalled that touring company and Dibben's name, but the rest was utterly incomprehensible. I took out that faded print.

"All this is highly confidential, but here's a photograph we found among Dibben's possessions—the man who'd been calling himself Colonel Marquis."

In a moment she had changed. In her eyes was a quick apprehension as I held that photograph out. I smiled, and, I hope, charmingly.

"You're not allergic to photographs?"

"What do you mean?"

"I once knew a woman who was," I said. "I'm allergic to telegrams. Show me one of those little yellow envelopes and I'm hot and cold all over."

She gave that print a quick glance. What she saw was reassuring her.

"It's very badly faded," she said. "And am I supposed to recognise it?"

"It couldn't possibly be Seeway?"

She looked at it again, and frowned. She held it the other way to make the recumbent figure upright.

"I couldn't say," she said. "But David was surely so much bigger—taller and slimmer."

"Well, there we are," I said. "We could only hope, and we were wrong."

I got to my feet. I told her how grateful I was, and how good it was of her to let me take so much of her time.

"You'll let me know if you discover anything about David? I'd so love to see him."

"I will," I said, and drew back to let her go through the door. "I've seen your husband, by the way. Purely unofficially. I happened to be going by a strawberry field yesterday morning and hoped to buy a basket. Apparently I was out of order. Is he tall, your husband? Blonde and blue-eyed and very brown?"

"That would be Richard," she said. I didn't look at her face, but there were innumerable things in her voice.

"Use your own judgment about telling him confidentially of this visit of mine," I said. "I don't know if the advice is of any use to you, but I also am an extremely happily married person. Nevertheless I've often found it tactful to keep my own counsel about certain episodes in my past."

"How clever you are!" she told me, and gave a little laugh. "Perhaps I shall take your advice."

"There's only just one thing," I went on. "It's just possible I may have to see you again, and your husband might happen to be here. Or Chief Superintendent Wharton might decide to see you himself."

I could almost feel her eyes on me. I went hurriedly on.

"He's quite easy to get along with. More of the gimlet-eyed type than myself, though. Looks very harassed and forlorn, but don't let that deceive you. I'd hate myself, to tell him a lie."

I still hadn't looked at her and it was as if I'd been talking to a second self. But I did turn when we were at the car.

"Lovely place you have here. Wish to heaven I could get out of town and live in something like it. And very kind indeed of you to see me."

"Yes," she said, and I knew it must be rarely that a woman like her could be at a loss for words.

I turned back from the very door of the car.

"Don't let ghosts frighten you," I told her quietly. "There's only one thing to do with ghosts. Face up to them."

Her eyes met mine and then she was turning away. Her tongue was nervously moistening her lips again. The car moved off, and when I looked back from the end of the drive she had gone.

CHAPTER TWELVE
PRODEN ONCE MORE

WHARTON was out when I got back, so I called in a stenographer and dictated a report while the whole of that interview was still vivid in my mind. When I returned from snatching a quick lunch, I found him in, and he'd just finished reading those typewritten sheets.

"One of your best," he was good enough to tell me. "Opens up a whole lot of new ideas, though."

"Such as?"

"Well, this Hugh Proden. According to her, he was a regular Mephistopheles. Turned up at Bassingford and got himself in well with the old lady and got rid of Seeway and married his girl and came in for the old lady's money. And you're still not sure if that ex-wife of his was biased or not?"

"Naturally she was biased," I said. "She couldn't help being. All the same, I'd rather trust her evidence than Proden's. That makes Proden out to be a prodigious liar. And if you refer to that report of mine after I got back from Bassingford the first time, you'll find question marks against a couple of things. One was that he said he didn't know Dibben and yet he'd given very much of a start as soon as I mentioned the name. The other was that his description of Dibben was at variance with a couple of other descriptions, just as if he'd been trying to put me off the scent."

"I know," he said, though I doubted if he did. "So just one little idea. Could he have killed Dibben? Was he the one who was interested in those photographs of Major and Mrs. Rome?"

"How could he be?" I said. "She divorced *him*. It was she who stood in danger of the King's Proctor. And whatever Proden is, he isn't a blackmailer. You can't keep on hoodwinking local opinion, and local opinion says he's a wealthy man. And, in my judgment, he isn't the type."

George grunted.

"I don't know that I wouldn't like to run my rule over him, for all that. Not that we haven't got a better suspect or two."

"If you do see him, you might contrive to look into his alibi for the murder night," I said. "You'll see in that second Bassingford report of mine that there was just a trifling coincidence. I don't claim it's more than that, but he went in his car to stay for a day or two with someone near Doncaster, and on the same evening as Dibben was killed. You might think it worth checking."

"Maybe I will," he said. "But he hasn't a motive like a few other people. This Colonel Caverly-Hare, for instance. What about *him*?"

"Could be," I said. "But only if he'd discovered in some amazing way who Marquis really was. And if Marquis was putting on the bite for a second time."

"Yes," he said. "It's all very tricky. It wants the very devil of a lot of thinking over. We don't want to jump too soon. After all, you seem to have left that Mrs. Caverly-Hare in a pretty nervous state. Maybe she and her husband may decide to talk of their own free will. That was your own idea?"

"Something of the sort," I said. "All the same, I can't get away from what seems more and more an undeniable fact—that Dibben had his own tracks well covered. I'm inclining to the idea of an inside job. Three people did know who he was."

"Yes," he said, "but I don't see Cleaver as a killer. I can see him rubbing his hands and talking about Providence after Dibben was killed, but not doing the job. Unstone? Maybe yes. I think Dibben had found out some peculation or double-crossing, and that's why he'd begun to handle a lot of vital business himself. Maybe Unstone was scared he'd find out about that Guildford business. Maybe he and Rappham put their heads together and decided they'd like to run the business themselves. Didn't like Dibben taking all that cut. Maybe they knew they'd have Cleaver's blessing."

"If so, that telephone call I happened to take was just a blind," I said. "I can't bring myself to think it was. Think of those vital two words—*he'll pay*. If it had been a blind, Rappham would have talked trivialities. We know those two words actually gave the game away."

There was something in that that he couldn't counter, but when I began suggesting that we were rather neglecting Rappham, he didn't agree. Rappham wasn't making a move without its being watched.

"All in good time," he said, and tried to make it genial. "You go gadding about the countryside. I spend half my time at that telephone keeping an eye on best part of fifty men. Men at Manchester, men at Stapley Green, men on the tails of our three friends. Looks as if I ought to put some more on that Caverly-Hare's tail, and on Proden's."

"You go and see Proden yourself," I told him placatingly. "Do a bit of gadding about yourself. Or run down to Maddenham."

That last hadn't been put too convincingly, but he hadn't seemed to notice. He said he might run down to Bassingford that evening if he could make time to read through those reports of mine again. As for myself, there wasn't an immediate job on hand. I was to have an hour or two off and report back later in the evening.

Bernice was out when I got to the flat, so I made myself some tea. Then the mail came up—just the one letter. It was from Clandon, and posted that morning.

"Dear Mr. Travers,

"I've decided, somewhat reluctantly I admit, to take your advice about letting that little commission of mine lie fallow for a bit. You may think me several kinds of a fool, but I wasn't so comfortable as I might have seemed about that talk with your Superintendent Wharton. I suppose it's a persistence of one's boyhood apprehension of the police, but I confess that I was scared stiff. Even the average honest citizen can't help a few qualms about coming into contact with the law, or so one reads, but to come into direct contact with Scotland Yard proved too much for me.

"I'm sure I must owe you people some money, so please send me your bill. It probably won't be settled for another ten days or so, as I'm just off for the balance of my holiday. I had to take the rest of the three weeks earlier in the year to help out another member of the firm. I shan't be going far. Just cruising around off the main tracks in that little car of mine. I'll be dropping a card now and again to Sussex Street in the rare event of the law wanting me again.

"Very many thanks indeed.

"Yours with good wishes,

"H. Clandon."

Quite a nice letter, I thought, and a sensible one, and I didn't somehow think Wharton would be wanting to see Henry Clandon again. So I put the letter in a handy drawer and rang Norris and told him the gist of it. Then I put on some comfortable slippers, reached for *The Times*, propped my long legs against the mantelpiece and took my mind off the Dibben-Marquis case with a cross-word puzzle. It was the harder kind, and I'd worked my way through about two thirds of it when the telephone went. George Wharton was on the line.

"You're in then," he said. "I'd rather like you to pop over. Something I'd like to suggest."

So I went back to the Yard. In the corridor from Wharton's room I met Molly Flynn. A pretty girl, Molly, and smart as they come. I've been in one or two cases where Wharton has planted her with first-class results. And I didn't see now where she could have come from unless it was Wharton's room. I asked him bluntly as soon as I went in.

"Ah, that," he said speciously. "Forgot to tell you that. All rigged up this morning after you'd gone. Weeks, Ltd. had an advertisement in the *Telegraph*. Various items and one for a receptionist for a high-class country hotel. Took us all the morning to coach her for the part and rig up testimonials. This afternoon she went round and saw Unstone."

"Any luck?"

"Don't know yet. Sounded to me as if this afternoon was a kind of try-out. She's reporting again at ten in the morning."

"Sounds hopeful," I said.

"Trust Molly to put on a good act. She'd a hard-luck story that'd brought tears into anyone's eyes. Willing to do anything—you know the kind of thing. Hope she didn't overdo it."

"It's too good to be true," I said. "But what'll you do if Unstone takes her on as a spotter? Arrange for a weekend couple of our own to go down to this hotel?"

"That's it," he said. "Get Rappham on the job and pick him up red-handed. But about this evening. Proden didn't have an idea you were in any way connected with us?"

I said he almost certainly had no idea. I'd been exactly what I was—an acting operative from the Broad Street Detective Agency.

"Then I think I'd like you to come along," he said. "It may be a bit of a jolt if he sees you walk in with me. And you'll be able to check up on any discrepancies."

Wharton had taken care to find out if Proden was back from that Doncaster trip, and the appointment was for six o'clock. There was no need for hurry, and as we drove slowly through the town I could point out the *Gazette* office, and the cinema that had once been the Theatre Royal.

"That reminds me," he said. "That man Finney you saw. Didn't he hint when he saw you last that he might have something else for you?"

"I didn't quite believe him," I said. "Finney's made a pound or two in not too hard a way and I think he was stringing me along. Wanted to keep a good client on his books, so to speak. Besides, if he'd really found anything for me, he'd have rung me or written."

A couple of minutes and we were at Beaulieu. It was a delightfully pleasant evening after the heat of the day, and there in the deck-chair under the cedar tree at the far side of that enormous front lawn was Proden, and reading what looked like a newspaper.

"On the look-out for you, George," I said, and sure enough, as soon as our car had come to a stop Proden was peering across and getting to his feet. We had just got through the gate when he was on us. There was no surprise, only a smile at the sight of me. But he'd had me under his eye for best part of a minute, and if I'd been anything of a shock, which I doubted, there'd been time for recovery.

"Hallo, Travers," he said. "What brings you here?"

"Roped in by the law," I said. "This is Chief Superintendent Wharton."

"How're you, sir?" Wharton said, and let a quick eye rove round. "Handsome place you've got here."

"Well, I like it," Proden said, "and I suppose that's what really matters."

"Nice to be some people," Wharton told him roguishly. "Lucky for you you weren't born to be a copper."

Proden laughed. From the word go, everything was being nice and friendly. Would we prefer to talk out of doors or in the house? George said he was allergic to midges, and Proden said maybe he was right. So it was the house for us, and that room which I'd already seen. And what would we have to drink?

"A temptation," George said, "but you know how it is. I suppose you could say I'm here on business. Mr. Travers looks a bit thirsty, though."

A smooth way of putting me outside the law. So I had a long whisky-soda and Proden had the same. George wouldn't even have a cigarette or cigar, but he did light his pipe.

But there we were: snug as three bugs in a rug, as George would put it. And he was getting straight into that Seeway business.

"Must have been a shock when you read about your old friend Dibben, Mr. Proden?"

"My God, you're right!" Proden told him. "But he never was any friend of mine. You must have heard all that from Mr. Travers."

"True enough," George told him archly. "But what the soldier said isn't evidence. That's why I've had to bother you myself."

So Proden went back to that week when the *Under My Thumb* company had been in Bassingford. He skated rather more lightly over the Seeway business, and insisted there could be no possible connection between it and the presence of Dibben in Bassingford.

"Wait a minute," Wharton said. "There's something that may be news to you. Something that we've unearthed. Seeway left Bassingford. So did Dibben—when the week was over. But Dibben didn't go on to Colchester with the touring company. He was absent for a whole week. He didn't rejoin the company till it got to Ipswich. Something, I was told, to do with a sick relative."

"Yes," Proden said. "There's something I seem to remember. Just give me a second and I think I'll have it."

He hardly needed the second. He even remembered that it had been in the newspapers. Something to do with a sister who was ill.

"I take it you've found out whether or not that was true?" he was asking Wharton. "I remember now that there was some mention of it on the Saturday night, before the company left. That was on the Sunday morning, of course."

"It's true enough," Wharton said. "At least there was a sister and she was ill. In fact she died not long afterwards." He shrugged his shoulders and gave me a look. "Another dead end, then. No use thinking that Seeway might have left here with Dibben."

"Good heavens, no!" Proden told him. He was even finding the idea a bit amusing. "I know why Seeway left. He was sick to death of Bassingford and, as I told Mr. Travers, in rather bad odour with his aunt. I tried to dissuade him and smooth things over, but he was his own enemy, if you know what I mean. If he hadn't had money of his own, it might have been different."

"I get you," Wharton told him. "But what was your private idea about where he went to?"

"I'm practically sure he went to one of the colonies. I've been thinking about it a good deal since Mr. Travers was here, and things have sort of come back. He was often talking about the colonies and finding some sort of job there. Later, of course, when nobody heard from him, we thought he must have got himself into the war and been killed. That was why I could hardly believe Mr. Travers when he assured me Seeway was alive in 1943. What I asked myself was why he'd never communicated with anyone after that. All I could assume again was that he'd been killed soon after this client of Mr. Travers saw him and spoke to him."

"And spoke about Dibben."

"I know," he said. His hands rose and fell. "It's positively staggering. It makes no kind of sense. All I can say is that if there was anything underhand or fishy going on during that week here between David Seeway and Dibben, I never suspected it. And—I don't want to be rude, mind you—I still can't credit it."

"Well, it's a mystery." Wharton sighed heavily. "Maybe we'll never solve it, but there it is. Mr. Travers approached us with what he knew about Dibben and we were casting about for people who'd known Dibben, and this Seeway business seemed a connection."

He leaned forward, eyes wrinkled in the same bewilderment.

"Just what sort of a chap was this Seeway?"

What he heard varied scarcely in a word from what he'd read in my report. As for Proden, there was the same implied regret at having to be so frank about a blood relation.

"A tremendous degeneration during the wars," he said. "I hadn't been in England for best part of twenty years, and what

I saw left rather a nasty taste in the mouth. No manners, sir. A lot of noise and crudity, and most of the fine old things gone. Things like respect for elders and thinking of others in preference to one's self."

"Don't I know it," Wharton told him, and gave a preliminary shuffle in his seat. It was the cue for me to enter.

"Doesn't look as if Mr. Proden can tell us anything further."

"No," Wharton said, and rather heavily. Then he was giving a little chuckle. "There's only one thing. If he's not going to be bothered again, I ought perhaps to take his alibi."

Proden looked as if he couldn't trust his ears. Wharton's face sobered.

"Just the merest formality in your case, Mr. Proden. Everyone even remotely connected with the man Dibben has had to furnish an alibi." He gave another little chuckle. "As I tell people, it's only the guilty who're scared by the word alibi. In your case it's merely a certainty that you'll be crossed off the list of those that still have to be bothered."

"Sounds as if you're doing Mr. Proden a favour," I said. "Well, aren't I? We don't want to come here pestering him again?"

"Wait a minute," Proden cut in. "I don't follow this alibi business. An alibi for what?"

"For the night of Dibben's murder," Wharton told him. "I don't mind telling you that it was at about a quarter-past seven when that little affair took place on the eighth."

"A quarter-past seven." Proden frowned reflectively. "Wonder where I was at half-past seven. I think I must have been between Royston and Huntingdon."

He explained. An old friend from Ceylon was now living near Doncaster at a village called Uffley Moor, and he usually saw him every year. Things happened to be quiet in Bassingford and he'd decided to run up there for a bit of a change. He'd intended to leave either very early indeed in the morning or else in the late afternoon, and to avoid the main traffic on the Great North Road. Then a business engagement had held him back and he hadn't been able to leave till about half-past six in the evening. He'd reached Uffley Moor soon after half-past ten that night.

"What is it?" I said. "About a hundred and forty miles?"

"Just about," he said. "I drove straight through. Had a puncture at a little village just through Grantham—place called Dallery—and right close to a garage. Then I stopped at a little pub just after Newark and had a drink. Forget what that place was called, but I know the pub was the Bricklayers' Arms. On the left-hand side just short of the village. That's all, I think, except that I was at Uffley Moor well before eleven."

"Pretty good going," I said. "You must have averaged well over thirty on the road."

"She's still a nice little car," he said. "1939 Austin Ten. Been well looked after. Just a bit heavy on petrol now. Not that that matters now rationing's off. Like to have a look at her?"

"Don't let's talk about cars," Wharton said as he hoisted himself from the easy chair. "Travers is a maniac on that topic."

"Won't take a second," Proden told him. "But sure you won't have a drink, just for the road?"

"I'll stay obstinate," Wharton said. "And I'm in just a bit of a hurry."

"A quick spot for you, Travers?"

I wouldn't have another, and out we went to the garage. The doors were open and I had a quick look at that car, not that there was anything much to see. All I could say was that it certainly looked in good enough condition.

"We didn't get one thing from Mr. Proden," Wharton said impatiently. "No use having an alibi and not giving it a quick check. What's the name of your friend at this Uffley Moor place, Mr. Proden?"

Proden made a wry face. The name was Harraway, of the Old Rectory. But he didn't like the idea of his being bothered.

"Don't worry," Wharton told him. "We do these things tactfully. Your friend won't even know he's been questioned. And it'll be by the local police. Some cock-and-bull yarn or other, just to get information."

So that was that. Wharton didn't even bother to make a note in his book, and the three of us walked together to the gate.

Wharton shook hands and the thanks were effusive. Proden actually looked a bit embarrassed.

The car moved on, and through the town. Just across the bridge, Wharton got out his notebook and had the car stop.

"Let's get everything down while it's in our minds. That chap remembered a bit too much for me. Sounded just a bit too pat."

He took it all down and the car moved on. I asked him what he'd thought of Proden.

"Smooth," he said. "Smooth as they make 'em. Off the top shelf, as you'd put it, but I don't know. Can't say I cottoned to him. And, according to you, he's a first-class liar."

"Not according to me," I said. "According to his wife."

"Same thing," he said, and grunted. "A pity about that alibi. I'll lay a fiver it's as tight as a drum."

"Even if it weren't, I don't see why he should have killed Dibben. There isn't a vestige of motive. We haven't found a suspicion of one from either end—his or Dibben's."

He gave another grunt.

"Make him out as bad as you can," I said, "and that leaves him a pretty unscrupulous character who was highly successful in getting hold of his aunt's money and Seeway's girl. Not that Seeway appears to have wanted her all that much. But that's the devil of a long way from making him a murderer. It's ten years ago since he got what he was scheming for. All that, Dibben included, belongs to the past."

"Don't I know it?" he told me, and glared. Then he said he wanted to do a bit of thinking, and we were well on the way to town when I remembered something.

"Pity we didn't look in on old Finney while we were at Bass-ngford," I said. "I'd have liked you to see him. And there's just the chance he might have picked up something after all."

"Plenty of time," he said. "We can always find Finney."

We came in by Holloway and Camden Town, and he dropped me at the flat. What we did in the morning, he said, might depend on the luck that Molly Flynn had with Unstone. We left it that he'd give me a ring when he wanted me. I told him to ring Broad Street. It was high time I put in an hour at the office.

The car moved off and I guessed the first thing he'd do at the Yard would be to set in motion a testing of that alibi of Proden's, and for the life of me I couldn't see what good it would do except in the matter of elimination. Important enough in its way. Too much lumber clutters up a case, and to me Proden was merely lumber: a man without a motive and useful only as a faint echo of a problematic Seeway and the dead Dibben. And in both those matters he had been pumped dry. If he'd told lies, then it was understandable. Only by blackening Seeway could he make his own actions of twelve years ago look natural and inevitable.

My hopes weren't pinned on Proden. I was looking forward to something far more sensational—the fair chance that Molly Flynn might sufficiently ingratiate herself with Unstone as to be placed as a spotter. I could see us planting a supposedly unmarried couple in that hotel for a quiet week-end, and Molly giving the tip to Unstone, and Rappham turning up with his camera, and I even wondered if Wharton would have him taken red-handed, as he'd put it, or would let the play be acted out till it possibly included Cleaver. But that would mean a longish wait perhaps, which wasn't so exhilarating a thought.

I woke in the morning with the anticipation of all that on my mind. By the time I left for Broad Street Wharton hadn't rung I put in an hour with Norris and I wasn't anticipating a call till after eleven o'clock, which would give time for Molly to report from Spenser Street. It was at exactly half-past ten that the call was unexpectedly to come.

Chapter Thirteen
EVERYBODY TALKS

WHARTON was playing one of his little jokes. He told me lugubriously that Molly Flynn had reported at Spenser Street, as arranged, only to be told that the post was filled.

"A pity," I said. "You think she overdid it?"

"Don't think so," George said. "Either they had ideas about her or else they're lying low."

Then he was giving me one of his quizzical looks.

"A good job we had another string to our bow."

Then, of course, he had to tell about it. In spite of Matthews' wasted visit, he'd thought that the Downland Court Hotel still held a good few possibilities. The former owner had been seen—a man named Catterick who now had a hotel at Sandford-on-Sea—and he supplied the name of the employee who had been taken on through Weeks, Ltd. It was a receptionist, a woman named Clarice Glenn. There was even more to it than that, for Catterick remembered that Clarice Glenn had left his employ-ment in the September of that 1947 to marry the local veterinary surgeon. No hint had naturally been given to Catterick as to the purport of the enquiry and, according to him, Clarice Glenn had been not only competent but a pleasant person to have about the place.

Matthews had got into touch with her. Her name was now Smallwood and she had a boy of two. Her husband's busi-ness seemed to be flourishing, and she herself was well spoken of locally, and all those things had necessitated some wary approaches on the part of Matthews. He had noticed a consider-able alarm at the sight of his warrant card, and even more at the mention of the Downland Court Hotel, and even the excuse that her help was wanted in connection with some people who might have stayed at the hotel during her employment there had not wholly removed the alarm. Curiously enough, it was her husband who had said she ought to help the police, and he had been perfectly happy about her coming to the Yard.

"And when's that?" I said.

"This morning. Due here in a few minutes."

Before I'd time to ask what line he proposed to take, the buzzer went. Matthews was a bit early, and in a couple of minutes I was having a look at Clarice Smallwood. She was a smartly dressed, good-looking woman of just over thirty, and there was still something of apprehension in the look she gave as she came through the door, and the smile that answered Wharton's own as he held out his hand.

"Very good of you to come here and help us, Mrs. Small-wood. Sergeant Matthews will have told you all about the kind of thing we want."

I'd held the chair for her. The stenographer was unobtrusive in his corner. Wharton was all smiles and affability and the sun was coming cheerfully through the windows, and yet she wasn't at ease. Wharton donned his spectacles.

"So you're married now, Mrs. Smallwood, and have a boy, so they tell me. I'm a grandfather myself, as you probably guessed by the look of me."

There was a considerable deal more of that, and slowly the nervousness began to go. George got down to business. He was peering over his spectacle tops as he held out that photograph.

"Well, we mustn't keep you waiting, Mrs. Smallwood. You'll be wanting to get out and do some shopping perhaps, before you go back to Bickhurst. So will you have a look at this photograph and this hotel bill and tell us, if you can, whether you remember anything about this Major and Mrs. Rome?"

She had glanced at that photograph before he had mentioned the names. She gave him a quick, nervous look.

"I'm sorry, but I don't really know anything about them."

"But you haven't really looked," he told her. "Look again, Mrs. Smallwood. Look at the writing on that bill. Isn't that your own?"

"I don't know," she said. "It's such a long while ago."

Wharton leaned forward.

"Mrs. Smallwood, why don't you be reasonable? You know about those two people. You know about that bill. We don't want to have to bring in your husband or make a public scandal. We're asking you to tell us confidentially just what you did about that photograph and that bill. Whatever it was—and I may tell you we have more than a shrewd idea—you're not going to be prosecuted for it. You give us the information we want, and we'll proceed to forget all about it. You can go back to Bickhurst with something at last off your conscience. It has been on your conscience, hasn't it?"

That was when she began to cry. It was three or four minutes before she was giving her eyes a last dab. It was another half-hour before we had all we needed.

Hers had been a hard-luck case that Unstone must have welcomed: a woman of training and experience who'd had a series of misfortunes that had taken practically her last shilling. She claimed to have hated the idea of doing what Unstone had suggested, and that the people she had known as Major and Mrs. Rome were the only ones she had ever reported. And it had been something she had overheard that had made her ring Unstone, just in case. Then all she had had to do was arrange about the arrival of a man who called himself Rawlings, and give him a room as near as possible to that of the Romes. None had been free on either side, but she had arranged for one that faced the Romes' room. That was all, except supplying the duplicate bill. Later she received twenty pounds from Unstone by registered letter.

Wharton described Rappham and there was never a doubt that he was Rawlings. Unstone, she said, had never been to the hotel, nor had anyone resembling Cleaver. Unstone had also taken quite well the news of her marriage, and he had never bothered her since. Doubtless he had relied for security upon the fact that she'd never be likely to say a word to her husband, or that any attempt to make trouble might bring some nasty publicity to herself.

"You'll go home a happy woman," Wharton told her. "All these years you've had it on your mind, and now at last it's off. All we shall need from you is a confidential statement."

That brought a new alarm, but at last she went out with Matthews.

"And what now, George?" I said.

"Wait till she's made that statement," he told me. "Then use it as a leverage for our two friends at Maddenham. That'll be after lunch."

It was just after two o'clock when we left, and the Caverly-Hares would be expecting us. I asked him if he had any more tricks tucked up his sleeve, and his look was pained and reproachful. All he admitted was an enquiry into Proden's alibi. I offered to bet him we should find it water-tight, and I was a fool to make the offer. When I win, George generally forgets to pay.

"Don't know," he said, "but you're probably right. I didn't like the way he wanted you to look at that car."

"How do you mean?"

He clicked his tongue exasperatedly.

"Why is it you sometimes can't see your nose in front of your face? He wanted you to see the car number, didn't he? He wanted that alibi gone into."

"Very well," I said. "He wanted the alibi gone into. So why won't you bet it's water-tight?"

He clicked his tongue again.

"Because that isn't the end of it. We'll suppose it *is* water-tight, and that's why he wanted us to find it so. Then what do we do? We wipe him off the list. He's in the clear for the Dibben killing. But suppose he's been up to something else. Something as far back as that Seeway disappearance, for instance, and a tie-up with Dibben. Wouldn't it be a smart move to let us wipe him off for the 1951 killing and so forget about anything that might have happened in 1939?"

I said he was a bit too Machiavellian for me, and that was how we left it. He began reading again that report of mine on that interview with Rosamund Caverly-Hare and I was looking at the scenery. When we were through Sittingbourne he gave me a bit more news. He'd sounded her about that visit of mine, and she'd reported it to her husband. He seemed to think that was going to make things much easier. Again I didn't quite see it. Not that that worried me. That afternoon would be George's headache, and at the moment he was looking a long way from anxious.

We turned right a few miles from Canterbury and took a short cut and it was well before four o'clock when we drew in at the drive of the Old Grange. The lady herself was at the open door when we got out, and Wharton was his most affable self. The three of us were chatting as we went into that room where I'd had that first interview. Rosamund said she'd call her husband: she knew he was somewhere about.

"Wants an impressive entrance," I whispered to George.

He was looking round the room. He'd just told me it was a posh sort of place when we heard the steps outside and got up from our chairs. His hand was out before Caverly-Hare was hardly in the room.

"Sorry about these clothes, but afraid I'm rather busy," the Colonel told him. If Wharton caught the shade of aloofness, he certainly concealed the fact. He admitted a liking for shorts himself, and claimed also to be a fairly busy man. Then he remembered to introduce myself, and I mentioned that meeting in the shed on the strawberry field, and finally we got sorted out into our chairs.

"What was it exactly you wanted to see us about?" the Colonel asked him stiffly. "If it's still this man Seeway, I'm afraid I can't help you."

I was watching the lady, and she was watching him.

"Hadn't we better wait, darling, and hear all that from Superintendent Wharton himself?"

"As a matter of fact," Wharton said, "we're here on a matter which seems to have no connection with Seeway. But it does seem to be connected with the death of that man Dibben whom Mr. Travers mentioned when he was here. We can't be overheard, by the way?"

"Can't we come straight to the point—if there is a point?" Caverly-Hare told him.

He was sitting there, elbows on his chair, lips rather set and eyes coldly on Wharton. In his tone there wasn't exactly a superiority, only that same touch of aloofness and a certain impatience.

"There's a point, all right," Wharton told him, and gave a reflective pursing of the lips as he took the envelope from the leather portfolio. "But I have to explain that man Dibben who was murdered. We have evidence that he was a blackmailer, operating through an employment agency which he owned.

You've seen that last fact, perhaps, in the newspapers. That's why I'd like you to look at this photograph."

She knew what was coming. She looked at that photograph and yet I doubt if her eyes saw anything but a blur. Her husband reached across and took it from her hand. Maybe he had heard about it, but to him it was new. His eyes narrowed as he gave it back to Wharton.

"Well, what do you propose to do about it?"

There was something ridiculously bellicose in the challenge. Wharton put the print back and produced the hotel bill.

"Apparently you won't want to see this," he said. "Your wife has almost certainly seen it before. Just a duplicate of the hotel bill for that week-end at the Downland Court Hotel. This morning I interviewed the very receptionist who provided it for the blackmailers. You may remember her: a rather good-looking, tallish girl—"

"Does that matter?"

"Matter?" Wharton said.

"Yes, matter. Why can't you get to the point. Assuming all this is true, then what're you going to do about it?"

"Don't know," Wharton said dryly. "Probably nothing at all."

The Colonel stared. I looked at his wife and she, too, was looking as if she couldn't credit what Wharton had said.

"Naturally what I do will depend on you and your wife," Wharton told him. "Everything we're saying, by the way, is highly confidential, that's why I took the risk of saying I'd probably do nothing. I'm not the King's Proctor. I'm here on a murder case. You help me and I'll help you. You tell me frankly all about the way you were blackmailed."

"It was not my husband, it was I," she said. "He was away, and I didn't want to worry him. I paid the money. He knew nothing about it till after we were married."

"Well, that's frank enough," Wharton said, and swivelled round in his chair to face her. "Suppose, Mrs. Caverly-Hare, that you start at the very beginning. Why you took the risk of going to that hotel, and so on."

It began, she said, when Richard was suddenly ordered to India. That made them take a chance. Then, after that chance, things began to happen. His orders were changed back to Germany, and she received a solicitor's letter. As far as she remembered it merely said that the firm would like to see her on a matter of some urgency. It was on the Cleaver and Hewes notepaper and signed by Cleaver.

She was then living at a Kensington flat. An appointment was fixed and she was assuming that the urgent business was something to do with the divorce. It was—with a difference. Cleaver informed her he was acting for a client whose name he could not reveal, and then he produced the photograph. He talked a lot of legal jargon, the gist of which was that unless she was prepared to pay his client, the King's Proctor would be informed. A few days were given her in which to think things over, and then she decided to pay. She realised some securities and handed Cleaver the sum of fifteen hundred pounds in cash. There was no receipt, and all she received was the photograph and its negative. Cleaver assured her that the matter was considered by his client as settled for good and all.

"Who did you think this client of his was?" I asked her.

"Hugh Proden," she said. "He'd made difficulties about the divorce. I don't think I'd ever have obtained a divorce if I hadn't engaged a firm of detectives to watch him."

"This man Cleaver," Wharton said. "He kept his word about not bothering you again?"

"Yes," she said. "For a long time we were very worried, but he did keep his word."

"I wouldn't exactly call it worried," Caverly-Hare told her. "It was just a question of knowing what to do if a scoundrel like that tried the same game again."

"And what would you have done?"

"It all depended. If he came here, I'd have knocked hell out of him and told him to do his damndest."

"Well, that's one way of handling things," Wharton told him. "And there's nothing else that either of you can tell me?"

"Nothing," he said. "But I'd still like to know just where we stand."

"Well, first I'd like you to make official statements. They'll be highly confidential, of course. I may be able to bring a case without using them. I can't promise, but I'll do my best."

"A case against whom? Hugh Proden?"

Wharton put him right. Proden hadn't been concerned in the matter at all.

"The whole thing was a highly organised racket, worked through spotters at various hotels. The spotters were planted by an employment agency, the real brains of which was this man Marquis. His real name was Dibben. You've read about it, as I said, in the papers. Cleaver was in it and the man who took the photograph and followed you after you left the hotel. Dibben got the biggest share of the fifteen hundred pounds. Then, a few days ago, on the night of the eighth, to be exact, Dibben was murdered. And that reminds me. Where were you, Colonel, on the night of the eighth? Say at about seven-fifteen?"

"I?" he said. "What have I got to do with it?"

Wharton peered amiably from over the tops of the spectacles.

"Didn't you have a good reason for killing him?"

"Good God, man, use some sense! I never heard of the fellow till I saw his name in the papers."

"Maybe," Wharton told him evenly. "All the same, I'll have to know where you were."

He trotted out the old arguments, and I could only admire his patience. I'm a reasonably patient man myself, but I knew I should have resented much of the attitude and the tone of Colonel Caverly-Hare; at least to the extent of asking who in hell he imagined he was.

"So there you are, sir," Wharton was saying. "So tell us where you were."

"If you must know, I drove a lorry load of stuff to Covent Garden. My man was taken ill at the beginning of the month and I did the job."

"Fine," Wharton said, and produced his notebook. "You left here, when?"

"Don't know exactly. Roughly at about five o'clock."

"And you got there at?"

"Somewhere round seven."

"Name of the firm?"

"James Hopper. I saw the foreman, a man named Gander."

"And you were back here at?"

"Don't remember. Probably round about half-past ten. I had a meal in town. Rather a decent little pub sort of place, the Stratford, in Long Acre."

"Pardon my butting in," I said, "but I was under the impression that you people who used Covent Garden always got there at some unearthly hour in the morning."

"Some do," he said. "Depends on the kind of thing you're taking up. Mine happened to be delivery of contract stuff."

"Well, that's that," Wharton said, and got to his feet. "Only one thing to do now, and that's to take those official statements. Would you prefer to do it here, or is there some other room?"

It was nearer seven o'clock than six when we got away. Towards the last, Caverly-Hare had shown himself far more amenable. He'd even seemed hurt that we'd not accepted a drink.

Rosamund Caverly-Hare had walked with me down the steps towards the car, and I'd guessed that she'd wanted a private word with me.

"You've heard nothing about David Seeway?" she'd finally asked, and I could only tell her that we knew nothing. We were still hoping, I said, that out of all the enquiries, even those of that very evening, we should discover if he were still alive.

"You'll let me know?"

"Yes," I'd said. "I'll be happy to let you know."

"It's worried me. That he should be connected with that dreadful man Dibben. You're sure you can't be wrong?"

I'd had to tell her I couldn't possibly be wrong. I did add the reassuring rider that connection needn't by any means assume a part in that blackmail racket. And that had been that. The car moved on, and there was no sign of her or her husband when it turned into the lane.

"Not too profitable an afternoon," I told George. "We've only got what we hoped to get."

"Don't know," he said. "Better wait till we've gone into that alibi."

It was just something that had to be done, even if it seemed a waste of time. George agreed, but he didn't agree when I said that Caverly-Hare would never have stunned a man and strangled him. He was the sort of highly superior, play-the-game, self-opinionated sahib who'd regard himself as a private executioner: who'd have walked into that house, put a bullet in Dibben's head, and calmly walked out again and be damned to everyone. And there remained the problem as to how he could have become aware of Marquis's part in the blackmail racket. That, to me at least, put Caverly-Hare well out of the suspect class. Not that I wouldn't have welcomed the chance to make him at least in some way involved. I'd liked his wife, but I'd hated the sight of him. His particular brand of snobbery has always made my hackles rise.

"What happens now to the gang?" I was asking George. "You think you've got enough on them to bring them in?"

"Plenty," he said. "Don't know how it strikes you, though, but this blackmail business seems to be getting us further and further from the Dibben murder. Once we've gone into that Caverly-What's-his-name's alibi, we'll turn that side of it over to Jewle."

I liked the idea. All that evening I'd felt that we were wandering off the track. What if Rosamund Proden *had* been blackmailed? What if the gang got five years or seven?

A satisfactory sort of side-line, perhaps, but was it getting us nearer to who killed Dibben? I didn't feel that it was. There did, of course, remain the possibility that the murder had been what I'd called an inside job. All three of the gang had at least reasonable motives for seeing Dibben out of things, and Unstone especially might by some double-crossing or peculation have got himself into a corner from which only the removal of Dibben could extricate him.

"Rappham," I said. "I've never really clapped eyes on him. Wonder what yarns he'd have to tell if we saw him?"

In a few minutes I was seeing why George was thinking of turning that blackmail side of things over to Jewle. And that Jewle would inherit quite a considerable headache. Unstone could hardly wriggle clear, but Rappham might swear that he was merely a kind of employee who had acted in perfectly good faith. As for Cleaver, he could fall back on that anonymous client. Or he could brazenly claim that he had been acting on behalf of Rosamund Proden herself. She had had nothing in writing, and even that negative and print had been destroyed.

"I know," Wharton said. "But don't worry about our friend Frederick Rappham. Plenty of ways and means of roping him in."

There was no news for us at the Yard, so I went home to a belated meal. A letter had come by that evening's post and it turned out to be from Finney.

"DEAR SIR,

"You told me to let you know if I found anything out about that Mr. Seeway, and I've remembered what it was I couldn't remember the other night. It was something Jim Barnes told me just after that touring company was here that we were talking about, so if you're this way any time after tomorrow, I think I'll have something for you.

"Yours respectfully,

"J. FINNEY."

Jim Barnes was that commissionaire who'd died fairly recently—the man who'd tapped on Proden's door that Saturday night twelve years ago, and had found the door unaccountably locked. That was all I knew about him, but since he was dead it couldn't be to him that Finney was going for verification of whatever it was that he'd remembered. But I didn't worry my head about that. I was too mentally tired, and sufficient unto the day would be the information thereof.

Chapter Fourteen
TO AND FRO

When I woke the next morning and groped as usual for my glasses, a something was suddenly in my mind. I don't want to stress the obvious, but it's curious how oddly one's brain will sometimes work. Many a time I've gone to bed after a stiffish crossword puzzle with a tricky clue still unsolved, and I've woke in the morning with the answer pat as pie. The subconscious mind—that used to be the jargon term, but maybe you've had the same experience often enough. But what I woke with that morning was not the answer to a tricky clue. It was merely a something that Wharton had said as we were going through the first suburbs on our way back from Maddenham—that I needn't worry too much about Frederick Rappham. And *Frederick* was what they call the operative word.

I switched on the electric kettle, got back into bed and lay there thinking. It was at Cambridge that a man had appeared in the wings of the theatre twelve years ago, and had brazenly—Widgeon's own words—walked on to the stage during rehearsal and spoken to Dibben. Dibben had called him *Fred*. And the Fred of Widgeon's description had been the Rappham of twelve years ago. Fred and Dibben had gone out together, and Dibben had been late in returning. I'd gathered that he'd kept the whole company waiting.

So far, so good; but just what did that discovery mean? Five minutes later I still didn't know. All I knew was that before that blackmail business had started Dibben had been acquainted with Rappham. Was Rappham even at that time a private detective? And if so, had Dibben been employing him? I didn't know but somehow or other I knew that I was going to find out.

So the first thing I did that morning at the Yard was to put things up to Wharton. He seemed interested, even if he thought the connection a bit far-fetched. But when I'd agreed that the world had quite a number of Freds, he was still interested enough to ask what I was thinking of doing. I told him I'd like at least to get Rappham positively identified.

"What about that man of Summer's at Stapley Green that night?" I said. "Has he seen Rappham since and identified him as the one who played that trick on him?"

Wharton said he had. Rappham was the man who'd called himself Brewer and had gone boldly through the gate of the corner house.

"What about the gate? Did Summer get Rappham's prints from it?"

"Rappham didn't touch the actual gate," he said. "He lifted the latch. Summer missed that point till it was too late and the prints had been smeared."

He said he had Rappham's prints in any case, so no great harm had been done. And, unfortunately for us, Rappham was without a record. I said I merely asked because I might manage to get Rappham's prints myself that morning.

A few minutes later I was on my way to Enfield, and I wasn't feeling too hopeful. But I was doing something, and that was the main point. If Rappham had been the Fred of that Cambridge theatre, then I had some chance of making what I'd always felt was the right approach to the murder of Dibben—an approach not from now to then but from then to now. Dibben's murder, as some strange hunch was always telling me, had happened as a result of unknown events in 1939, and to discover all I could about those events seemed curiously vital. But I wasn't too hopeful, as I've said. We'd uncovered a blackmail racket that had successfully operated for the best part of ten years and had numbered in its fleecings some scores of people. The haystack, in fact, might have scores of needles. What were our few suspects—Caverly-Hare, Rappham, Unstone, Proden perhaps, and Cleaver, even the mysterious Seeway—compared with those unknown victims, any one of whom might have done that murder job. Common sense and the law of averages said that we might not yet have discovered even the right haystack. So I was hopeful and no more. And what Widgeon and I were going to do was at least an interlude and a kind of relaxation, and I'd always liked playing at Indians.

That was rather how Widgeon took it. He seemed quite amused at playing the part of a Scotland Yard man. He even taught me something about darkening the hair that showed below his hat and making himself look twenty years younger.

"But only a walking-on part," I told him. "I do the talking and you just keep your eyes on him. And don't exaggerate the grimness."

We had a quick rehearsal. Half an hour later we were drawing up the car just short of Crane Street. One of Wharton's men came across. Rappham had left his office about an hour previously, and all we could do was wait. And that had better be in Crane Street facing north, with the hope that he'd come back the same way and Widgeon could have a front view of him.

We settled down to it and I didn't tell Widgeon that we might be there for best part of the day. But we were lucky. In under half an hour I spotted someone I thought was Rappham, and Widgeon had the glasses on him. He kept coming our way, and turned into the building that housed his office.

"Well, what about it?"

"I'm practically sure it's the same man," Widgeon said. "Naturally he's older, but he has the same kind of face."

"Right," I said, and began manoeuvring my legs out of the car. "Let's go and have a closer view."

Rappham was on the first floor; a couple of smallish rooms, apparently, and facing us on that first landing. I knocked at the door and almost at once it was opened.

"Mr. Rappham?"

"Yes," he said. Me he knew, there wasn't a doubt about that; his eyes went beyond me to Widgeon.

"Scotland Yard," I said. "We'd like a few words with you."

I hoped it was bravado, but there was a smile on his foxy face as he waved a hand and drew back from the door. His hair had a faint tinge of red and was greying at the temples. His skin had a sallowness and his clean-shaven jaws were spotted with some kind of acne.

"We shan't keep you long," I said, and gave him my warrant card. He waved it away.

"That's all right, sir. I've seen you before, at the Old Bailey."

"Not helping to hang one of your clients, I hope."

That was a fine joke. He was still chuckling as he asked us to sit down.

"Snug little place you have here," I said. "Been here long?"

"Quite a few years," he told me, and his face sobered. "First time, though, I've had a visit from the Yard."

Every now and again he'd been having a look at Widgeon. He couldn't help asking if he was a colleague of mine. I introduced him as Sergeant Widgeon, and the name conveyed nothing.

"I'm really here to ask for your help," I said. "You were acquainted with the late Archibald Marquis."

"Marquis?" he said, and did some pondering. Then he caught my eye. Something told him not to overplay the role.

"Oh, him," he said. "That chap who was murdered at Stapley Green. Used to be a comedian named Dibben."

Then he was staring, and he certainly did it well.

"Just a minute, sir. Did you say that I knew him?"

"Didn't you?" I asked him blandly.

"Never saw him in my life. Never heard his name till I read all about it in the papers."

Widgeon had given that prearranged cough of recognition. I had to do some quick thinking. You can't rush bull-headed at a brick wall of ignorance.

"You're a curious chap," I said. "A private detective for most of your life and still thinking that we're fools."

"Me?" He spread his palms indignantly. "I *would* be a fool if I thought anything like that. You people know it all."

"Too generous of you," I said, "but nice to hear, all the same. And to realise that you know we know a whole lot about yourself that quite a few people don't."

He shrugged his shoulders.

"That don't worry me, sir. If you people had ever had anything on me, you'd have been after me long ago. Always keep your nose clean, that's my motto. You may get dirty jobs—divorce, and all that—but you can do 'em in a clean way."

"Very praise-worthy of you," I told him. "But to get back to Marquis who used to be Dibben, and let's make it the spring of 1939. You did a job for Dibben. You saw him about it at Cambridge, at the theatre during a rehearsal, or rather there was an immediate adjournment and you went out with Dibben to talk things over. All I want you to do is tell me what that job was."

He'd listened, he'd been puzzled, he'd been almost amused. Now he spread his palms again.

"As far as I'm concerned, sir, you're talking double-dutch. Must have got me mixed up with some other man."

"Very well," I said. "If that's how you want to play it, you must do so. But suppose we have you on the stand at the reopened inquest, and confront you with a witness who'll swear you were the man whom Dibben addressed as Fred and who saw him at that theatre?"

He gave a little indignant snort.

"You do that, sir, and I'll tell him he's a liar to his face. The last time I was in Cambridge was twenty years ago. Might be more."

"A pity," I said. "But that won't be all. I shall be there myself. You know when Dibben was killed, by the way?"

"Don't remember. It wasn't long ago, though."

"It was on the eighth," I said. "His body was found on the afternoon of the ninth. I shall be prepared to swear that you rang him that afternoon. I ought to know because I was the one who answered you."

It was a bit of a facer. But for only the merest moment. There was the same incredulity, the puzzlement, the thought of some practical joke.

"You don't kid me with that, sir," He leaned back with a little chuckle. "How could I have rung him if I'd never heard of him!"

"Just one of life's mysteries," I said. "But I'll still be prepared to swear. And there's more to come. You yourself were at Stapley green at eight o'clock that evening of the ninth, just as you'd told me—thinking I was Dibben—on the telephone."

"Now, just a minute, sir." It was as if there was precisely so much he could stand and no more. "Eight o'clock, you say, on the ninth?"

"That's right. And a witness will identify you. Your name, for the special occasion, was Mr. Brewer."

"Sounds like a nightmare, far as I'm concerned." He was shaking his head with a nice bewilderment. Then he remembered something. There was a pad on his desk and he flipped the pages back. He gave a smile.

"Here we are, sir. At eight o'clock that evening I was miles from Stapley Green. I was actually having supper with a friend of mine. One of my clients."

"Just a minute," I said.

I got out my notebook, wrote something on a page, ripped the page out and folded it.

"Mind telling me the name of this client?"

There was a moment's hesitation.

"Why should I? He was a Mr. Unstone, and I was at his house at Ealing."

"Look at that," I said, and passed him the paper.

"Well I'm damned!" he said, and I couldn't for the life of me tell if the stare was faked. "How on earth did you know that?"

"Ways and means," I told him airily, and got up from that damnable hard chair. "Won't keep you any longer. But we might just get it all clear. You never knew Dibben or Marquis. You haven't been to Cambridge for over twenty years. You didn't telephone him on the ninth. You weren't at Stapley Green that night. O.K.?"

"Sure it's O.K. And I can prove it."

"That's fine," I said, and reached out for that sheet of paper that had Unstone's name and slipped it into my pocket. "Business pretty good?"

"Can't grumble," he said, and shot me a look.

"Might be a good time to sell out," I said, as his hand went forward to the door. "Or get a good manager."

"Manager?" he said. "Why should I want a manager? I've always managed to run things myself."

"Maybe," I said, and motioned for Widgeon to go ahead. "Life's pretty uncertain, though. My advice to you is to sell."

Through the door, I turned. In those small grey eyes of his was a sudden uncertainty.

"Get the best price you can," I told him. "My idea is that in a mighty short time you're going to take a very long holiday. And you know where it *won't* be?"

The hard grey eyes were still on me as he half shook his head.

"The Downland Court Hotel," I told him gently and followed Widgeon down the stairs.

"So there we are," I said to Wharton. "Widgeon positively identifies him as the man who saw Dibben that day at Cambridge. Probably Rappham's now busy making another alibi."

"You think you did right to scare him?"

I said there was just the chance that he might try to bolt.

"You never know," he said. "The more brazen they are, the quicker they crack. And if he doesn't—then what?"

"That'll be Jewle's worry," I said, and showed him that letter I had from Finney. "What I'd like to do is slip along to Bassingford after lunch and hear what Finney's unearthed. Any news about Proden's alibi?"

"The trouble with me is I'm too damned kind-hearted, or I'd have taken that bet of yours," he told me. "The alibi's all right. His housekeeper says he started at about six-thirty and the Yorkshire end says he arrived when he said." He and Jewle were due for a conference, so I wrote a report on the Rappham interview and noted expressly that a copy should go to Jewle. Then I went back to the flat and had a service lunch. The day had turned cloudy and none too warm, so I changed into a brown suit instead of the thin grey. As I emptied the pockets I saw that paper on which I'd written Unstone's name, and I slipped it into a drawer. I don't know why I did it. The waste-paper basket was handy, and I ought to have screwed it into a ball and dropped it in. But I just didn't. Maybe I was absent-minded and thinking of something else. And, if so, it was a good job that I was, *for that piece of paper was virtually to solve the case.*

Too hard for you? Well, maybe it is, but it'll do you no harm to try to think it out.

I drove my own car to Bassingford. I'd offered to take Bernice, but she knows what things are like when I'm on a case, and had booked for a matinée with some friends. It was about four o'clock when I got to Finney's house and I think I must have disturbed him in a nap, for he looked a bit bleary-eyed as he opened the door.

"It's you, sir," he said, and brightened up at once. "Wasn't expectin' you so soon."

We went into his parlour and he drew back the curtains. He wanted to know if I'd have a cup of tea, but I said I wouldn't.

"In a hurry again, I reckon," he told me. "You want to take things more easy. But about what I wrote you."

I made an excuse to close the window. The way he was bellowing at me would have made his news the property of the street.

"Don't like draughts myself," he said. "Don't like bein' stuffy neither. That's why I had the window open and the curtains drawn. But about this Seeway . . ."

What he had to say was uttered with an air of portentousness and swollen with considerable padding. I guessed he was judging the reward by the time it took to impart the news. For there certainly wasn't much, and maybe I'd better refresh your memory or the one solitary fact might seem precious little for the couple of pounds I gave him.

Jim Barnes—and him you'll certainly have remembered—was the commissionaire-handyman. One of his functions was to see that the theatre was locked for the night, and then he'd tap at the manager's door, poke his head in, say that everything was in order, and ask if there was anything further to do. On that particular night—Saturday, 31st March 1939—he heard voices in the manager's room as he neared it from the stairs. The voices ceased as he neared still more and there was no sound as he tapped at the door; and when he went to open that door, it was locked. But Proden came to the door. He didn't open it. He heard Barnes' report through the closed door and told him he could go. So Barnes went.

Barnes lived in the same street as Finney, and two doors away made him almost a next-door neighbour, which was how Finney came to be told—and casually it must have been, or Finney wouldn't have almost forgotten it—that Barnes had nearly reached home when he began to wonder. We all wonder when we have left a house: about a possibly running tap or a fire left on, or an unlocked door. And it was an unfastened window about which Barnes was worrying and wondering. So he went back. The streets were now deserted and he cut through Frenchman's Alley into the Market Square, and it was then he saw Proden with young Seeway. Seeway was definitely drunk, and Proden had difficulty in getting him into the car that was drawn up at the kerb by the stage door.

The car moved off and up the slope towards Beaulieu. Barnes went in the side passage and saw that the window was shut after all, and then he went home.

"Made a rare fool o' myself last night, Jack."

That was the way the event had been introduced to Finney, with, "Don't say anything to anybody, but . . ." and there'd followed the mention of Seeway's name. But Barnes hadn't told Finney what he was later to tell the cashier, that he suspected that some sort of celebration had been going on in the manager's office after the final show. I'd heard that part of it from the cashier myself, and now it seemed as if Barnes' guess had been right. There had been drinking up in that room, and Seeway—the man who couldn't stand his liquor—had been so drunk that Proden had had difficulty in getting him into the car.

It was just for that that I gave Finney a couple of pound-notes, and I knew myself for a fool as I did it. But when I told him to go on thinking, I was hoping to heaven that never again would he bring me to Bassingford on little more than a fool's errand. Then I drove on into the town and circled round to that tea-shop, and over my pot of tea and macaroon I was wondering if I ought to call on that ex-cashier, Mrs. Gaul, again. Then I decided against it. What she'd told me had been confirmed and I doubted if she could tell me the slightest thing more.

I was looking for the waitress and my bill when I saw some-one entering the door. At first I couldn't believe my eyes, then I knew that it was really Clandon. Then he saw me and made for my table.'

"Good lord!" I said. "What brings you here?"

"As a matter of fact I've been putting in a couple of days at Aldburgh," he said. "Pretty chilly there today so I thought I'd cut inland. And I've been wanting a good look at this Bassing-ford place."

Then he was giving that diffident smile of his.

"What about you? Or is that question out of bounds?"

"Yes and no," I said. "Still enquiring into that Seeway-Dibben business. Seeking clues, so to speak, and finding none."

"I oughtn't to say it, but there was something quite ridicu-lous at the back of my mind when I came here. I parked my car up the road there, in the Square, and I must have been staring at everyone I met. You know, sort of hoping I'd meet Seeway."

"Quite a rational feeling," I told him. "One's always hoping for these strange coincidences."

The waitress came and took his order and gave me my bill.

"Talking about Seeway," he went on, "I've got to own up to a rather shame-making feeling. That business about hunting him out and trying to pay him back for what he did for me seems a bit mawkish when you look at it in cold blood. A bit cheap and patronising, somehow."

"Maybe you're right," I said. "But it might have been nice to have met him again, just to see how things had gone with him."

"I know," he said. "But getting mixed up with the police rather shook me. I told you that in my letter."

"I wouldn't let it worry me," I told him. "If Seeway's alive, we'll find him sooner or later; then I'll give you a private tip."

"You've been awfully decent over all this."

"Rubbish!" I said. "I haven't done a thing I haven't been paid for. Where're you bound for when you leave here, by the way? I only ask it because there's very little to see in Bassingford."

"I'm not staying," he said. "My real objective is Cambridge. Someone at Aldburgh told me I oughtn't to miss the Fitzwilliam."

"That somebody was right," I said. "It's about the nicest museum I know. And don't miss the porcelain figures on the landing when you go up the steps from the hall."

"Thanks," he said. "I'll look out for them first thing. Perhaps we might have lunch together when I finally get back to town."

I said I'd be delighted. We gave each other a farewell smile and nod and I paid my bill and went out to the car. It had been nice seeing Clandon again, so I wasn't feeling too dispirited as I drove back to town. I wasn't in any great hurry, and it was well after seven o'clock when I walked into Wharton's room. Sergeant Matthews was there. Wharton, he said, was at Stapley Green.

"Anything done yet about that Caverly-Hare alibi?" I asked him.

"A wash-out," he said. "He got to Covent Garden just before seven and saw that foreman. He unloaded the lorry and checked and tipped the foreman's man to look after the lorry while he got a meal at that pub place. That was O.K., too. Then he collected the lorry at about a quarter-past eight and got home when he said—about half-past ten."

I gave a Whartonian grunt and said one good suspect had gone. I told him what I'd done at Bassingford and said it wasn't worth a report, so perhaps he'd pass it on to Wharton.

"I wouldn't worry any more about that Seeway," he told me. "The Old General's trying a new tack."

He gave me a bit of a grin as he realised he'd come out with Wharton's Yard nickname.

"What's he up to now?" I said.

"Just one of those INFORMATION WANTED advertisements," he said. "Coming out in all the papers. Between you and me, sir, that's what he ought to have done from the first."

Chapter Fifteen
THE COSSINGHAM AFFAIR

I GOT up rather late that next morning, if seven o'clock can be considered late, and I had to bustle about to be round at the Yard at half-past eight. But Wharton had only just arrived.

"Not much doing at Bassingford yesterday," he said.

I owned it had been almost a wasted afternoon. We'd known already that the young Seeway hadn't been able to carry much liquor.

"I know," he said, "but isn't there a little discrepancy? Didn't that Mrs. Caverly-Hare contradict most of what you heard from Proden? And what he told me?"

"True enough," I said, "but I did point out that she had every reason to be biased. Any stone's good enough for a dog, and she certainly hated Proden like sin."

"She could have abused Proden without defending Seeway?"

"Not in that particular context," I said. "I wanted to find out if she'd ever heard from Seeway, so I talked about him. All I could say about him was what I'd heard from Proden, and she immediately began to deny or modify everything Proden had told me."

He shrugged his shoulders. His hand went out to one of the newspapers on the side table.

"You've seen this about our friend Clandon?"

I must have been staring. He passed me the paper, finger at the place.

"HOLD-UP IN COUNTRY LANE
MOTORIST SHOT RY GUNMAN

"A man armed with a revolver last night attacked a Mr. Henry Clandon who was travelling in his car towards Cambridge on the Cossingham-Frickley road. The man apparently thumbed the car for a lift and, when Mr. Clandon drew it to a halt, he produced the revolver and ordered him to get out.

"Mr. Clandon made as if to ignore the order, whereupon the man fired, and, but for a movement of the car when the brake was released, the bullet might have proved fatal. As it was, it gave Clandon a nasty wound in the shoulder and chest, and the impact momentarily knocked him out. When he came to, the man had gone, but his wallet was missing with quite a considerable sum in notes. A bag in the rear of the car containing clothes and personal belongings was untouched.

"Mr. Clandon attempted to drive the car on to Cossingham to warn the police, but he almost immediately collapsed again. Fortunately the car was moving only slowly and came to rest almost undamaged against a bank. There it was later seen by a local farmer who was returning from Cambridge in his car.

"Mr. Clandon, who was taken to Cossingham Cottage Hospital, was able to furnish a description of the man, and a search of the neighbourhood was immediately begun."

I'd done some more staring as soon as I'd begun to read. As I told George, it was extraordinary that I should have run across Clandon in Bassingford and heard about his trip to Cambridge.

"Wonder what time this shooting took place?" I said. "I left him having his tea at about a quarter-past five."

"I don't like all these coincidences," George told me. "Bassingford keeps cropping up too much for my liking. It mightn't be a bad idea if you went along to this Cossingham place and got the ins and outs."

"But this affair couldn't have anything to do with the case," I said. "How on earth was anyone to know that Clandon was even remotely concerned? There couldn't have been a leakage at Broad Street, and if there was, why attempt to kill Clandon? All he did was commission us to find Seeway. He knew nothing about either Seeway or Dibben."

"All the same, I don't like it," George said dourly.

"Naturally I'll run along there if you think I ought to," I told him. "But after what he told me, I see him as just an ordinary citizen travelling from one place to another. That makes it just an ordinary hold-up."

"With the addition of a gun—and shooting."

"Granted," I said. "Mind if we look at a large-scale map? I'd like to see what road he was actually on, and why."

The map showed that Clandon had taken a short-cut that was little more than a country lane. As I worked it out, he had travelled about twenty miles after leaving Bassingford, and was intending to get to Cambridge well before dark.

"Why take that so-called short-cut?" George asked me, and jabbed a finger on the map. "He was on the main road to Great Chesterford and then he could leave it for this other good road straight to Cambridge. He could have travelled quicker. How can a short-cut be a short-cut when it doesn't get you anywhere more quickly. And goes a longer way round."

"Don't know," I said. "It's something I'll have to ask him. If they'll let me see him."

"You'll see him," he told me. "I'll give that hospital a ring. And you might drop in on the local police."

I had a police car and driver and I sat in the back and read the reports in a couple of other papers. I needn't have bought them. Except for the headlines, they varied in never a word from what I'd already seen. Obviously there had been the same agency report, and received too late for individual enquiry.

But the Cossingham police were to tell me a whole lot more. The attack had been in a lonely wooded stretch of lane about two miles from Cossingham, and the time was about nine o'clock. It had been a dull day and the spot chosen had made the light very far from good, and things had happened so quickly that Clandon had been able to give only the sketchiest description of the man. He had been about thirty-five to forty and was shortish and sturdily built. He'd had a spiv-like moustache and a rather pointed nose, and had been wearing a grubby waterproof and had his snap-brim hat well over his eyes.

"Any hopes of collaring him?"

"Precious little," the sergeant said. "It was over an hour before we could get a statement and he'd be miles away by then. Not that we aren't trying."

"What about the wound?"

"Clean through the fleshy part here"—he was pointing to his right shoulder—"then right across the chest. Plenty of blood but not very deep."

"The bullet?"

"Clean through and out just below the near-side window."

"And no finger-prints?"

"Never a hope."

"Must have been a clever lad," I said. "But why did he shoot?"

"Don't know," he said, "unless he thought Clandon was after a gun of his own when he shifted the brake to move the car on."

"Ordinary travellers don't carry guns," I said. "That doesn't make him so clever. But what was Clandon like this morning?"

"He'll be all right. Just under observation, as they call it. Three or four days and he'll be allowed to go home. Funny he should be a friend of yours, sir, and you connected with the Yard?"

"Don't know," I said. "Even coppers sometimes get hurt."

I told him I'd almost certainly be back. Outside the little hospital gate a uniformed constable had a look at my card and let me through. The matron was expecting me.

"He had quite a fair night," she said. "The doctor was quite pleased. All the same, you're not to stay more than ten minutes."

She opened the door for me and I stepped into that private ward. Clandon was lying with eyes closed, but at the sound of me his eyes opened. He stirred, made a grimace, and gave a sheepish grin.

"I know," I said. "I've had some of it. Hurts like hell when you forget. And how're you feeling after all the fun?"

"Not too bad," he said. "Mustn't breathe too deeply or move suddenly, that's all."

"Not too good a business, though. I read about it in the paper this morning and didn't happen to be so busy that I couldn't look you up."

I drew the one chair up at the end of the bed where we could see each other without squinting.

"What'd you do with yourself after I left you yesterday afternoon?"

"Had a look round the town," he said. "Ordered dinner at the White Hart and filled in the time at the cinema."

"Wasn't there a Western on?"

"Didn't get round to that," he said. "I saw the News and then a most appalling thing called *Getting Her Man*, or something. I actually went out before it was over."

"What time did you actually leave the town?"

"About a quarter-past eight. I know it was about nine o'clock when this cove held me up."

"So they're telling me," I said. "But what made you take that little side road?"

The grin was again a bit sheepish.

"To tell you the truth, I was lost. I'd been a bit casual about the map and knew I had to take a fork to the left and I simply took the wrong fork. I guessed something was wrong, but I kept driving on; sort of hoping for the best. Then I ran across that lane that said it was six miles to Cossingham, so I took it."

"Damn bad luck for you. What about Cambridge? You'd booked at a hotel?"

"The Blue Boar. I'd told them I might not be in till after nine."

I said I hoped they get the gunman. Clandon thought he'd really been after the car, not the money. The impact of the bullet had sent him off his balance and he'd cracked his skull against the dashboard, and that must have alarmed the man, and he'd grabbed the wallet and gone.

"What about money? Want any?"

"Uncommonly good of you," he said, "but I don't think so. And I'm expecting one of my colleagues to be along after lunch."

"Nothing at all you want?"

"Can't think of anything. Two or three days and I ought to be getting back to town. I'd rather convalesce, if there's any convalescing to do, in my own flat than a hotel."

"True enough," I said. "And your own doctor can keep an eye on you."

There was a sound at the door. The matron was there and a nurse with something on a tray.

"No, no," I told them reproachfully. "It can't be ten minutes already!"

I was told it was more like a quarter of an hour. And out I had to go. I told Clandon from the door that I'd look him up when he got back to town, and the door was closed on me. A word or two with the matron and I was getting back to the local police.

"Any chance of seeing the car?" I was asking the sergeant.

He went with me to an open garage in the station yard, and there was that smart little post-war car I'd last seen outside the office in Broad Street. The near front bumper had been driven back against the wing where it had hit that bank, but an hour or so's work would put it right. Just below the window was the hole where the bullet had gone through the thinnish metal of the car body.

"Must have been a pretty hefty slug," I said. "What from, do you think? A Webley or a Colt?"

One or the other, he thought. Then he got in the driving seat for me and I checked the angle of the wound. The alignment looked perfect for the exit hole of the bullet. "Not much blood," I said. "A little on the steering wheel."

"Most of it got absorbed by his clothes," he said. "These wheel marks came off that, and his hands."

There seemed nothing else to see. I asked if he'd show me on the map the exact place where the hold-up had been. That was something he couldn't do. Clandon had moved the car on after the attack, and he didn't know just how far. And the road was dry and the tyres had left no marks. But he'd send a man with me on a motor-bike and show where the car had hit the bank.

I could have found that place for myself, for the bumper had torn a strip of rough turf from the bank. But I stood there where the car had been and looked along the lane by which Clandon had come, and it seemed to me that he couldn't have driven that car more than at the most for a hundred yards, for at that distance down the lane were the overhanging trees that had made the gloom for the hold-up. And that tallied some-how with the way I'd visualised the happening. If Clandon had waited a few minutes more till he'd recovered from the shock of the bullet and that crack on the skull, then he might have got that car of his to Cossingham. As it was, he hadn't lasted more than a hundred yards. After all, the same kind of thing had once happened to myself.

I drove on towards Bassingford and tried to take the route by which Clandon had come to that narrow lane. I found the sign-post he had seen and turned left into a rather wider lane. I followed it for six miles or so, and came out at a fork to the main road that he had left. I turned the car right. Two miles to my left, according to the map, would be the fork he should have taken, and the direct road that would have brought him to Cambridge.

I let the driver take the wheel and I did a bit of thinking, and it seemed to me that I'd had quite a pleasant country morning for just nothing at all. Everything had fitted, and I could treat myself to a pious I-told-you-so. And I *had* told Wharton so. How in the name of common sense could that hold-up have been other than the ordinary? It was inconceivable that there should have been any leakage by Broad Street, and I, in any case, had handled the Clandon job entirely by myself. One might go so far as to say that where the Dibben murder was concerned, Clandon simply didn't exist. What Wharton then had wanted me to find that morning, heaven alone knew, and, whatever it was, I certainly hadn't found it.

But I wasn't grumbling. I'd had a pleasant morning and I was proposing to spin out the morning to best part of a day. Wharton wanted an investigation and he should have one, and so the car was parked in the Market Square at Bassingford and I told the driver to take his time over lunch, and then I saw to a lunch myself at the White Hart. It was actually on, but first I stood myself a beer in the private bar.

"Mr. Proden in this morning?" I asked the barman.

"Not this morning, sir," he told me. "Usually is in, though, but perhaps he's away."

I had my meal and then saw the manager in his office. I described Clandon to him and he remembered he'd booked a dinner the previous evening. He sent for a waiter and the waiter confirmed that Clandon had entered the dining-room at about a quarter-past seven, and had had a beer with his dinner, and coffee afterwards in the lounge. From the way he told his tale I guessed that Clandon had tipped him well.

It was then just after two o'clock and I went out to the cinema. In the foyer I had a look at the time-table and compared it with what I knew of Clandon's movements. Presumably he'd left the tea-shop at about five-thirty. He'd had a look at the town and he might have gone into the church, but all that couldn't have taken more than a few minutes. Then he'd booked dinner and it was at about five or ten minutes to six that he'd entered the cinema. And he'd seen only the News Reel and the second feature, and had left soon after seven.

And there it all was on that time-table.

5.55. Pathé Gazette.
6.10. Getting Her Man.
7.20. Homestead Creek.

After that it seemed almost a shame to have taken the day, for a day it almost was by the time we were back at the Yard. Wharton wasn't in and I own that it was with a certain ironic joy that I wrote a meticulous report. Matthews came in while I was at it, and Wharton must have put ideas in his head, for he, too, seemed disappointed about the Cossingham trip. But he had some news of his own. There was an idea that things were stirring among the blackmail trio. It began just after Widgeon and I left Rappham's office the previous morning.

Rappham left a few minutes later and hopped a bus at the end of Crane Street. He got off at Selfridges and proceeded to lose his tail. That was easy enough and the real significance was that he should know he had a tail at all. That, by the way, was at about eleven o'clock.

But he hadn't allowed for the fact that Unstone's office was also under observation, and he was seen there, coming in the back way from Castle Street, at just before half-past eleven. He stayed with Unstone till just after midday and left by the back way. And again he hadn't taken into account the fact that Cleaver was under observation, for he was seen in Raglan Court at soon after half-past twelve, and he was in Cleaver's office for about twenty minutes. The next seen of him was when he got off another bus at the end of Crane Street and went up to his own office. He was there till after four o'clock and then went to his home—19 Stafford Road, Paddington. He was there till about seven o'clock and then spent the next three hours at the Hen and Chickens in Vidlow Street.

But Unstone had also been shaken. He had seen Cleaver at soon after two o'clock that afternoon, and that evening he had stayed very late in his office. The receptionist had left at five, but it was almost nine o'clock when Unstone left for his home in Ealing, and he had not gone out again that night.

"What about this morning?"

"Rappham didn't turn up at his office till nearly midday," he said. "Last I heard, he was still there. Unstone was a bit late, too."

"Both of them married?"

"Rappham isn't. He's got a lady friend at the Hen and Chickens. He's living in rooms. Unstone's a widower. Got a married daughter living in Acton. Nice little place he's got at Ealing. One of those posh service flats. Stands him back about three-fifty."

"What about Cleaver? He getting restless, too?"

"He's still on the beam," he said. "Regular as clockwork. Gets to his office at half-past nine and leaves at five. Hops a bus at the end of Chancery Lane for Liverpool Street and catches the five-thirty-five for Brentwood. Lives at a private hotel there."

At six o'clock there was no sign of Wharton. Matthews had an idea he'd gone out on some urgent call or other. I saw no point in hanging around, so I went home to the flat. I hadn't been there an hour when he was calling me.

"Rappham's gone," he said. "Don't know how he did it, but he must have got out of that building. Jewle's after somebody's blood."

I said I'd come along. There'd been nothing explosive about Wharton himself as he gave me that news, and I was thinking of the Frenchman's adage and the fortitude with which we can bear the misfortunes of others. But I wasn't sorry that Rappham had bolted, provided always that he was picked up again. And there seemed at least one way to do that, as I was to tell Wharton. I ought to have known it was something already up his sleeve.

"That's being taken care of," he told me. "If that barmaid at the Hen and Chickens is going to join him, there'll be no slipping up a second time."

Then he was giving some other news. Unstone, too, looked like making a bolt.

"He had a few minutes in his bank this afternoon, so I've been having a word with the manager. He telephoned the manager yesterday afternoon that he was withdrawing his balance and this afternoon he did it."

"How much?"

"About eleven hundred pounds," George said. "Took it chiefly in fivers. But he'll have some more salted away somewhere."

There was nothing for me to do, and then it turned out he hadn't even looked at that Cossingham report of mine and I had to give him the outlines.

"Everything seems all right," he said. "Don't see why he hung about Bassingford, though. Anyone'd have thought he'd have had a quick look and pushed on to Cambridge."

I didn't see it like that. As I told him, Clandon might have thought there was more to see in Bassingford than there actually was. That was why he'd told the Cambridge hotel he wouldn't be in till after dinner. And once he'd done that, he'd had to spin out his time in Bassingford.

"Got a short memory, haven't you?" he was firing at me.

"What do you mean?"

"Didn't Clandon go to Bassingford not so long ago to see one of his firm's clients about a manuscript?"

"I know," I said. "But if you look at the same report again, you'll see he added that it was a very hurried visit, and he told you the same thing. That implies he went straight to the author's house and then back."

"Maybe." He shrugged his shoulders and I picked up my hat. I said I'd be pushing along and, as usual, I'd be on tap.

"Looks as if we might have to try things from a different angle," he told me. "Still, I'll think it over and let you know in the morning."

I said good night, and then he added a further something as I was practically through the door.

"Plenty of banks, were there, in that lane where Clandon was found in his car?"

I stood there with my hand on the knob of the door, and for a moment or two he had me on the wrong leg.

"Don't think there were," I said. "Most of the way it had the usual grass verges and shallow ditches."

"That's what I thought," he told me, and the wave of the hand might have been one of dismissal. "A pretty handy thing, that bank."

Chapter Sixteen
CONCERNING AN ALIBI

THAT remark of George Wharton's was the first thing that came to me the next morning when I woke, and it found me of the same opinion with which I'd gone to bed the previous night. George, it still seemed to me, had been a bit too hopeful that I might find something at Cossingham and therefore a bit too piqued that I'd had a day as wasted as I'd foreshadowed. And therefore he'd had to make at least a point or two of his own; to throw out a hint that I hadn't been, shall we say, as observant as George Wharton would have been, had he made that Cossingham call. As for the handiness of that bank, well, why deny it? Clandon must have known himself to be on the verge of a collapse and he had seen that low bank and turned the car deliberately into it. Or he might have been trying to pull up at the side of the lane, and the car fortuitously came to a stop at a bank which just happened to be there.

As for the implications behind the remark of George Wharton's, they could only be that Clandon had driven the car fairly safely into that bank to give the impression that he had collapsed. And that was fantastic. A man with a bullet wound in his shoulder and a deeply scored chest doesn't need to fake a collapse. But there was a still better answer. Clandon had been driving along a lane which he had never before seen in his life. How could he then anticipate that ahead of him there would be a low bank? So no, I told myself. Wharton was just trying to be clever. And he hadn't wanted me to have too good a conceit of myself.

I reported at the Yard, but I might just as well have stayed at home. At ten o'clock George was having a conference with what he called the Big Bugs or the Higher-Ups, and an hour and a half later I heard the result. Everything was now to be banked on a breakdown by Rappham and Unstone, with either or both supplying the names of other blackmail victims, among whom, presumably, we were to find the Dibben murderer. I hated the very sound of it. I always did hate those lulls in a case when a promising trail just peters out and one casts about for a new one. And now there was only one satisfaction. George, with the Big Bugs, was deferential to a degree. But there was quite another George: the one who let the Big Bugs talk and plan and who all the time had his private ideas. That was the George who had almost winked as he told me about that new hunt for new suspects.

"Jewle's in charge," he said, "and I'm in a sort of advisory capacity. What we'd better do is lie low and see how the cat jumps. If you get any ideas, you let me know, and I'll pass anything along."

I couldn't grumble. I was still on the pay-roll with little to do but think. And I didn't have too much time for that, for that same evening George rang me at the flat.

"Unstone's off," he said. "Boarded the Liverpool-Belfast boat-train at six. Jewle's on the train."

"Where'll he collect him? At Liverpool?"

"That's it," he said. "Let him get actually on the boat."

"What's Unstone's idea? Slipping across the border to Eire?"

"Wouldn't be surprised. We'll know more by the morning."

I was round at the Yard pretty early. Jewle was actually with Wharton, so I had things at first hand. What I didn't like was that Unstone had never looked like talking. Jewle said that in an hour or two he was due to appear, and that might alter things.

"What can you hold him for?"

Jewle grinned. Almost anything ought to do. Unstone had shaved off that needle-pointed treasure of a moustache and had been wearing glasses, and there'd been the money in a false bottom of his bag.

"Well hold him all right till we pick up Rappham," he said. "Then we can play one off against the other. One of 'em will talk."

There wasn't any news of Rappham, but Jewle had his hopes on that barmaid at the Hen and Chickens. She was fairly new there and, according to Jewle, Rappham had fallen for her pretty heavily and she for him. Her letters would be checked and telephone calls.

There had been never a reply to that advertisement about Seeway, so there was I at a loose end again. Later in the morning I rang Cossington. The matron told me the doctor was very pleased with Clandon, and that if things went on as well, then Clandon would be home in a couple of days. The garage people were doing those small repairs to his car, and they would probably drive him to town.

It was that last remark that must have put an idea into my head, for thinking about cars made me think about Proden's car and that trip of his to Doncaster. I stress that it was merely a something about which to think, with, behind it, of course, a wish to end that lull in the case. Even when I had finished thinking and had come to a decision, it still wasn't much more than that. But it did have some germ of hope.

Why, I had asked myself, had Proden been so frank about that alibi? Why had he remembered so accurately, and so much? Why, when he was arriving so late, had he stopped for a drink? Why, indeed, had he so managed his affairs as to have arrived at all at the ungodly hour of eleven at night? And was it merely a coincidence that that curious night journey had been undertaken on that very evening when Dibben-Marquis had been killed?

Most of that had been chewed upon by Wharton and myself. His idea had been that Proden had been on a legitimate journey and had been glad for us to prove it so. Proden's had been—still according to George—a kind of ingratiation: the wish to have us regard him as a man of unquestionable integrity, and, by such an acceptance, to wipe him clean off the Dibben suspect list. But only because such a removal would keep us from enquiring into a mysterious and earlier something else.

About that I'd never been happy and, now that I had thought it over again, I was even less happy than before. And it seemed to me, though I'd never tell him so, that the enquiry into the Proden alibi had been just a bit perfunctory. Mind you, there had been a logic about George's conclusions. A man is known to leave a place at six-thirty in a car whose average speed on the road could never be more than thirty-five miles an hour. He does the journey of a hundred and fifty or so miles in four hours and a half, and, allowing for the two short stoppages, the timing is exact. Why, then, trouble to check those stoppages?

And yet, as I said, I didn't know. In our time we'd broken alibis even more tight than that. And always at the back of my mind was one thing. Why should Proden, when I first interviewed him at Bassingford, have started involuntarily at the mention of Dibben's name, and only to claim when in practically the same split second he had recovered himself that the name was one he had utterly forgotten. I had had to drag out of him every bit of information about Dibben, and yet that name for the merest moment had been very much of a shock.

So I saw George Wharton. I said I was rather tired of inaction and would he mind if I had a thorough enquiry into that alibi of Proden's. I expected him to flare up, but he didn't. Maybe he was as bored as I was. Maybe he was like a parent who gladly hands over a shilling to have his offspring safe for an hour or two in the local cinema, but he did ask just what I was proposing to do.

"Go over the whole of the route," I said. "The first stop he mentioned was the devil of a way on the road. Why shouldn't he have left Bassingford, had a fast car ready a few miles north, dashed back to Stapley Green and then back to his own car, and then pushed his own car on hell for leather to make up for lost time? If he killed Dibben and left Stapley Green almost at once, he'd have had a hundred and sixty miles to do in three hours and a half. It sounds impossible, but I'm not so sure."

"Yes, but why? Why should he kill Dibben?"

I didn't know. Maybe it was the frankness that brought the patronage. George shrugged his shoulders. If I wanted to amuse myself that way, there was little reason why I shouldn't. That was what I read into his tone before we settled things. And I have to admit that when they were settled, I wasn't feeling half so happy as when I had walked into his room.

I had with me a man called Steed. Matthews had picked him for me. He was youngish and keen, he said, and he'd had his eyes on him for quite a time.

We set off in the morning soon after nine and the first stop was Bassingford. We made it exactly ten o'clock when we left, and then we headed north for Royston and Huntingdon. On the easy stretches we kept the car at about fifty, which would be Proden's best speed, and that brought our average to just over thirty-five, what with the speed limit of large villages and small towns and the crawling behind heavy traffic where the road wound and turned. We left Peterborough on our right and had to slow to a crawl through Stamford, and then came the twenty-one miles to Grantham. A mile or two through the town was the strip of ribbon development that had once been the hamlet of Dallery.

We slowed the car, and there on the left was the garage near which Proden had probably had his puncture.

The speedometer showed a trip of eighty-two miles from Bassingford and we had made it in two hours and twenty minutes. If Proden had travelled at that same speed of thirty-five an hour, then he should have reached that garage at about nine o'clock on the night of the tenth. That was what we had to check.

The garage was a smallish place with four pumps and a fairish run-in. The workshop had a pit and didn't look equipped for major repairs, and, when I went in, a middle-aged man was working on a pre-war Morris. I asked if I could see the owner. He *was* the owner.

"Scotland Yard," I said, and gave him my card. He didn't bat an eyelid as he looked at it and handed it back.

"We're trying to trace a man who came through here on the night of Thursday the eighth," I said, and I described Proden and his car. "He claims to have had a puncture quite near here, and that you repaired it."

He remembered.

"It weren't really a puncture," he said. "The tyre was flat, or practically flat, but Charlie tested the valve and that's all it was. We fitted a new valve and blew her up and off he went."

"That's fine," I said. "And what time did he get here?"

He rubbed his chin. He reckoned it was about nine. Then he was going out to the yard hollering to Charlie. In a couple of minutes he was back. It was just before nine o'clock, he said, and Charlie ought to know. Charlie was his son, and the garage was closed for the night at nine o'clock. I thanked him, took on three gallons for the good of the house, and moved the car on. But only for a mile.

"That's one theory gone by the board," I told Steed. "The housekeeper says Proden left at six-thirty. He had to do some pretty good driving to get to that garage at just before nine o'clock. It's simply impossible that he could have been at Stapley Green when Dibben was killed."

"Then what do we do now, sir?"

"Don't know," I said. "Better push on, perhaps, now we've started. Get through Newark and look for that pub where he had a drink."

It was only fifteen miles and soon after one o'clock we were at the Bricklayers' Arms. It stood nicely back from the road as Proden had said, with plenty of room to draw in a dozen cars. I thought perhaps we might get a snack there, and we did: a small meat pie apiece and tomatoes and a pint of beer, and we had it at a table in the saloon bar. Only one man was there and he had the air of a regular. He was an elderly, morose sort of cove, and when his mug was empty he rapped with it on the bar, and in came the landlord from the other bar and filled the mug, and never a word had been said. I had a word with him about the weather, and all I got was an aye and a grunt.

We finished our snack. I rapped on the bar and the landlord came in and I paid him. Then I gave him my warrant card and said my piece. I caught the eye of the morose man and he was staring at me from under his bushy, grey eyebrows.

"That'll be him what did the arguing," he told the landlord. "I knew he was a liar as soon as he opened his mouth."

It took some deft work to get the story told. Proden had called in at that pub on his way back from Doncaster, and he had prefaced some remark with: "When I dropped in here for a quick drink on Thursday night . . ."

Our morose friend—his name was Albert Moss—immediately took him up.

"It weren't on Thursday. It was Wednesday."

As I reconstructed it, Proden had smiled placatingly. He'd suavely insisted it was a Thursday.

"Couldn't have been Thursday," Moss had told him, "because I was in here when you come. Just before half-past nine, it was."

Proden had left it like that. Moss drove the point home.

"Couldn't have been Thursday because I wasn't in on Thursday. Thursday night's club night and I always have my pint before eight o'clock and don't come back."

Proden had shrugged his shoulders and given the landlord a suggestive look.

"That's all right, Albert," the landlord had said. "Reckon you've made a mistake for once. The gentleman ought to know."

He'd tipped a wink which Albert caught. Albert had even accepted a pint from Proden and kept his mouth shut about Thursdays and Wednesdays. But as soon as Proden had driven off, he began again. He rounded on the landlord for taking Proden's side. The landlord told him it did a house no good to have arguments, and a customer had always to be right.

"But he wasn't right," I said.

"No, sir, he certainly wasn't. Albert was right. It was a Wednesday night he popped in here. All of a hurry he was. Weren't in longer than it takes to drink a double whisky."

That was the gist of it all. A few minutes later we were drawing the car up again and talking things over, and we were like a man whose spade has turned up some long hidden coins, and whose quick wonder is whether those coins are gold or copper.

"It seems a fact that he did go to that pub on the Wednesday," Steed said. "Why shouldn't we nip back, sir, and try that garage again. And now I come to think of it, there was something suspicious about that puncture. Why shouldn't he have unscrewed a valve himself and let the tyre down on purpose?"

We drove back the fifteen miles and we saw Charlie. In the cubby-hole that was used as an office, he checked up on the old-fashioned cash-register. The last entry for the night of Wednesday the seventh was—Valve 1s. 6d.

"Did he happen to call in again three or four days later?" I said.

He didn't remember. If he'd called, he hadn't seen him himself. I asked if I could speak to his father.

"Come to think of it, I believe he did," the father told us. "Be about half-past eleven in the morning. I think he had four gallons and a pint of oil."

"Then think very carefully," I said. "We have an idea he was trying to create the impression that it was on the Thursday that he had that leaking valve and not on the Wednesday, so when you were putting in those four gallons, did he make any reference to the Thursday?"

"Don't know that he didn't," he said. "I know he mentioned that valve and how he ought to have tested it himself. I'd say he mentioned the Thursday. Can't remember exactly how, though."

I said that with any luck we'd be back that way that night, and maybe he'd think it over. Then we moved off again. Doncaster was fifty miles or so ahead, but we didn't take it fast. There was far too much to think about.

What was a certainty was that we were on to something big. Proden had made that journey from Bassingford to at least as far as the Bricklayers' Arms at Little Sawbury on the Wednesday night.

"If he turned round there and went back to Bassingford," Steed said, "that wouldn't give him an alibi for the Thursday. It would give him an alibi for the same night—the Wednesday."

That was obvious. And it didn't account for the fact that Proden had tried at the garage and the pub to establish it as a fact that it had been on the Thursday that he had been at both places. And then I had it. I ought to have had it at once, for it had stared me in the face.

"This is it," I said, "and we'll test it at Doncaster. He drove that car to Doncaster on the Wednesday. He trusted to the fact that if ever he were a suspect for Dibben's murder, it'd be days or weeks afterwards and what the garage people and the pub would remember was the last thing he'd put in their minds."

"That Albert Moss must have been a shock to him?" Steed told me with a grin.

"You're right," I said. "But Proden must have thought he'd get away with it or he'd never have told us about the Bricklayers' Arms. So what we've got to do when we get to Doncaster is to look up trains. I think Proden parked the car somewhere in Doncaster on the Wednesday night and came back to Bassingford by train the following day. Then he pretended to leave Bassingford in the same car at half-past six on the Thursday, but he didn't. He took the train for town, and that train goes through Stapley Green. He got off there, killed Dibben, then took the Tube from Stapley Green to King's Cross and caught the express for Doncaster. He picked up his car and drove to Uffley Moor and got there at about eleven o'clock."

The first thing I did at Doncaster was to make for the Enquiry Bureau at the main station, and I found two perfect trains. The express for the north left King's Cross at ten minutes to eight, and the first stop was Doncaster, where it arrived at ten forty-five. A train left Bassingford at six forty-five and stopped at Stapley Green at ten past seven.

We parked the car and looked about for an all-night garage. It had to be reasonably near the station, since every minute would count, and we found one that was not two hundred yards away, and on the road which Proden must have taken for Uffley Moor. It was a huge place and I didn't expect quick results. The manager told me, in fact, that I'd better come back in an hour and he might have the information ready for me, so Steed and I went back into the town and got ourselves some tea. When we returned to that garage, we had a facer. No car of that number had checked in on the Wednesday night.

I asked what records they kept and he showed me the entry book. What they took was the make of car, its number, the client's name, time of leaving and time the car was wanted.

"You don't by any chance look at the licence?"

He seemed puzzled.

"Just an idea," I said. "It's just possible that the car I want may have had false plates. If so, the licence would have been faked."

"Sheer luck if we ever look at a licence," he told me. "If the holder had slipped or there wasn't a licence, we might call the owner's attention to it. That wouldn't happen once in a thousand times."

"Well, do this for me," I said. "I'm sorry to be such a nuisance, but, believe me, it's highly important. Get me information about any Austin Tens of about 1939 that did come in at about half-past ten on that Wednesday night. And it would have to show in the book as taken out at about the same time the following night."

He got to work on the book. In a couple of minutes he had what I wanted. A black Austin Ten met the requirements and it number was NJ 8517. The owner was a Mr. Black. I asked to see the man who'd taken the car over on the Wednesday night. Luckily he was on day duty after the night duty of the previous week.

I wasn't worrying about the car: it was a description of Black that I was after, and the man wasn't a lot of help. It was no use forcing information, and all I got was that Black had worn glasses, had a dark and rather untidy moustache, was tallish walked with a slight limp and had a Scotch accent. And all that except for the height, was just no use at all. Glasses are the first disguise most people turn to, and the limp and the accent were easy enough to assume.

As for Proden's cavalry moustache, that might have been combed down and darkened.

A quarter of an hour later we were leaving Doncaster. In a way we'd had a day successful beyond the most fantastic hopes, and that unsatisfying half-hour at the garage was little more than a loose end. But all that was in the first flush, as it were, of discovery. As we drove south there were more loose ends.

"Someone must have slipped up over that housekeeper's evidence," Steed said. "Wouldn't she swear he took his car out at half-past six on the Thursday?"

"There's just the chance there were two cars," I said and liked it far less when I'd said it. Proden couldn't have had time to acquire another car that resembled his own, for Dibben had been killed only a day or so after I'd paid that first call on him. And both cars would have had to go to Doncaster, and I didn't see how a manipulation could have been worked. But it did give me an idea. At Newark I called on the local police and had a call put through to that Doncaster garage. The manager had gone, but the deputy on duty got hold of the man I'd seen.

"Going back to that Austin Ten," I said. "Can you recall anything peculiar about it, or the bodywork, or anything? Wear marks or scratches? Bent bumper or anything peculiar about the tyres? Anything that'd make you recognise the car again, whatever its number-plates?"

He seemed to be thinking it over. Then he said it was curious I should ask the question, because just above the rear bumper the bodywork had a dent as if the car had backed into something. He'd thought of asking Black if he'd like the dent taken out. It was part of everyone's job to spot things like that and mention them to the client. It was one way of getting work. But he hadn't mentioned it. He'd just forgotten it, and that was that.

We drove on again and I was trying to see Proden's car again, and for the life of me I couldn't recall any dent. I had first seen that car from the back, and I'd thought it in immaculate condition. But maybe that dent had been pretty small.

We stopped at Dallery and saw that garage proprietor again, but he'd remembered nothing else. There was no need this time

174 | CHRISTOPHER BUSH

to drive round by Bassingford, and we came on through Ware and the Cambridge arterial. It was about half-past nine when we drew in at the Yard. Wharton was in his room.

Chapter Seventeen
DISCOVERY

WHARTON was flabbergasted. He owned we'd done a good job, but he couldn't help telling me that but for my cantankerous friend at the Bricklayers' Arms we might have come home as wise as we'd started. For we'd slipped up badly at that first call at the garage. We'd enquired about an hour, not a day.

I couldn't let him get away with that, especially in front of Matthews.

"Did you ever think in terms of a day? Not that I know of. I set out to test an alibi for the Thursday night. None of us even dreamed it'd bring us to the Wednesday night." He mumbled something and turned on Matthews. Who'd done that checking on the Beaulieu housekeeper? Matthews said it was Waller, and he was a good man. Wharton brought out the Proden file. He found what he wanted and began grimly to read.

"10.30 a.m. Went to Beaulieu, Bassingford, as instructed. Saw the housekeeper, a Mrs. Purdie, who said that Mr. Proden was playing golf and I might find him on the local course. I said I wouldn't bother him, but I might see him later. I said I'd call to see him at about seven o'clock on the evening of the eighth and had found nobody in. She said I must have just missed him as he'd left in his car for a short holiday near Doncaster at about half-past six. I said were you here and she said yes. I gave my name as Wallace and said I'd probably be seeing Proden later."

"What's wrong with that?" I said. "It reads to me like a perfect report."

Whatever he was going to say, he didn't say it. He gave a grunt and put the report back.

"She won't run away," I said. "She can always be questioned again. And we know there's a catch somewhere. She couldn't possibly have seen that car leave its garage, and for the simple reason that it wasn't there."

"Then what about the gardener?" His tone was mildness itself. "He's a full-time man. If the garage was empty he'd have known it on the Thursday. And where was the housekeeper on the Wednesday night that she didn't know Proden wasn't sleeping at the house?"

I said they weren't questions that couldn't be answered. Then he was hedging. You couldn't question that housekeeper and gardener without Proden hearing of it, and the very nature of the enquiries would let him know we were on to the faked alibi.

"No reason we shouldn't try," I said. "I'm perfectly willing to have a shot at it. It's something that's certainly got to be done. And I'd like a good look at his car to try to find that dent. Both'd be easy if he happens to be playing golf."

To cut a long argument short, it was arranged that I should go to Bassingford in the morning. A man would be sent ahead and he'd contact me at the White Hart at eleven o'clock.

"Anything happen today?" I asked. "Anything about Rappham or Unstone?"

Nothing happened. Unstone was still being held and there'd been no movement yet by Rappham's lady friend at the Hen and Chickens. Then, almost as an afterthought, Wharton was giving me a letter. It had come by that evening's post.

"DEAR SIRS,

"About the David Seeway you were asking for in the advertisement, I knew him at Bassingford before the war and then I met him in the army not long before the war ended. He was calling himself Davidson, and made out at first he wasn't Seeway and then he had to own up. He said he'd fallen out with his aunt and had wanted to cut loose from Bassingford, so he had changed his name.

"Then I ran into him about a week ago in London and he told me he'd opened a tourist agency in Belgium with another man and they were doing pretty well. He was looking prosperous enough and we had a drink or two at the Swallow in Courtney Street.

"If there is any reward for this, please put a notice to that effect in the Personal column of the *Telegraph* and I will arrange to collect.

"Yours truly,

"ANZIO.

"P.S. I may remember something more by then."

There was no address and no date, but it had been posted that afternoon in the West Central district. It was on a sheet of fair quality paper torn from a block, and the writing was upright, roundish and neat, as if each letter had been carefully formed.

"An extraordinary event," I told George. "This is the first we've heard of Seeway since Clandon saw him in Sicily. Even if this letter isn't genuine, it's still something." He was wanting to know what I thought of it. I said it read quite well, and as if written by someone whom Seeway might have regarded as an equal.

"No prints on it," he said.

That wasn't so good. The gentleman with the nom-de-plume of Anzio might have a record, and that, of course, fitted in with the request for a notice in the *Telegraph* if there was a reward.

"Can't afford to disregard it," George said. "We've got into touch with the Belgians and they're going to do what they can."

It looked attractive to me, and I said so. And if Seeway were really in London a week ago, maybe he had been mixed up somehow in the Dibben murder, if only as an accomplice of Proden. George wasn't so sure. According to him, the letter told too much of what we didn't want to know and too little of what we did. My idea about that was that Anzio was a pretty shrewd customer. He was going to be sure about a reward before he parted with everything he knew, and hence the hint in the postscript.

I couldn't help sleeping well that night, and in the morning there was no need to rush round to the Yard. But George did give me a ring just before I left for Bassingford. Once more he was advising the extremest caution. On no account must Proden be given the slightest hint that we suspected his alibi.

I'd had a brief run of luck, and it was to continue. Before I contacted Wharton's man in Bassingford, I'd had no idea how I could get the information I wanted and at the same time keep within the cautionary bounds that Wharton had set. And then it all turned out as easy as could be. Wharton's man simply said that Proden was away and the house shut up, but the gardener was still there.

"Did you find out where Proden was?"

"I thought I hadn't better," he said. "All I did was carry my bag and go round to the back door and then this gardener stopped me. Said everyone was away, and it wasn't any use my knocking."

I drove on to Beaulieu. The gardener was weeding flower-beds at the front of the house.

"Mr. Proden in?"

"As a matter of fact, sir, he's away. The house is shut up and they won't be back for at least another week."

I passed him my cigarette case and he held his lighter for mine.

"It doesn't really matter," I said. "I just happened to be this way. What's he actually doing? On a holiday?"

"That's it, sir. There's a nice little bungalow down at Wood-sea, and the guvnor plays golf on the course there and has a swim and so on. The sea's almost at the end of the garden."

"Very nice, too," I said. "And you're the only one left behind."

"Oh, I got a holiday out of it all right, sir," he told me, and grinned. "Mrs. Purdie, she's the housekeeper, and me had all the Wednesday and Thursday there. The guv'nor hired a car for us and I tidied up the garden and she saw to the bungalow and then we came back the Thursday afternoon late. I didn't actually come back except to bring her, so that was as good as two days' holiday."

"A yearly event, is it?"

"Well, ever since the war. Never know when we're going, though. It depends on the weather. Been pretty good this year, so the guv'nor thought he'd go early."

"Wouldn't mind a few days myself," I said, "now it's turned hot again. But that Thursday when you came back. Wasn't that the day Mr. Proden went up to Doncaster? I called to see him a day or two after. You remember."

"That's right, sir. That was the Thursday. He was here when I brought Mrs. Purdie back, and that'd be about six. He spoke to me at the gate and reckoned he'd soon be off."

"And I'll be off, too," I said. "No need to give him any message. I just happened to be this way and thought I'd drop in."

I drove the car out of the town to the north and then circled round. I sent Wharton's man back to town and went to the local police station and got Wharton on the line from there. He seemed uncommonly pleased at what I'd found out.

"What about my running over to this Woodsea place?" I said "It's only about fifty miles."

He told me to hold the line. In two or three minutes he was saying that Woodsea was a pretty small place and I might be spotted. What he'd do would be to send Matthews down, but only for a look at the car. If that dent was found, we'd have enough on Proden without risking a chat with the housekeeper

I asked about reporting back and he said there was no great hurry even if there was something in the wind. That barmaid at the Hen and Chickens had asked for the day off to see her sister who was supposed to be ill in Ashford. She was still at her lodgings and they were waiting for her to emerge. If anything happened that called for me, he'd give me a ring. He himself would be seeing the C.C. and there might be a conference at once on the action to be taken against Proden.

So I had lunch at Bassingford and then made a leisurely way home. And I hoped in a way it would be my last trip, for that once interesting road to Bassingford had become so familiar that I could almost have driven it with shut eyes. And with Proden practically booked for the Dibben murder, it was as if the zest had gone from the case. All that remained was th

Seeway-Dibben mystery, and now, with a chance of picking up both Rappham and Seeway himself, it looked as if a day or two might bring the answer even to that.

Bernice and I were just finishing dinner that evening when Wharton rang.

"Matthews is due in at any time," he said. "He's got what we wanted. Don't know if you'd like to see him."

I said I'd be along, and then he rang off before I could ask him about Rappham. I actually got to the Yard as Matthew's car was coming in, and we walked up the stairs together.

"The dent's there," he said. "You have to see it in a certain light or else you'd never spot it."

I heard more when he was running over things with Wharton. It was a high-class little bungalow at Woodsea, he said, and about a quarter of a mile along the inlet. It had its own strip of beach and a little boathouse with quite a nice little motor-boat. When he'd spied out the land, the garage was empty, so he'd taken a chance at the golf course at Frimley, about three miles away. He tracked down Proden, who was playing in a foursome, and then had slipped back to the club-house and found the car.

"That motor-boat," Wharton said. "Pretty handy, would it be, if he wanted to make a getaway?"

Matthews thought it very handy indeed, though where he might make for was harder to guess.

"Better get along there in the morning and have the bungalow watched," Wharton said. "Not that anything's going to be done about Proden—not yet. What they want is a motive."

They were the Big Bugs of Wharton's afternoon conference. What we'd got was good, but not good enough. The proving of a faked alibi didn't necessarily connect Proden with Dibben's murder—that was how they'd seen it.

"It's their headache," Wharton told us. "It's up to them to decide when the cat jumps. All we can do is go plodding along and try to get what they want."

The buzzer went. What was happening we couldn't gather, but it was a good three minutes before Wharton hung up.

"That barmaid, Irene Drew," he said. "She took the eight-five from London Bridge. Booked for Folkestone and had one heavy case with her. Jewle's on the train."

"What's the idea?" Matthews said. "Hoping to slip across to France?"

Wharton wouldn't hazard a guess. My guess was that she'd be meeting Rappham and both of them lying low, and then slipping into France by one of the new day trips.

"About that housekeeper of Proden's," Wharton said. "What's a feasible explanation of why she needn't have seen Proden actually start?"

"She'd just got back from Woodsea," I said. "Her room would be at the back and Proden could call that he was just off. That's all there'd be to it."

"Or Proden might have asked her to slip along to the pillar-box with a letter," Matthews said. "Or to take a note to that cinema manager."

We talked around it and Proden's alibi and the slowness of the Belgian police and everything to pass the time for Wharton. Then at nine o'clock even he recognised we were only talking, and Matthews got away for a meal and I went home to wait for a possible call. Bernice had one of her headaches and went to bed early. I sat on, and it was almost eleven when the telephone went.

"She went straight to a hotel," Wharton was telling me. "The Excelsior, near the station. A chap resembling Rappham's been there since Rappham gave us the slip. Started to grow a moustache and altered himself a bit. They're watching his room."

There'd be nothing else that night, so I went to bed, and it was one of those nights when I just couldn't sleep. The case kept revolving in my mind and every fact came back monotonously in its turn. I wondered what we should get from Rappham, and I knew it wouldn't be I who'd try to do the extracting. After that interview of mine with Widgeon in his office, he'd keep his mouth shut for sheer spite rather than spill a single word. I wondered what the job had been that he'd done for Dibben: the job on which he'd come to report that far-off day in Cambridge. I wondered if it would give us a clue to the Dibben-Seeway mystery and why Seeway—or Davidson—had mentioned Dibben's name that day in a hospital in Sicily. And if Seeway had then been calling himself Davidson, there was the additional mystery of why he had given his real name to Clandon. And if Proden had killed Dibben—and whatever the Big Bugs might think, that looked a certainty—then what had been the motive? Those were the things that kept revolving, and when at last I got to sleep it was only to wake again and find them revolving still.

I woke for the last time at five o'clock and I felt it was hopeless to try to sleep again. So I lay on for a bit and then crept to the bathroom. I lingered out my dressing and made myself a cup of tea. I walked to Leicester Square and bought a paper that would be different from my own, and I came back and made a cup of tea for Bernice. Her head was still none too good, so I rang down for one service breakfast. I read the paper till it came, and when I had taken my time over what was on the tray, it was still only a little after seven. And then I could no longer keep thought at bay, and things began once more revolving in my mind.

I got round to Rappham, and it was curious in a way that I should have wondered about his prints, and if Wharton or Summer had ever discovered anything about those prints that had been found on the outer knob of that French window at Redgates. It was absurd, of course, to think that those prints might have been Rappham's, and that made me remember that I had Rappham's prints myself, on that page from my notebook on which I'd written Unstone's name. I opened the drawer and there it was.

I glanced at my watch and it was about a quarter past seven. It must have been instinctively and to kill time that I got out the grey powder and brush insufflator. In a couple of minutes I was looking at a handsome set of Rappham's prints. Then I shrugged my shoulders. Handsome or not, the Yard had them, too, and I wasn't going to make myself so much of a fool as to take them along for testing.

I put that paper back in the drawer. Or rather, I didn't. I saw another paper, and a quick glance at it made it that letter of Clandon's: the one where he'd said he had decided to drop the Seeway-Dibben affair just as I'd advised him. I was putting that letter back when I glanced at my watch again, and only ten minutes had gone since I last looked. Maybe it was with the idea of killing a bit more time that I began dusting that letter with grey powder. I had done one side of that sheet of paper and had brought up a print or two of my own, and then suddenly I was realising an astounding something. At once I was dusting the other side of that paper. I took my own prints and compared, and everything was in order. But one thing wasn't. *Except for my own, there were no other prints.*

I must have sat and stared at that sheet of notepaper. You see the implications? It should have had prints where it had been taken from a rack or drawer, where a left hand had held it while the right hand wrote, and where Clandon's fingers had folded it for the envelope, and yet it didn't have a single print. Why, then, had he gloved his hands through every process of handling it? There seemed only one answer—that he was anxious I should not identify his prints. But since the letter had been written after Wharton's visit, it was not of myself but of Scotland Yard that he had been afraid. And that meant only one thing, *that Henry Clandon had a record.*

I couldn't believe it, yet there it was, staring me in the face. And I knew there was only one thing to do—to get Clandon's prints and send them to the Yard. So I looked in my note-book where I thought I'd jotted down the telephone number of the Cossingham hospital, and there the number was. It was about five minutes before I was speaking to the matron.

"Mr. Clandon has gone home," she said. "He left early yesterday morning. The garage people drove him in his car."

"How was he?"

"The doctor was very pleased," she said. "There's nothing now that his own doctor can't see to. Just the stitches to remove and that should be all."

I ought to have remembered that Clandon would probably be home, but two or three days had slipped by and Clandon had been almost forgotten. But when I began to think about calling that morning at his flat, I suddenly began to have a whole series of moral qualms. That letter of his hadn't been marked confidential, but it had nevertheless been a letter from a client to the Agency. And Clandon was something of a friend, and I hated to sneak up on him and make a friendly call the excuse to get his prints. It was an attitude that Wharton would regard as worse than weakness, but I wasn't George Wharton.

Then I began to waver. I could ask Clandon confidentially to explain the absence of prints on that letter, and I was telling myself that he'd surely have some reasonable explanation. Then I was wavering the other way. What reasonable explanation could there possibly be? And then it suddenly came to me that I didn't have to go to Clandon's flat to get his prints. *I already had his prints*. And within half an hour I could have them checked at the Yard. And what I did then would have to depend on what that check disclosed.

I slipped round to the garage and got my car, and in ten minutes I was at Broad Street. It was just too early for Norris, and the night man was still on duty when I let myself into the office and unlocked the safe. Just as a precaution we keep all contracts for six months after expiration, and there was the contract that Clandon had signed. As far as I remembered, only my prints and his were on it, not that that mattered. It was his prints that would be spotted if the Bureau had a record.

It was still early when I got round to the Yard. The Chief Superintendent wasn't in, but I saw an inspector whom I knew and then hung about to await results. I had them in ten minutes and I knew by his face that something was afoot.

"You've got these yourself," he told me. "We tried to check them for you over that Marquis job."

I must have stared. I was trying to remember what prints we had had.

"You know," he said. "The ones on the knob of that french window at Stapley Green."

Chapter Eighteen
FROM THE HORSE'S MOUTH

I PUT that contract carefully in my pocket and wandered out to the main entrance and then across the road and along to the Embankment. All I could think was that somehow we had been wrong about Proden, and it was Henry Clandon who had killed Dibben!

But that was panic-thinking, even if it took me a few minutes to realise it. The shock of that discovery had gone, and as I began to go slowly and carefully back to the things that had happened, I knew, and with a curious warmth of pleasure, that Clandon could never have killed Dibben. Dibben had been killed on the evening of the eighth, and it had not been till the morning of the ninth that I had let Clandon know that I was on Dibben's tracks, and that he was supposed to be living at Stapley Green and calling himself Colonel Marquis. And so Dibben was dead hours before Clandon had known that he actually still existed.

And yet there was the inescapable fact that those prints on the knob of that french window were Clandon's. At some time on the ninth Clandon had gone to that house at Stapley Green, and after I had given him the information and before that time in the afternoon when I had gone there myself that curiosity had been too much for him. The man who had hired a dog had been seized with the itch to bark for himself. So he had probably discovered, much as I had myself, the house of a Colonel Marquis, and had gone to investigate. He had found the house with no one at home, and had ventured to wander round to the back. And when I thought that, I suddenly groped for my glasses. *If Clandon had been at that window, then he must have seen Marquis's body.* Why, then, had he not admitted as much? There was reason perhaps why he should not inform the police; he might not wish, for instance, to admit that rather officious curiosity. But why had he not admitted it to me in confidence? Why had he received the news of Marquis's death with a pretence of enormous surprise?

I didn't argue it out. Something else was far too suddenly in my mind. What possible satisfaction could Clandon get from a visit to Marquis! Surely curiosity or officiousness could not have gone so far, or self-conceit have deluded him into thinking he could induce Marquis to tell him why Seeway had mentioned his name that day in Sicily? Or even to tell him of Seeway's whereabouts if he knew them? And Clandon certainly had not gone to Stapley Green to identify Marquis, for Marquis-Dibben was a someone whom he had never seen. Or had he?

And then my fingers were fumbling at my glasses again. Something had hit me with the force of a navvy's hammer, and I turned away from the river and was making for the Yard. I don't remember crossing the road, but I do remember going into Wharton's room and accepting him for granted when I saw him there. He gave me a good-morning and then he must have seen something on my face.

"What's the matter? Not feeling too fit?"

"Not that," I said, and hung up my hat. "I've just discovered something. *Henry Clandon is David Seeway.*"

As simple as that, and under our noses for days. Why had the army no knowledge of a Seeway in Sicily? Because there hadn't been a Seeway. Why had the mysterious Seeway mentioned Dibben's name to Clandon? Because he hadn't. There'd been no Seeway and no mention of Dibben. It was true that Clandon had been in that hospital with a wound in the stomach, but the rest was sheer imagination. It might sound ridiculous, but Clandon had approached the Broad Street Detective Agency to find himself! And therefore the important thing about that commission had not been the finding of Seeway, *but the finding of Dibben.*

And Seeway-Clandon *had* known Dibben. He had gone to Stapley Green to try to see him and identify him. And he had seen him—dead on his office floor—and had identified him. Then two things naturally followed. There was no need for the Agency to go on with the search for Seeway since the real object had been arrived at—the finding of Dibben. So Clandon had written me a letter which fitted happily in with the suggestion I'd already made—that he should drop the whole matter for at least a time.

"Then Clandon was Anzio," George said. "He wrote that anonymous letter."

"Must have done," I said. "It was a final dissociation of Clandon from Seeway. An attempt to get us to Belgium and well off the real track."

"You go to his flat and arrest him," I said, "and where will that get us? The only public mischief he's actually caused is over that hold-up at Cossingham. And that wasn't faked. He was shot and there isn't a doubt about it. I admit he saw Dibben dead and didn't inform the police, and he wrote the Anzio letter and told a few lies about Chile, but they're comparative trivialities when you come to weigh them up. Only Clandon can tell us what we want to know. Why Proden killed Dibben, for instance. Why Clandon wanted Dibben found."

George simmered down.

"What's the best thing to do? Go and see him?"

"I think so," I said. "Mention arrest as a sideline, but make him talk."

"You get him," George said. "Spin him some yarn."

So I spoke to Clandon. I asked how he was and I didn't make it too gushing or too austere. And he didn't sound too perturbed when I said there were one or two little things about which Wharton would like his help, and might we come round.

"There we are, George," I said as I rang off. "Any time we like."

"Right," he said, and I didn't like that Coliseum smile. "Give me ten minutes, and God help him if he doesn't tell the truth."

Clandon told the truth. He let us in himself and, but for the bandaged shoulder, he was looking his normal self. I gave him a second good-morning, and then Wharton pricked the bubble with half a dozen or so of words.

"Sit down, Mr. Seeway, and start telling us the truth."

I don't say I've got the words all right, but the gist of the story is there, and at least it's in chronological order. I leave out the interruptions, the hesitations, the stammerings, the apologies, and I give you in my own words what Clandon said. It's a story that needs no embellishments. It had a flavour of the fantastic, or it would have had if I had never had that interview with Rosamund Caverly-Hare. Proden had mesmerised her, too. That background she had given me was a kind of cement that fastened the jig-saw pieces firmly into place.

It was the arrival of Hugh Proden from Ceylon that began the whole thing, and his object had undoubtedly been from the very first to secure for himself at least a share of his aunt's money, so he oozed that natural charm and set himself to dominate the Beaulieu household. In less than no time he had ingratiated himself with the aunt and had David Seeway hanging on his words and aping his very mannerisms.

That in those days Seeway was callow and something of a cub was undoubted, and that he had to tread warily with that Puritanic bigot of an aunt. Proden played a double game. Ostensibly he was on Seeway's side. He tried to make him—and Seeway was grateful—a man of the world, but he enlarged those minor scrapes into which Seeway had precipitated himself till the aunt had reached a point where at any time she might think of a disinheriting. She had certainly spoken to Seeway and warned him.

Out of that inability of Seeway's to stand much drink, and that fracas in the White Hart, Proden evolved his final scheme. Something, too, had probably emerged from the opinions he had formed of Archie Dibben during that week of the *Under My Thumb* company in Bassingford. And there I must make an insertion. In the years that followed, Clandon-Seeway had had plenty of time and reason to think things over. It was after he had had that quick glimpse of Dibben—about which you have yet to hear—that he made the reconstruction which that morning he was giving us. That reconstruction was this.

What happened was not originally intended. All that Proden wanted was to create a scandal that would cause a final break between Seeway and his aunt. So he approached Dibben. A trick was to be played on Seeway. The way Proden would put it to Dibben would have been something like this: that on Seeway's own behalf and for Seeway's own good he was going to put a thorough scare into him. It was 31st March and the trick was to have the nature of an April Fool character, and it was this.

After the final show, Proden would have Dibben in his office for a drink. Seeway was to be there, too, but Seeway would either have had a drink or two already, or the one drink he had had would be slightly doped. But there were the three men of the world having a drink and a few yarns, and then Dibben was gradually to be a bit tipsy himself and definitely cantankerous. He was so to rile Seeway or insult him that Seeway could do no other than strike him. Seeway himself—to hark back again—had utterly forgotten what it was that Dibben had said. His wits were so fuddled that he hardly remembered striking Dibben at all. But there was Dibben on the floor. There was Proden, through the haze of tobacco smoke, bending over him, and at last looking up with an ominous licking of the lips.

"My God, he's dead! You've killed him!"

But Dibben had done the job almost too well. He'd had the capsule in his mouth with the dyed water or red ink, and had crushed it when he fell. The blood was oozing apparently from his mouth, and never had a man looked more dead. Was that when the major scheme had come to Proden's mind? Might it not at least be tried? No great harm would be done if Seeway refused to credit the things that would have to be done. So Proden tried it.

Dibben was left in the office when Jim Barnes had gone, and Proden took Seeway down to the handily placed car. The fuddled brain of Seeway scarcely comprehended what Proden was trying to tell him, but Proden would put everything right. That was what he knew. And maybe Proden doped another drink for him and took care to be at his bedside the next morning to wake him or be there as soon as he woke.

Incredible it might be, but Seeway was like putty in Proden's fingers. What had happened to the dead body of Dibben he refused to say, but there was a mention of something of the sort that had happened to a friend of his in Ceylon, and talk about Seeway and himself standing by each other. Scandal had to be avoided, and the fact that the killing had been an accident made no difference to that. But always there had to be the insistence that now Proden had taken the first steps to dispose of Dibben's body, Proden himself was involved. Loyalty to Proden, then, as well as safety for Seeway himself.

So Seeway left Bassingford at the earliest moment, and that he had later communicated with Proden we had known from what I'd heard in that interview with Rosamund Caverly-Hare. Proden had said the body had never been found—he himself had seen to that—and it had been assumed that Dibben—always a cantankerous person to handle—had left the company in a fit of pique. But for safety's sake Seeway had better take another name. Maybe he'd better go to one of the colonies, or contrive somehow to drop out altogether. Corresponding was dangerous to both of them, and any personal meeting would be more so. And Seeway did change his name, and he did drop out: at least he joined the Forces and tried to wipe Bassingford and what had happened from his mind.

And what about Dibben? Proden must have told him that night when he returned to the office that Seeway hadn't credited that he was dead. The trick would have to have more of a grim earnestness. Dibben was induced to be absent from the company for a week, and with a reasonable excuse. Maybe Proden tried to induce him, under talk of his own influence in Town, to quit the company altogether. That we would never know. But when Dibben was absent for only the week, Proden must have been in a constant state of alarm. At any moment Seeway might discover that Dibben was alive. But Proden had only a very few weeks in which to be anxious. Dibben himself began to take a hand.

Conjecture? Maybe, but that was how we saw things. Dibben became suspicious of that Bassingford stunt, and the far too serious conclusions to which Proden had later carried it. Maybe Proden had been incautious and had paid him too heavily, but what looked certain was that Dibben had employed Rappham to make careful enquiries. Rappham couldn't help hearing about the sudden departure of Seeway and the difference that departure was likely to make in the affairs of Proden. That was why he was so cock-a-hoop that day at Cambridge when he reported to Dibben what he'd discovered.

Did Dibben blackmail Proden at once? Or did he wait till the aunt was dead and Proden had come in for her money? My idea was that he began the blackmailing at once. He certainly left the stage and, though he'd inherited that employment agency from his sister, I didn't think he'd have waited for over a year before applying pressure to Proden. Dibben himself was out for a complete change of life, and the one-time star of a town production who knew only too well he'd never reach those heights again, was to undergo a metamorphosis. Dibben had gone. In his place was the retired colonel, the moneyed man of leisure with a craze for golf and a fund of Indian anecdotes and always a drink and a handsome cigar for his cronies.

Seeway was demobilised. What he had said about his entry into the publishing business was implicitly true. The years had sobered him down, but in any case it was something he had always wanted to do. But even that utter cutting of himself adrift from Bassingford and the past couldn't remove from his mind the remembering of what had happened that long-distant night. It was, as they say, on his conscience. He had even thought of employing private detectives to discover if Dibben had left any dependants so that he might make some secret restitution. And then the extraordinary thing happened.

It was about three weeks before that visit of Clandon to the agency and he was travelling on the Underground in a crowded compartment. He himself was standing jammed in a crowd by the central door when he noticed a man who was a foot or two from him. It should be stated that, in furtherance of that scheme of his, Proden had thrown Seeway very much into the company of Dibben during that week in Bassingford. Clandon had a good look at a man who seemed curiously familiar in spite of the beard and the differences of over ten years. He spotted that mole and, as he told us, he went hot and cold all over, for he knew somehow that the man was Dibben. And then the train slowed for Leicester Square Station and the man got out. Clandon himself was on his way to an urgent appointment, but even then he considered following the man. By the time he had made up his mind to get off the train, it was on the move again.

It was after that that he began to do his thinking. Then he knew he had to discover whether Dibben was the man of the train, and that was why he came to the Broad Street Detective Agency. It had taken him days, he said, to prepare and rehearse the tale he had told me. If Dibben were really dead, then he couldn't tell the truth. If he were alive, then he was prepared to handle the situation himself once he was found.

And that was what he did. As soon as I'd told him that Dibben was probably Marquis and living at Stapley Green, he had gone to Stapley Green and made enquiries at the post office. That sent him to Redgates. Through that french window he identified the dead man as the man he'd seen in the train. And from where he had stood he had seen the ends of the cord that was round the dead man's neck.

That was both a fright and a complication. He decided to await events, and then he used that suggestion of mine, and a pretended nervousness of the law, to withdraw from things altogether. But it had come to him far too late that he might have left prints on that window, and that was why the letter to me had been written with gloved hands. And he had sent that anonymous letter to the Yard so that "Anzio" should be thought a suspect, and that the prints were his.

But meanwhile he had made his own plans for retribution. And it was seeming to him as if his own life might be in some danger if, as he thought, Proden had killed Dibben to keep his mouth shut. That may sound like cloak-and-dagger stuff, but it sounded real enough to me as he sat telling his story to Wharton and myself. And that fear of what Proden might do made him take a holiday in no one place, and before the end of it he was hoping that the murder of Dibben might be pinned on Proden. If it were, then he was proposing to come forward with his story.

And he was proposing to scare Proden into some kind of action, so he rang him from Aldburgh. It must have been a nasty moment for Proden when a voice said it was David Seeway speaking.

"I happen to know who killed Dibben. Think it over, Proden; I may have to ask you to do something about it."

Then he rang off. A day later he rang him again, building up on the same bluff.

"I want twenty thousand pounds, Proden. That's only chicken feed compared with what I'd have had from my aunt. You'd better start getting it ready."

When he rang for the third and last time, Proden asked him to come to Beaulieu at eight o'clock the following night when the money would be ready. Clandon said he might and he mightn't, but Proden had better be in, all the same. Then he thought things over. He had now a moral ascendency over Proden that didn't admit of fear, and he had with him a little Italian 6.3 millimetre gun that would be unnoticed in his pocket. And then he had the bad luck to run into me at Bassingford, but I had seemed uncommonly credulous and had gone back to town.

He went to Beaulieu and Proden admitted him. They went into that lounge and Clandon, knowing the house held only Proden and himself, was well on his guard. Proden had his story ready. Dibben had not been actually killed that night, he said, but he had had a stroke due to the blow that kept him for months between life and death, and when he had at last recovered, then Seeway's whereabouts were unknown, and all he could presume was that he had been killed in the war. As for that idea that he himself had murdered Dibben, the police were aware that no such thing could have happened. They knew he had an unquestionable alibi. And with regard to making restitution, the word itself was an unfortunate one. Proden, in fact, expressed himself as only too ready to hand over any sum whatever that Seeway considered right. That should finally remove any idea that there'd been a conspiracy. Proden said he didn't want to sound gushing, but he was honestly glad that Seeway was alive and he hoped, now that misconceptions had been removed, to see Seeway and himself back on the old terms of twelve years ago.

"That bit about the police exonerating him from anything to do with Dibben's murder took the wind out of my sails," Clandon said. "And he was turning on all the old charm and directing it full at me so that I hadn't really a chance to think. It was all plausible, I know that now, but then it was just enough to make me wonder if I'd been wrong all along. I was fool enough to admit I'd been bluffing about knowing he'd killed Dibben, and that was when he caught me clean off guard. He said there was something he'd like to show me and he went to a table drawer just behind me. Lucky for me I looked round. What he had was a damn great gun with a silencer on it."

Clandon acted from sheer instinct. If he had been a second later, a bullet would have been in his head. As it was, he went forward and pushed back the chair into Proden as he fell. Proden came forward over the chair and Clandon closed with him. The gun went off and the bullet ripped through the fleshy part of Clandon's shoulder and across his chest. But he kneed Proden in the body and Proden doubled up and let the gun fall. Clandon brought out his own gun.

"What I'm going to do I don't know," he told Proden, "but if that twenty thousand isn't in my hands at this address within two days I'm going to the police."

There was plenty of blood, but that wound had scarcely begun to hurt. Clandon picked up Proden's gun and went out to his car. After what he had told me, he knew he had to drive towards Cambridge. It was a road on which he'd once known each tree and almost each blade of grass. But the wound had begun to hurt and he drove very steadily with the left hand. Then he began to wonder if he were hurt worse than he knew, and in any case that wound would have to be treated. That was why he faked the hold-up.

"Creating a public mischief," Wharton told him. "I ought to bring you in for it straight away. And you really expect us to believe this yarn of yours?"

"I think I do," Clandon told him evenly. "It's the truth. I can't tell it in any other way."

Wharton grunted.

"You want us to believe you were fool enough to swallow that yarn of his hook, line and sinker! That you'd killed Dibben and he'd disposed of the body! You didn't think about a simple case of manslaughter. You just bolted and left him in charge of the roost."

"Yes," he said. "And I still can't tell it any other way. But think of yourself at the age I was then, Superintendent. Don't you ever wince at the things you did and the ideas you had? Proden was almost a god. He took me to town, had me at his club, taught me how to dress, what to eat and drink—the whole run of things. What he told me was law. And that about Dibben wasn't too much to believe. I'd knocked him down. I'd seen the blood at his mouth. I was fuddled, even most of the next day, and then things had gone so far I couldn't step back."

"Where'd you go when you left Bassingford?"

"To France. Took my car with me. And remember I had money. And youth can be pretty resilient. It wasn't too hard to acquire an easy conscience. I hadn't really killed Dibben. It was only an accident. All I'd done wrong was be a party to concealing the body, and I couldn't do a thing about that without betraying Proden."

"You never once smelt a rat?"

"Never. I was more than grateful to Proden. I wasn't worrying about my aunt and her money. I had money of my own. When the war came I hadn't any time to do any thinking."

"Why didn't you get into touch with Proden when you were demobilised?"

"Would you have done?" he said. "The war did something to me, as it did to most people. That business at Bassingford and even myself before the war was pretty disreputable. I'd acquired a new name and a new personality and I preferred to keep it that way."

"What about that Rosamund girl you were engaged to? You didn't make enquiries about her?"

"Why should I?" he said. "I was never in love with her or she with me. I admit I did take a chance one day and went to Bassingford and learned she'd married Proden and divorced him, but that conveyed nothing to me. And I hated the sight of Bassingford. I never wanted to go there again. I never thought I would—till that day when I caught sight of Dibben.”

“Well, I don’t know what I’m going to do about you,” Wharton said, and got to his feet. “Maybe nothing at all. I can’t say. But you’re going to Scotland Yard to make an official statement. Confidential, of course, but every word you’ve told us here. More if you can think of it.”

“When do you want it?”

“Now,” Wharton told him. “And you needn’t worry about washing behind your ears.”

Chapter Nineteen
ROUNDED OFF

IT WAS after lunch when I saw Wharton again. Clandon’s statement had been taken and before I could ask if there had been any additions or differences, he was giving me some news. Rappham had been brought in from Folkestone that morning and Jewle said he was prepared to talk. Rappham’s line was that he was merely an unsuspecting agent of Unstone’s, and always with the idea that the investigations he made and the photographs he took were for divorce cases pure and simple. He swore he had never received a penny except the usual fees of a private enquiry agent.

“I’m having him in in a minute or two,” Wharton said. “Think I’ll pretend to swallow that gaff of his and get him to clear up that little business about Dibben and Bassingford.”

“Wonder how Dibben first ran across him?” I said.

“Rappham may have been advertising in those days,” Wharton said. “But don’t worry, Rappham’ll tell us.”

“You’d like me here?”

“Why not?” he told me. “Jewle’s got him thinking his neck’s at stake. The sight of you won’t close his mouth.”

So Rappham was brought in. He'd shaved off that new moustache of his and but for a darkening under the eyes he looked much the same as when I'd seen him last. He gave me a glance and no more. I was sitting well back, in any case. It was Wharton who had the limelight.

And you'd have thought Rappham was his erring, prodigal brother. Rappham had made a statement, he said, and he wanted to believe it. Maybe he'd like a further sign of Rappham's good faith. We knew a whole lot now about Rappham's earliest association with Marquis-Dibben, but perhaps Rappham would like to give us his version of things. Then George was peering at him over the tops of his antiquated spectacles.

"No lies, mind you. Dibben may be dead, but we've ways and means of checking up. So start talking."

Rappham talked. He'd first run across Dibben, he said, when Dibben's wife was divorcing him, and Dibben had employed him to try to get evidence against the wife. Then Dibben had approached him about that Bassingford business. Dibben, and I thought Rappham was telling the truth, had given just enough information and no more. Dibben claimed, in fact, that Seeway was a distant relation of his and that he suspected Proden of being up to some mischief. What Rappham did was just what we'd guessed, and he'd continued his investigations for some time after that Cambridge visit, and then Dibben had paid him off. One thing Rappham had tried to do was to pick up Seeway's traces, but all he had discovered was that Proden had received a letter from France, and France was too big a haystack in which to look for a needle.

"We'll want all that in the form of a statement," Wharton said, and that was the last I was to see for some time of Fred Rappham.

"That ties that up," Wharton told me. "The next job is collecting Proden."

I said that'd be a bit ticklish. Proden must have gone to Woodsea so as to be ready for a getaway. That shooting of Seeway and Seeway's threats had scared the life out of him.

"If he does bolt he won't get far," Wharton said. "Bet you a new hat the Big Bugs give us the order to move in."

"Maybe they will," I said. "They've got what they wanted—a motive. But one thing I was wondering about. Why did Dibben have that print of himself in that same secret compartment where he had the ones of the Romes?"

George let himself go. He talks about my theorising, but now he was in an expansive mood. He'd seen and heard so much in the last few hours that he must have thought himself omniscient.

"That's simple," he said. "I'll lay that blackmailing of Proden was the first job Dibben did. Sort of founded the Dibben fortune. Gave him and Unstone ideas about that employment agency, so he kept it as a kind of souvenir after he'd used it to put the bite on Proden. Dibben probably had a photographer pal to take it later, and kidded Proden it'd been taken the night of the scheme."

That last bit was a trifle far-fetched, but I didn't say so. I said he still hadn't answered the question about the other photographs.

"She'd been Proden's wife, hadn't she?" he said. "All belonging to the same family, so keep them in the same drawer. And maybe he had ideas about using them a second time."

I asked him what line he was going to take about motive when he had that conference.

"Child's play," he told me airily. "You scared him talking about Seeway and Dibben. He simply had to guess your client was Seeway, so he had to close Dibben's mouth before Seeway could get at him."

"Yes," I said. "That's as good a motive as any. Wonder what he actually took out of that safe besides a double set of books."

"No use guessing," he said, "and Proden won't tell us. Probably he was only after that print of Dibben lying there with the blood coming out of his mouth. If so, he had no luck."

"Rappham might possibly know something," I said.

"Maybe," he said. "Either him or Unstone. But Cleaver won't."

"Why not?"

"He's finished with talking," he told me. "Took an overdose of something last night. They found him dead at that hotel of his this morning."

It was about noon when we set out for Woodsea, and half-past one when we got there. Wharton had rung me about it overnight, and why he wanted me to be there I didn't know. I'd thought that all that would be needed was an arrest, but apparently it wasn't going to be that way. Maybe the Higher-Ups still thought the evidence too circumstantial: they wanted everything handed them on a gold platter, and Wharton was to sign, seal and deliver by extorting a confession. But, as I said, I didn't know, and he didn't tell me.

Matthews contacted us just short of the village. Proden had been playing golf all morning and by now had probably had his lunch. I couldn't help wondering what sort of game Proden had played.

"Right," Wharton said. "Pass the word round. Half an hour ought to finish it."

That bungalow—I'd prefer to call it a house on one floor—stood on the rise above the inlet. It had plenty of ground, as did its neighbours, and across the two hundred yards of water were more bungalows along the opposite rise. Proden's was an expensive-looking place, trim and recently painted. The doors of the brick garage were open and we could see his car. Wharton drew up ours against the gates. He locked it and pocketed the keys.

It was the housekeeper who opened the front door.

"Mr. Proden in?"

"I think so," she said. "What name is it, please?"

"Just two old friends who want to surprise him," Wharton told her, and stepped past her into the tiny hall. She gave him a quick look and turned to the door at the right. Wharton's hand went out.

"That's all right. We'll let ourselves in."

Proden was reading a newspaper, legs well out and cigar in full blast. A decanter, a siphon and a half-emptied glass were on a low table within reach. Through the wide window was a fine view of the inlet, and beyond it to the right was the darker blue of the sea. Below the steeply terraced lawn were tall clumps of blue hydrangeas. Not a bad spot, I thought, to spend a sunny June.

Proden's head turned idly at the sound of the opening door. In his look there seemed a momentary panic, then he was getting to his feet. The charm was switched on: the pleasant modulation of a voice and the nice adjustment of a smile.

"This *is* a surprise!" He gave me a quick nod and the faintest smile. "What brings you this way, Superintendent?"

"Just a little business," Wharton told him, and parked his bulk on the arm of an easy chair. "Sit down, Mr. Proden. There're one or two questions we've got to ask you."

"But surely! I thought we'd gone into everything the last time we met."

"Things have altered since then."

"Really?" The eyebrows lifted in polite enquiry. "But let me offer both of you a drink. What will you have?"

"Nothing," Wharton told him brusquely. "All we want, Mr. Proden, are the answers to a few questions. I ought to tell you, by the way, that we've seen David Seeway."

"Seeway," he said slowly and the word had regret and pity. "Poor David. I suppose he told you about shooting himself?"

Wharton stared. My own eyebrows must have lifted. "Yes," Proden said. "He rang me and asked if he might see me, and naturally I said I'd be delighted. Then he came out with some cock-and-bull story about me killing that man Dibben. I naturally told him about that alibi of mine—I could see he was a bit excited and needed humouring—and then he switched to some extraordinary yarn about something that was supposed to have happened years ago in Bassingford."

"That's interesting," Wharton said. "And what did happen at Bassingford?"

"Well, he'd had one of those rowdy arguments of his with the man Dibben and ended by knocking him down. I took him home and he was far too drunk to remember things properly.

He actually accused me of cooking up some scheme or other with Dibben to make him leave Bassingford." He gave an airy, dismissing wave of the hand.

"That gives you an idea of the rubbish it was, but according to this mad idea of his I'd made out that Dibben was dead and he'd killed him, and that I'd disposed of the body!" The chuckle went and he was nodding soberly at Wharton. "If he told you the same thing, you probably thought him a bit mental."

Wharton's comment was a grunt.

"But this shooting affair. What's your version?"

"Version?" For a moment he looked hurt. "My dear sir, it won't be a version. It'll be the truth. I simply laughed at him and that must have infuriated him because he suddenly produced a gun. I told him not to be a fool and I managed to get my hands on him. Then the gun went off. I told him to get out or I'd call the police. It may sound a bit callous, but I was absolutely furious."

"Funny!" Wharton said. "He claims you produced the gun—a Webley with a silencer. When he left, he took that gun. Threw it into a pond after he'd put a bullet through the side of his car. We recovered it yesterday, so how do you account for that?"

"Planted, my dear sir—planted. He had to concoct some tale or other and bolster it up. I've never owned a Webley in my life. Far too hard on the pull."

"Well, that's your story," Wharton told him evenly. "But about this alibi of yours. One or two queer things have come to light."

As I listened I couldn't help thinking that it was Proden who was mad. He had all the egomaniac's assurance: the incredibility that he should not be believed. There were the deft answers, the bland accusations of lying, the same looks of pain and reproach that a statement of his own should even need a questioning.

"So everyone's a fool or a rogue or a liar," Wharton told him bluntly. "The whole battalion's out of step but you. That Dallery garage made a wrong entry; Moss muddled his dates; it wasn't your car at the Doncaster garage and the man saw the same dent in someone else's car. I'm afraid it won't do."

"Mind if I say something?" I said. "I wonder if Mr. Proden would give me one tiny piece of information. I was the one who investigated that alibi of yours, Mr. Proden. I also made careful enquiries about road conditions on the evenings of the seventh and the eighth. On the eighth, the night you claim you travelled, emergency road repairs were being done for about two miles and there had to be a very wide detour for traffic going north, like that car of yours. Very well then. Tell us exactly where you had to make that detour."

Proden's eyes narrowed. He gave a shrug of the shoulders.

"My dear Travers, you surely wouldn't expect me to remember a mere episode like that in a journey of a hundred and fifty miles?"

"On the contrary," I said. "I claim, and twelve honest jurors would claim, that you couldn't possibly help remembering it. It was a very roundabout detour. So think carefully, Mr. Proden. I don't need to tell you what depends on it."

He was frowning in thought.

"Yes, I think I remember," he said slowly. "Mind if I have just one look at the map?"

"Why not?"

But he didn't look at a map. He slipped between Wharton and myself and was out of the verandah door like a streak.

I made for the window and I caught just a glimpse of him before the tall hydrangeas hid him.

"No need for panic," Wharton told me imperturbably, and quietly made for the door. "He won't get far."

He brought out his pipe and began sucking at the cold stem as we stood on that verandah. Then almost at once there was the splutter of an engine, and a quick chug-chug below to our left. That little motor-boat came into sight from behind the hydrangea clumps and the spray was already hurtling across its bows.

Wharton nudged me, and pointed. Across from the far shore of the inlet a bigger boat was roaring towards that boat of Proden's. Wharton chuckled. Then he was grasping my arm.

"What the hell's he up to!"

It was Proden he meant. That smaller boat made a violent turn. It seemed to head straight for the larger boat. That larger boat caught it amidships and we heard the crash from where we stood. The bigger boat reeled, then righted itself as its engines spluttered to quiet, but Proden's boat was no longer there. Someone was diving from the bigger boat. Wharton scuttled down the steps from the verandah and he was muttering furiously to himself as I followed at his heels.

They didn't recover Proden's body till three days later. Wharton cracked his usual gag about saving the tax-payers' money, but I knew he'd rather have brought Proden in. I didn't see his report to the Big Bugs. He gave me quite a lot of praise—I do know that—but he showed a queer disinclination to talk about that final scene of ours with Proden.

And that certainly suited me. If we had talked things over and patted each other on the back, he might have put one very awkward question.

"Smart bit of work yours, making those road repair enquiries. And, by the way, where exactly *was* that detour?"

What could I have said? Any stone to throw at a mad dog? Quoted his own quip about lies and the sacred name of justice? I don't know. I might have had some luck, of course. The road *might* have been up that night, and there *might* have been a detour. Maybe you were that way yourself that night. If so, I'd be highly obliged if you'd let me know.

THE END

Printed in Great Britain
by Amazon

32691323R00119